Chosen

Spiderwize
Remus House
Coltsfoot Drive
Woodston
Peterborough
PE2 9BF

www.spiderwize.com

Edited by Jenni Bannister
Layout and cover design by Camilla Design

ISBN: 978-1-908128-91-1

CHOSEN

Sheila Caldwell

For Matthew

CONTENTS

ACKNOWLEDGMENTS

I would like to thank Pauline Turner for her welcome critique, and the curator in the Romano-Germanic museum in Cologne for his patience over a very sensitive topic.

Great thanks also to my husband Charles for his encouragement and support.

FOREWORD

The inspiration for this book began while I was undertaking a creative writing course as part of an Open University Degree. For an assignment, we were asked to write 500 words suggested by a selection of prompts, one of them being – 'The work of a Rat Catcher.' While searching through various articles online, I came across information about the Black Death in Europe and was amazed to find that this plague was responsible for killing 30-60% of the European population in the Middle Ages. A small etching or woodcut print showed people being burned, along with the words, '300 Jews burned alive in Cologne in 1349.' This grabbed my attention and I went on to research more about the fate of the Jewish population in the Germanic States at that time. It turns out that thousands of Jews perished through the ignorance of Christians who blamed them for starting the plague. While I knew about the Nazi Holocaust in Germany during the Second World War, I did not realise that there had been many previous acts of a similar nature throughout Europe.

The seed of a short story grew in my mind but over the months, this expanded into a novel after much research into Jewish customs, Jewish, Danish and German names, medieval maps and types of ships. I even travelled to Cologne and visited a museum there which had ancient maps on display. It was interesting to walk around the Altermarkt or market place and to see the town hall known as the Rathaus, and to visit the cathedral. It was hard to imagine huge numbers of merchant ships with sails on the Rhine in the distant past, as today it is mainly barges and pleasure boats filled with tourists that travel on the river.

I have written this historical fiction novel portraying a possible life story during the horrible times of the Black Death through my main character, a young tailor apprentice by the name of Aaron.

Sheila Caldwell

CHAPTER ONE

The Escape

For thou art an holy people to the Lord thy God:
the Lord thy God hath chosen thee to be a special people unto himself,
above all people that are on the face of the earth.
Deuteronomy 7:6

Cologne 1349

'The plague is getting worse,' Jerod voiced in hushed tones as he rinsed his hands in the wooden bowl. Leaning close to his wife's ear he whispered, 'There are so many deaths, that families are putting the bodies out in the streets. Apparently there's no more room in the graveyard and few people able to dig graves.'

Liora clutched his arm. 'Oh, how terrible! The poor things.'

'Hush, dear. We must trust in God to protect His chosen ones,' he whispered while drying his hands.

'I'm glad we live on the outskirts,' she answered quietly. 'So far our people haven't been affected like those in the centre.'

Jerod patted her arm. 'Just let's keep to the Jewish quarter meantime.'

She nodded. 'But... I'm afraid for our children.'

'We have to carry on as usual and trust that we will be safe,' her husband answered, giving her a reassuring smile that he did not feel, as he turned to go back to his workshop.

Liora nodded again. She did not feel comforted, but forced herself to act normally as she called to her elder daughter, 'Abigail, will you go for the bread please?'

'I'll go Mother,' offered Aaron, rushing through from the room where they all ate and slept. 'I've finished in the workshop now and Abigail's playing with Dorit.'

'You're very eager today. Perhaps there is some attraction at the bakehouse, hmm?'

'Er ... No, I could just do with a walk.' Aaron's face reddened, giving him away. 'I've been working inside with Father all morning.'

His mother smiled knowingly and handed him some coins. 'Very well, but come straight home. There are rumours that the plague is worsening.' As she watched her handsome, lanky son setting off she sighed, her heart feeling heavy. He was growing up so quickly; a young man now, showing interest in a girl.

Aaron smiled to himself. He would see Satis again. Just thinking about her gave him tingles as he hurried towards the bakehouse in the Jewish quarter, and sure enough, Satis was busy serving customers amid the delicious smell of newly-baked bread. She gave him a shy smile looking up through her thick dark lashes while her father was occupied, taking loaves and spicy buns from the oven. Aaron knew he was keeping his eye on him, so simply asked for the bread, feeling awkward and stepping from foot to foot all the while. His stomach turned over when Satis touched his fingers as she took his coins. Giving her a nod and a smile, he walked out into the sunshine unaware of the ground beneath his feet, clutching his loaf. Wanting to daydream about his first love, he forgot his mother's words and chose to dawdle a roundabout way home through one of his favourite places, the *Altermarkt*, where he often went with his father. They'd buy cloth from the exotic-looking turbaned mercers who came into the city plying their colourful wares. Someday, he would create a beautiful dress for Satis in sendal or brocade, not the usual muslins or worsteds that his father purchased for the locals. A deep ruby shade or sapphire blue would be perfect. Jewel colours would be …

Something penetrated his thoughts. He was brought to an abrupt halt as he turned into the market square. There was an unusual stillness; an eeriness about this place which was normally noisy with the bustling of people and animals. He realised it was silent around the *Dom*. There was no continual clink-clink of chisel against stone as masons worked to construct the huge Roman Catholic edifice which dominated the city. The wooden scaffolding clung like webs around the cathedral's structure, but there was no sign of any workmen.

There were just a few subdued buyers around the butchery and vegetable carts while the rest of the large market square stood empty apart from a number of deserted wooden stalls. Wind swirled dust around. Aaron's attention was drawn to a pile of rags heaped nearby on the cobblestones, and two men slowly digging a trench at the roadside. Then the realisation of what he was witnessing struck him. His throat constricted catching his breath as his whole body went rigid. It wasn't rags; it was dead bodies. *Dead bodies!* Real people; lying on top of each other, and now being heaved with little regard into a shallow hole and earth flung over them by the two men who looked work-weary and exhausted. Aaron's fifteen-year-old mind was horrified yet fascinated by the sight. He became aware of a stench in the area and shuddered as he caught sight of rats feeding on rotting food around the empty stalls. Excrement and blood buzzing with flies covered much of the pathways. He gulped down the bile rising in his throat. This was all new to him. His life was generally confined to the separate area where the Jewish community lived and worked, but when he had previously accompanied his father to the market, it had always been an exciting venture. He had heard his parents talk about the Black Death which was killing many people but had never actually seen anyone with this plague or the effects of it until now. As he turned to retrace his steps, a woman dropped to the ground before him. She had big black boils on her face. Blood was running from her nose and mouth. Aaron was horrified and clapped his hands over his mouth, but before his legs would move he heard voices coming towards him.

'Holy Mother of God, save us.' *Slap.* 'Holy Mother of God, forgive us.' *Slap.* 'Holy Mother of God, cleanse us.' *Slap.*

'Get back home boy! This is no place for you,' urged someone hurrying past.

Aaron stood transfixed watching the flagellants. Blood was running from open wounds on their naked backs where they flailed themselves with knotted leather thongs attached to a rough wooden handle. They chanted their prayers at each step and didn't appear to feel the pain, having a wild look in their eyes as they stumbled slowly onwards. Some followers were dabbing the wounds with rags and holding them to their hearts as though they were holy relics. Aaron watched open-mouthed as his shaking legs slowly retreated. He realised he'd involuntarily backed into a half-open doorway at the side of the imposing *Rathaus* and could hear men's raised voices inside.

'It has come to the Municipal Council's attention that the Jewish community has not been afflicted with this plague in the way that the rest of the city has.'

'They must be in league with the Devil. They're the only ones who seem to have escaped this curse,' someone shouted.

'Yeah, filthy Jews. I heard one's been seen dumping a dead body in a well. They're the ones poisoning us!' yelled another.

'Let's get 'em tonight. Round 'em up and burn 'em alive,' incited a third. 'Get a gang together. Torch the houses!'

'Them holy-holy ones out there cuttin' themselves have it wrong. It's not *God* who's punishin' us, it's those bloody Jews tryin' to poison us! Let's mark St. Bartholomew's Day with a *big* fire!'

Amid the cheers of agreement, Aaron heard, 'Gather together anything that will burn. Take what wood there is to be had in the now-deserted homes. Sadly the owners have no further need of it.'

He didn't wait to hear any more. He raced home and burst in on his mother preparing food. He slammed the door and leaned against it, panting.

'Aaron, Aaron, whatever is it?' she cried, shocked by the stricken look on his face. Quickly rubbing her hands on her apron, she ran over to him, gently unclenching his fingers and lifting away the loaf which was squashed against his heaving chest. His mouth worked soundlessly for a moment as he tried to gather his thoughts.

'The men...' he panted, 'they're going to burn us all... ALIVE... TONIGHT!' He slid to the floor, shuddering. Liora turned to scoop a ladle of water from the wooden bucket and held it shakily to his lips.

'Wh-what men, Aaron? Where? What exactly did they say?'

Aaron repeated what he'd seen and heard and his mother hugged him to her and knelt on the straw-covered floor rocking him. When his breathing had settled, she helped him to his feet.

'Now listen carefully. I want you to go next door to the shop. Tell your father that he must come quickly. Don't mention anything that you've heard in front of your sisters and come straight back. Go now!' she urged, shoving him towards the door.

Her husband appeared immediately, sensing by Aaron's white face that something was wrong.

'What is it, Liora? What's happened?'

'Oh, Jerod,' she sobbed, running into his arms, 'it's the Council. They are going to kill us. Burn us all *alive*.'

'How can this be? Where did you hear this?'

'Aaron overheard them planning to come tonight. They're preparing to burn us out. They think it's the *Jews* who are causing the plague.' Jerod looked at his son, who nodded.

'It's true, honestly Father. That's what I heard.'

Jerod struggled to digest this news.

'But some Jews have died too!' He shook his head in disbelief. 'We are not immune! Where will this end! They've killed off all the poor cripples and anyone simple minded or with a skin disease.' He threw up his hands. 'Now it's the Jews' turn!' Then he made a decision and sprang into action.

'Aaron, come here.'

'Yes, Father.'

'I want you to run to as many of our neighbours as you can and tell them your news. Tell them they must try to escape the city before nightfall. Don't be gone for long, we need you back here. Go!' Aaron nodded and ran out of the door towards the house adjoining theirs. Jerod turned to his wife. 'We must pack up what we can carry. Food, water and a few blankets and get away soon. I'm going to bury our valuables.' Liora nodded and set to packing up some food.

*

Aaron banged on their neighbour's door with such force that it burst open. The poor woman standing inside leapt in fright. 'I'm so sorry, but I've bad news,' he panted. 'You must pack up and escape the town before dark. The Council are planning to burn all the Jews. My father told me to tell you and for you to pass it on... *please*,' he added as the woman stood, shocked and open-mouthed. She nodded dumbly. He ran to the next house and repeated the instruction to be met with the same incredulous expression, but could see that the man there took him seriously.

'Th...thank you, I'll tell my wife and get the children ready.'

Aaron alerted more neighbours then with a sudden thought whispered, 'Satis!' and ran to the bakehouse.

Meanwhile, Jerod returned to his tailor's shop. He looked at his two daughters, Abigail aged eight and Dorit six, who were sitting happily playing on the floor with some scraps of material and yarns.

'Come, girls, we are all going on a surprise journey. Come help your mother to get your things together.' The girls jumped up excitedly but became quiet as they picked up on the tense atmosphere. They knew something serious was happening by their mother's set expression and the way both parents seemed suddenly to have burst into a flurry of activity. Jerod carefully wrapped the menorah candlestick, his treasured copy of the Torah and one of the mezuzah parchments and put them in a sack. He took some coins from his cash box and put them into his pouch, then slung the sack over his shoulder. Carrying a spade and the cash box which he'd wrapped in muslin, he walked to wasteland at the back of the houses, near the wall beside the synagogue. He hurriedly dug a hole in the grassy ground, laid the cash box in the bottom and placed the sack on top. Saying a quick prayer, he filled the hole with earth then turf and placed a flat stone on top. He measured that it was ten paces out from a support in the boundary wall. Satisfied with his task, he returned to the house.

'Hurry my darlings,' Liora urged the girls. 'Wear your warmest clothes and come back quickly to the table. We'll have some soup before we leave.' The girls nodded and ran to their small closet where they pulled out woollen pinafores which they donned over their existing clothes, then wrapped shawls around their shoulders. Each tugged on a woollen hat.

'Can I take my doll?' whimpered Dorit, clutching a small, carved wooden figure.

'Yes, yes. Just be quick. We must leave soon,' Liora urged. 'Here take these,' and she handed them each a bundle of hastily grabbed fruit and bread wrapped in some cloth. 'Where's Aaron? I wish he was back.'

Just at that, the door was thrust open and Aaron entered, out of breath. 'I went to about seven houses, I think,' he panted. 'And the bakehouse. They're all going to pass on the news.'

'Good lad,' nodded Jerod. 'Come outside with me for a minute,' and checking that no-one was about, he indicated where he'd buried the valuables. 'Remember this place; you may need these some day. Ten paces back. Think of the Ten Commandments.' Turning to face his son, he placed his hands on his shoulders. 'I want you to know that I am very proud of you and...' his voice cracked.

'I know, Father... I'll always try to make you proud of me,' Aaron assured him.

'You will be a great tailor one day.'

They returned to the house. Aaron gathered some food and a change of clothing into a bundle. He put the tools of his apprenticed trade – his scissors, needles, thread and chalk – into a leather pouch at his waist. Liora was ladling hot soup into wooden bowls.

'Drink this down quickly all of you. It may be some time before we eat again tonight.'

They all complied in silence.

'We better go right away,' Jerod urged when they'd finished. 'Now children, listen to me and do exactly as I say. We're going to walk out of here and find somewhere to hide, and then make our way to the next town once it's dark. Don't talk and be very good. God will guide us.'

They all nodded; eyes wide with apprehension at the prospect.

*

It was dusk as they walked out of the Jewish quarter, through the west gate in the city wall. Avoiding the main roadway, they took one of many tracks heading into the countryside. Jerod had an idea that they might be able to hide in one of the newly-deserted farmhouses about two miles out of the city. Aaron carried Dorit on his back for a while as she couldn't walk as fast as the others. As the sky darkened, they could see the shapes of other families fleeing the ghetto in all directions. Some were making their way along the track some distance behind themselves, pushing handcarts with children who were carrying bundles and sacks trailing alongside. Jerod could see the outline of some farm buildings ahead and pointed them out to his family.

'We'll rest there for a while and then move on under cover of darkness.'

A cry went up from further back the track, and the family looked round anxiously. They could see the lights of torches. The Council's men were already on the rampage. Jerod cursed under his breath. If he hadn't sent Aaron to the neighbours to raise the alarm, his family would have had a better chance.

'Quickly! Run to the buildings, everyone. We'll try to hide there.' They scrambled up a slope to a rough stone barn and discovered a pile of straw and old boxes inside. 'Climb in the boxes and we'll cover you with straw. Hurry now,' he urged.

The girls were soon hidden under heaps of straw, but Aaron insisted on staying with his parents. They watched the bobbing lights of flaming torches in the distance as the persecutors ran in pursuit along the track. In a matter of minutes there were screams and shouting and they knew that their friends had been overpowered.

Liora's hands rushed to her heart to stifle the panic rising in her chest. A line of torches bobbed slowly back towards the city with the captives, but a number of others were moving onwards towards the farm buildings.

'It's no good, we'll have to move,' cried Jerod, grabbing Abigail from her hiding place and heaving her up in his arm. 'You bring Dorit, Aaron.' Grasping Liora's hand with his free hand, he pulled her out of the doorway and they all fled into the darkness once more.

'My dolly, my dolly', wailed Dorit.

'Forget it, there's no time to go back now,' answered her father brusquely.

*

'I'm sure I saw a movement at that building ahead,' shouted one of the torch bearers.

'Well if there are any Jews hiding there, we'll burn them out,' panted another.

Six of the men reached the barn and searched inside and all around the outside.

'They've been here all right, and recently,' a shout came from one. 'They've left their bundles of food and look, here's a child's toy,' he said triumphantly. 'Let's go, they can't be far ahead.'

Someone touched his torch to the dry straw and the barn was ablaze in seconds.

Jerod and his family saw the flames light up the sky and hurried onwards, fear giving them strength. They stumbled into a copse of trees which by now was so darkened it was impossible to see ahead. They kept tripping over branches and getting caught by briars. Terrified and exhausted, they crouched down behind trees and boulders panting for breath.

'Spread out. Spread out. We might have a better chance,' ordered Jerod. Liora kept Dorit close to her, but the others scattered to find cover. Aaron shinned up an old tree as high as he could climb. They all heard and saw the men coming. Jerod counted eight burning torches and could hear rough voices cursing and coughing as they tried to hurry.   The family didn't have a chance. When the first two men came crashing into the woodland holding their flaming torches high, Dorit let out a shriek. She and Liora were instantly grabbed and hauled from their hiding place.

'No, no! Leave us alone!'

'Shut your noise or we'll finish you off now!' yelled Liora's captor as he proceeded to tie her hands behind her back.

Dorit was shrieking hysterically and was silenced by a hard slap to her face. She continued to shudder and whimper.

'Hush, darling. Stay close to me,' whispered Liora, trying her best to comfort the small girl pressed up against her leg.

'Get the other bastards, they can't be far,' shouted one of the men. Abigail was the next to be captured as she tried to make a run for it.

With the extra light from the other torches, it was just a matter of time before Jerod was discovered crouched in a hollow and hauled out. 'Thought you'd escape, did you? You filthy murdering Jews,' came the snarl from a face thrust into Jerod's.

'We've done nothing wrong. We've murdered no-one. Let - my - family - go!' he yelled, kicking and struggling with his opponents who were succeeding in tying him up.   The ringleader held his torch high and peered into Jerod's face. 'Are there any more of you?' he wheezed, his face glistening with sweat. 'Tell me!'

Jerod could see the tell-tale swellings on the man's neck and tried to rear away from him. 'There is no-one else,' he lied. 'You keep away from me. You have the Black Death.' At this, the captor spat on him. 'Now you can have it too,' he sneered, giving Jerod a shove forward on to the track. 'But you'll never even see the lumps as you'll be screaming to your God tonight when the flames burn the flesh from your bones and your eyes boil.'

Liora and the girls screamed hysterically at this, but the man just laughed maniacally and gave the order that they be escorted back to the town. He had a last look around the area holding his torch high but seemed satisfied that they'd captured everyone. Several men carried sharp pikes in addition to their torches, and they used these frequently to prod the helpless family onwards. Aaron watched in agony, his fist jammed in his mouth, as his beloved mother, father and sisters were led away. He felt a hot wetness on his leg as his bladder gave way.

*

At dawn, Aaron lay behind a fallen tree trunk where he'd crouched all night after slithering down from the tree. Curled into a tight ball, he still had his hands pressed over his ears where he'd clenched them to shut out the sounds drifting up from *Koln*. Paralysed with terror, he'd had no notion of time. At daylight, he painfully moved his limbs and tentatively half-stood up, expecting someone to discover him at any moment. Staggering to the edge of the copse, he looked out towards the city. The rosy pink of the sky was muddied by a thick pall of black smoke through which the church spires jabbed. He could faintly hear bells tolling out the time. The memories of last night played over and over in his head. *Could he have freed his family? Was he a coward to hide? Were they all really dead? Was God angry with him?*

'I'm only fifteen, God,' he whimpered. 'I couldn't fight... all these men.'

Brushing away the tears that brimmed and threatened to take him over, he straightened up, making the decision to move on. He knew he must get far away from this place.

*

Aaron ran more than he walked for the rest of that day. The need to get as far away as possible from the previous night's horrors kept him plunging onwards through fields and woods, keeping away from habitations, only stopping to catch his breath, slake his thirst in a stream or grab some blackberries or an apple. Whenever he stopped, he fancied he heard someone chasing him and the only way to block the memory of the screaming was to keep moving blindly onwards, onwards.

As the sun started to set, he saw a dovecote a short distance away in a field and made towards it. Inside it was dry, and although the ground was littered with pigeon droppings there was old straw and feathers and dried leaves that had blown in. He collapsed gasping and, pulling the straw over himself, fell into a fitful sleep punctuated by nightmare scenes.

He woke at daybreak, cold and stiff. The pigeons were cooing above, their feathers floating down while they fluttered and preened. Easing awkwardly to his feet, he went outside to relieve himself. A low mist covered the fields. *Good. I can move on. There's less chance of being seen in this.* Hunched over, he ran around the perimeter of the field making towards woodland on higher ground. Once among the trees, he felt safer and kept steadily scrambling onwards. Apart from some water, he found nothing to eat all that long day.

As dusk approached, it started to drizzle. He saw a building in a clearing with smoke rising lazily from the chimney hole. Aaron was intensely cold, aching and dizzy with hunger. His thoughts were drawn to warmth and food. Stumbling towards the house, no sooner had he scrambled a few steps when a loud barking caused his terror to return. He clambered into the nearest tree, scraping skin from his hands and knees, when a huge hairy hound leapt towards him, snarling and snapping at his heels. Numb with fear, convinced that 'the men' had caught up with him, he clung to the scratchy bark while the dog kept up its incessant barking and jumping.

'King! Stay now! What have you found?' The dog fell silent and nuzzled his master's hand. 'Good boy, good boy. You, up there! Get down NOW or you're dog meat!' shouted the figure, brandishing a staff. Aaron was shaking so much that he could neither speak nor move. The person below gave him a prod with his stick and Aaron toppled from the branches, landing at his feet. The dog owner was relieved to see that it was just a bedraggled, frightened lad, a few years younger than himself.

'Back boy,' he commanded the dog. 'Who are you? I don't recognise you,' he said, peering into Aaron's face in the gathering gloom.

'A…Aaron'.

'What are you doing on my land? Thinking of stealing, were you?'

'N…no, sir. I j…just...' but Aaron was overcome by a wave of dizziness and sank back in a faint.

He came round to find himself lying on the floor inside the house before a roaring fire. As he tried to get up, he was startled as the hound thumped down beside him.

'Just lie still. You're in a bad way.'

He was offered some water.

As Aaron gulped it, he looked into the blue eyes and serious face of a blonde-haired youth of around eighteen years. 'Don't try to talk just yet. I'll get you some stew. The dog won't harm you,' he added gruffly as King commenced to lick away the blood on Aaron's legs, then nuzzled the leather pouch at Aaron's side.

'My scissors; I'd forgotten. They're all I have left in the world.'

*

Over the course of the evening, Aaron learned that his host was called Ulrich. He had recently buried his father, mother, older sister, and two younger brothers. He himself had also suffered the plague, but was one of very few lucky ones to have recovered.

Aaron was feeling warmed and comfortable and Ulrich gave him a clean shirt and breeches and applied a soothing salve to his cuts and bruises.

'My mother used to make salves and tinctures from the flowers and herbs,' Ulrich offered sadly. 'The people in the villages around here appreciated her help.'

At the mention of Ulrich's mother, Aaron instantly thought of his own. He recalled her comforting him in her arms just days ago and the memory of the scent of her skin pricked at his senses. Tears slid down his cheeks as he began to talk of his ordeal and the probable horrific death of his family. At the mention of them being burned alive however, he burst into sporadic sobs as grief racked his body. Ulrich put an arm around him and Aaron turned into his shoulder and wept and wept. When finally he was spent, Ulrich, his own face wet with tears, laid him down on the floor on a rag rug near the hearth and covered him with a cloak. King tentatively nuzzled Aaron's neck as he slept, then lay at his side protectively.

CHAPTER TWO

Life with Ulrich

Ulrich had the idea that if Aaron would stay with him, they could work the farm and somehow manage through the winter. Next morning, he outlined a plan. 'I'd like you to stay here if you will. We can work together. I'm trying to keep all this going like my parents, but I can't work in the fields, keep the fire burning, cook *and* look after the horse, cow, goats and hens all on my own. What do you say? Will you stay?'

Aaron thought for a bit. 'What if the men are still chasing after me? Aren't you worried about having a Jew in the house?'

Ulrich smiled. 'I'll take that risk. The Council in *Koln* will have more to worry about than you. Besides, it's over two days ride away.'

'I'll be grateful to stay, Ulrich. 'I'll work hard for you.'

'You'll have to,' he replied. 'I've just been lighting the fire in the evenings but it'll be winter soon and we need to try to keep it going all the time or freeze. That means chopping piles of firewood and stacking it. Are you up to that?'

Aaron nodded. 'Of course. Just show me how it's done. I can put the animals in and out for you as well.'

'Great. I'll show you where the hens like to lay their eggs. Could you do some washing and sweeping as well?

'That's women's work!' retorted Aaron, frowning.

'Do you see any women here then?' answered Ulrich, waving his arms around.

Aaron shook his head and sighed. 'Alright, I'll do my best. What will we do about cooking? I only eat kosher food.'

'Stay here, and you eat what I provide.' Ulrich stood waiting with eyebrows raised.

Aaron considered this for a long moment. The alternative was hardship. 'I used to help my mother make vegetable soup and I've watched her make flat breads.'

'Things are looking up then,' Ulrich laughed and ruffled Aaron's dark head. 'You're turning out quite well for a little Jew boy,' he joked and ducked away from Aaron's retaliatory swipe. 'Come. I'll show you where to chop wood, and then I'm off to plough.'

He showed Aaron the axe and stump used as a chopping block and pointed to the pile of felled trees. They turned out the dairy cow and three goats into their fields and fed the hens. 'I'll milk the cow and goats in the evening,' said Ulrich as he led a huge shire horse from its stall into the yard. 'Have a look around. You'll soon find where things are.' He gave a wave and set off. 'I'll be back around midday.' Looking over at his dog he ordered, 'King - stay.'

The hound padded beside Aaron all morning.

*

The heavy wooden house was built on two levels. On the ground, there were three rooms, one with stalls for animals and the other was a store piled with sacks of vegetables and flour and other foodstuff. A cat lay curled in a corner. A small stone-built room with a stone shelf and hooks on the rafters from which hung rabbits and game birds provided a cold pantry. The upper floor was reached by an outside wooden stairway. A heavy door led into a long room the length of the house with a wide fireplace dominating the central area. A metal contraption which held a large cooking vessel could be swung over the fire which had a small oven on both sides, and a spit for roasting meat. A tinder box lay beside a heaped basket of logs near the fireplace. Three alcoves held wooden box beds. Only one now had a feather bed and blanket. The others had just bare wooden slats. A round tub made from half a large barrel served as a bath and a washtub. The water was poured down a hole under a trapdoor in one corner of the room along with sweepings and straw from the floor and the contents of the chamber pots. It all formed in a heap which Ulrich added to the animal manure for spreading on the fields. A simple table, the surface white from years of scrubbing, six chairs, two cupboards; one for eating and cooking utensils, the other containing jars of preserves and an old box containing some needles and thread, blocks of rough soap and candles. A wooden chest full of clothes completed the furniture. A stream running down the hillside close by provided water which had to be carried in buckets up the steps to the living area.

Aaron was determined to show Ulrich that he could cope with all his allocated chores, and set about cleaning out the fire and resetting it. He struggled for a while with the tinderbox, but eventually managed to set the kindling alight. He waited until it blazed up then added some large logs from the basket. The sight of the flames set his imagination working and he immediately thought of his family. Shuddering, he shook his head and forced himself to the tasks in hand. He'd helped his mother many times over the years to prepare vegetables, so that job wasn't so onerous. He brought turnips, carrots and onions from the storeroom where he also uncovered a sack of barley. He found salt in the cupboard. Soon soup was simmering in the pot over the fire, and spoons, wooden bowls and beakers were laid ready on the scrubbed top table.

'Right, now I'll chop some firewood,' he said to King, who seemed in agreement and stayed close to Aaron like a shadow, 'but first I need to find some cloth to wrap around my sore hands.' He raked in the box of clothing and found an old sheet. 'This has seen better days,' he remarked to the dog as he looked at the holes. 'I'll rip this and make bandages.'

The two hurried down the outside stair to the woodpile. King sat well back from the proceedings and watched as Aaron swung the axe and hit the logs awkwardly to start with, his grazed hands wrapped with rags. Then, gaining in confidence, he was soon filling a basket with decent logs.

When Ulrich returned, he was delighted to find the house filled with the aroma of soup and Aaron proudly busying himself serving it up.

'Well done, lad,' he affirmed giving Aaron a thump on the back. 'Good soup.' He slurped it down quickly and indicated the empty bowl. 'Another bowlful if you please.'

*

From the beginning, the two youths became firm friends. Time passed quickly enough as there was so much work to do around the house and yard. The days were getting shorter and Aaron was soon into a busy routine from before dawn till after dusk looking after the house and animals. He explored the food store and became more adventurous with his cooking. Ulrich supplied rabbits, pigeons and pheasants and the occasional old hen, and taught Aaron how to prepare them for the pot. He was squeamish at first, but didn't want to lose face in front of his benefactor so he tried his best and became quite good at skinning rabbits and plucking birds.

'Save the feathers,' ordered Ulrich, indicating a sack. 'You'll soon have enough for a pillow.'

One day, as the weather was turning colder, Ulrich stated, 'I'm going to ride into *Koln* tomorrow.'

At the mention of the city, Aaron trembled and looked up at Ulrich with frightened eyes.

'We need more provisions and *you* need a feather bed,' said Ulrich, prodding Aaron in the chest. 'I'll take the cow to barter. We have enough milk from the goats.'

'Oh, it's alright. I can sleep on the floor beside King,' said Aaron, not wanting to be any trouble.

'Nonsense. We have beds. I burned the bedding after the ... deaths. You know.' He put his head down for a moment. Then he straightened up pursing his lips. 'You deserve a decent place to sleep. You work hard.'

Aaron nodded and smiled his appreciation.

'Besides, I have a young lady to visit. I'll be gone for five days.' Ulrich added.

'Why are you visiting a lady?' queried Aaron.

'None of your business, young man,' answered his friend, punching him playfully on the shoulder. 'You'll be doing the same thing in a year or two,' he winked.

Aaron looked nonplussed.

That night, Ulrich decided it was time he had a good wash in the bath instead of the cursory daily cold water sluice in the stream.

'Fetch the buckets,' he ordered Aaron. They dragged the half barrel over in front of the fireplace and then went outside with buckets, filled them from the stream and tipped the water into the large cauldron over the fire. They repeated the process until the vessel was half full. Both ventured out into the cold once more to refill the buckets. When the water over the fire was very hot, they used another pan to ladle the hot water into the bath and added cold until it was a bearable temperature. Ulrich hunted for some soap, then stripped off and immersed himself in the hot bath with a sigh. He thoroughly lathered himself all over and enlisted Aaron to scrub his back.

'Do you want to go in next?' he offered as he stood up to dry off.

Aaron eyed the grey, scummy water. 'I'll have a bath when you are away.'

'Good idea,' answered Ulrich, laughing. 'Pile those dirty clothes of mine in then and you can give them a good scrubbing.'

Aaron sighed, but rolled up his sleeves and did his best to scrub and pummel the dirt from the clothes. Together they wrung out the wet washing then dragged the bath over the floor with much splashing and hilarity to the trapdoor, lifted it up and poured the black water down the hole. There were puddles everywhere which needed mopping up. They poured the last of the cold water into the tub to rinse the clothes, wrung them and finally hung them to dry over the chairs.

Early next morning, Ulrich was ready to set off in a cart pulled by Janus, the horse. The dairy cow was tied up to plod alongside; the breath from the animals creating puffy clouds in the frosty air. Aaron had packed three dozen eggs in straw into a crate for sale at the market along with two large crocks of goats' milk and two of cows' milk. Ulrich had wrapped up bread, rabbit meat and cheese, a stone bottle of ale and a few apples for the journey which would take almost two days. Putting coins into his pouch, he then packed a thick blanket and stacked some empty sacks on the seat at the front. He wore stout boots with a hooded cloak over two shirts and his breeches.

'W... will you try to find out what happened to ...?' but Ulrich knew what he was trying to say.

'Yes, of course. I'll ask around.'

'You won't tell anyone I'm here though, will you?'

Ulrich smiled kindly. 'No, little friend. It's our secret.'

He'd agreed to leave King behind as company and protection for the boy.   After waving him off, Aaron felt a deep pang on realising that he was going to be living alone for the first time in his life. Watching the cart disappear around a bend in the road, he swallowed hard and straightened up. He'd show Ulrich that he was responsible and could be trusted. He'd make Ulrich proud of him. Jerod came into his mind. He'd make his father proud too.

'I'll be good, Father. You'll see,' he whispered.

Aaron set about his tasks. He scattered grain for the hens, then went inside to the goat stall and milked the two nannies. Taking the bucket of warm milk upstairs, he set it on the table. Next, with much puffing and blowing, he managed to get the fire burning again from the still-glowing embers from the previous night. Piling more logs on, he soon had a comforting blaze. He swept the floor, shook the rag rug and poked the dirty straw down the hole in the corner. King accompanied him as he ran down the stairs to heave a new bale of straw up to the first floor. He separated some handfuls and scattered them around.

'There, that looks better,' he said, looking to King for approval. 'Let's have some porridge now, eh?'

King gave a bark of delight and watched Aaron as he stirred the barley meal and goats milk while it simmered in a pot on the fire. It was a short while later that they shared a companionable breakfast. Aaron was becoming accustomed to eating dairy foods and didn't think about his former Jewish food regime.

CHAPTER THREE

The Market

The journey to *Koln* was a long one for Ulrich. He had to go more slowly than usual because of the cow, and the weather had turned wet and blustery. He found shelter at dusk at his usual place in a wood and tethered the horse and cow on long ropes so they could crop the grass. He quickly milked the cow to keep her comfortable and it gave him a warm, nourishing drink. The rain had abated but it was cold and windy. It was the time of the full moon, which he always chose for travelling overnight to Cologne, but tonight the moon was hiding. He decided against trying to build a fire and just wrapped himself in his cloak and some canvas bags and settled down under a tree to enjoy his simple repast.

Looking around for a suitable place to sleep, he noticed just nearby a great old oak tree, with low spreading branches. The leaves were mostly torn away now but it afforded some decent shelter. He manhandled the cart for a short distance, pushing it underneath the overhanging branches and lay down inside on some sacks. Wrapping himself in his cloak and the blanket with more sacks on top, he was quite comfortable and out of the wind.

Next morning, he rose well before the sun was up. It was dry and the wind had lessened. He milked the cow and drank some of the warm, frothy milk along with the remainder of his bread and cheese. Feeling refreshed, he manoeuvred the cart back on to the track and knotted the cow's rope to the rear. Janus was then harnessed and moved into the shafts. Ulrich was soon on his way, hoping to reach Cologne by midday as he'd left so early.

*

The journey was uneventful and Ulrich was passing through the East Gate of the city as a bell started to chime twelve. Like Aaron, he was surprised at how few people were about instead of the usual bustle from hundreds of buyers and sellers. There were still a good number of traders who'd come in their ships, but only a straggle of sad-looking citizens. When he drove into the market square, however, a number of women moved towards him, pleased to see someone with fresh milk and eggs for sale. He sold his produce quickly and was pointed in the direction of a man who might be interested in buying his cow. This transaction was satisfactory and Ulrich was delighted that things were going smoothly. Now, he needed to buy provisions for himself so made his way over to the few traders touting their wares. He purchased sacks of barley meal, flour and hafer – a type of oatmeal – some salt, a honeycomb, two hams, a large sausage, lard and a bag of dried fruits. Then from the candle maker, he purchased a box of tallow candles and some soap. Next he went in search of a feather bed. It was then that he saw a brightly dressed, turbaned gentleman come into the square with two helpers carrying long rolls of cloth in bright colours. They laid down a large square of muslin on the ground where they displayed the satins, bernet, perse and sendal for the ladies to admire, along with the more mundane hessian, serge and muslin. There were also richly coloured and patterned rugs, cushions and bedding. Ulrich went over to have a look.

'Little point buying this material, beautiful though it is,' muttered a woman to her companion while handling a heavy, red satin.

'Mm, you're right,' answered her friend. 'Only the wealthy can wear clothes in bright colours. We have to have something warm that doesn't show the dirt!'

Her friend nodded in agreement. 'Do you have any brown serge to match our mud?' she asked the turbaned mercer and gave a grimace.

'Ah, beautiful ladies like you should wear beautiful colours. Blues and greens to match your eyes,' he replied, smiling and lifting material for them to handle. 'My friend, Jerod Levey the tailor will be pleased to make you something special, I'm sure.'

The two women shared a look, then one of them said, 'I'm afraid your friend the tailor and all his family are dead.'

'Oh, no ... this cannot be!' exclaimed the turbaned gentleman, shocked. 'Was it the plague that took them?'

The two ladies shuffled anxiously and handed back the cloth.

'No, didn't you know that all the Jews were burned?' whispered one.

'I...I can't believe this. Jerod, dead, and all his family... young Aaron... and all their friends...' His voice trailed off with the shock.

'Yes, it was a terrible night when it happened, but the authorities know what they're doing, I suppose,' voiced one of the women, then gave a sigh.

'Terrible, terrible,' repeated the other shaking her head. 'We have lost hundreds to the Black Death and now losing so many of the skilled people like the tailor and ...' she noticed Ulrich hovering nearby, listening to the conversation. 'We best be going.' She nudged her friend and they hurried off, thinking perhaps Ulrich was spying for the Council.

Ulrich approached the mercer and purchased a bolt of a smooth, brown woollen material and some thread. It occurred to him that Aaron could make them some new warm tunics and breeches for the winter. It saddened him to have the confirmation of the Levey family deaths and to see the grief in this black man's face.

He completed his necessary purchases deciding on a thick feather quilt and a straw-filled ticking mattress for Aaron. Now he wanted something pretty for Marta.

Wandering round the market, he found a boy selling trinkets. He chose a pretty necklace of blue beads which would match her eyes. With everything loaded into the cart covered with sacks, he set off out of the square to one of the tall tenement buildings which surrounded it. There were stables at the back of the houses and Ulrich tossed some coins to the young lad he knew there, to feed Janus and take care of his cart. As he visited Marta every few months, the lad knew him quite well.

'I'll look in tomorrow to check the horse. Mind that no-one touches my cart now. The things in there have to see me through the winter.'

The boy nodded and bowed. 'You can trust me sir.' He started to unharness the horse. 'I'll look after it sir.'

'You do that and I'll pay you well,' promised Ulrich, and strode off to knock on Marta's door.

*

Marta lived alone in a decent, two-roomed house on the ground floor of a four storey building. She had lived with her widowed father until recently, when he had succumbed to the plague.

'Ulrich! Oh, it's so good to see you,' she exclaimed, her face lighting up with pleasure. 'Come in, come in.'

Oh, it's good to see you too. Come here 'til I hold you,' he replied, pulling her into his arms.

They kissed and hugged passionately, their ardour growing.

'Hungry?' asked Marta, breathlessly.

'Yes... but for you first,' answered Ulrich, lifting her up and carrying her over to the bed.

*

Later, when they were enjoying a dinner of spiced sausage with gravy and carrots, Ulrich put down his tankard of ale, mopped up his gravy with a chunk of bread, licked his fingers and sat back, satisfied. Maybe now was a good time to broach the subject which was on his mind.

'I heard some women talking at the market about all the Jews being burned. Is that right?'

Marta's smile disappeared. 'Yes.'

'What happened?'

Marta fiddled with her fork for a moment. 'It was on St. Bartholomew's Day. The first I knew about it was when I was taking Frau Olgen's laundry to her. I've started taking in washing to get money for the rent and food.' She looked down at her hands and her voice dropped. Looking up again into Ulrich's face she carried on. 'I had just crossed the square and was going to walk over the green – you know, where the cows and geese graze.'

Ulrich nodded.

'Well, there was this huge heap of branches and wood. All sorts... broken furniture, doors, mattresses... ready to be lit as a bonfire. At first, I was excited, thinking it was going to be some sort of celebration as there were lots of people around, then I saw men and women... some that I knew, Jewish people... tied up... being herded in through the East Gate, screaming and...' she closed her eyes and sat with a hand over her mouth.

Jerod leaned forward and held her other hand. He waited for her to go on.

'The next thing I remember was the fire being lit. Then the men started... prodding the Jews forward into the flames. It was terrible. The people were screaming... writhing and struggling to escape of course, and no-one tried to help them. I didn't know why this was happening and couldn't bear to watch the suffering of all these men, women... and children. I... I hurried to deliver my bundle of washing. Frau Olgen told me that the Jews were responsible for starting the plague and had to be exterminated. She seemed to think it was justified.'

Ulrich sat shaking his head. 'I suppose your priest thought it was the proper Christian thing to do too.' His mouth was clenched tight and turned down at the corners.

Marta hung her head. 'He was there at the burning. I thought he would be praying for their souls, but he was cursing them... calling them children of Satan.'

'And do you think that too?'

'Oh, no!' she shook her head vehemently. 'How could all of those nice, hard working people that we know be working for the devil? At least, I don't think so,' she hesitated. 'And... and all of those little children...' She burst into tears.

Ulrich rocked her in his arms. 'Do you know how many were killed?

'Someone told me the next day that there were three hundred Jews burned.'

'Three hundred!' he exclaimed, sitting back with mouth open.

'I was told that some were burned in their own homes which were set alight and the doorways barred, while others ran to their synagogue. I heard they'd set that alight themselves... and died by their own hand... rather than have the Council's men do it.'

'It's unimaginable. Horrifying.'

'It... It was a night I can't get out of my mind. I just stayed inside with the door barricaded but that didn't blot out the sounds of screaming.'

'You poor, poor darling.' He held her close. 'And those poor people,' added Ulrich with a deep sigh.

'I don't want to see that priest again,' said Marta angrily. 'Our Lady in heaven must have been weeping oceans that night. Just because they don't share our faith doesn't make them all bad, does it?'

Ulrich shook his head. 'I think everyone should be able to decide what they want to believe for themselves. I'm not a Roman Catholic. I believe in the old ways of living by nature. I work with the seasons and plant by the moon. My parents brought me up that way, I suppose, but it seems natural to me. Live and let live.'

'I don't really understand what you mean,' answered Marta, 'but if a man of the Church can be as sadistic as our priest, I don't want to be part of that faith anymore.'

Ulrich sat holding her for a long time.

*

Aaron had an unexpected visitor while Ulrich was in Cologne. He was busy tending the animals when King suddenly rose with a growl and ran to the stall door.

'Stay King,' ordered Aaron, and the dog obediently sat, but continued with a low rumbling growl.

A voice called, 'Farmer, farmer! Is anyone at home?'

Feeling very afraid, Aaron tiptoed out of the goats' stall and peeped around the door holding King back by the scruff of his neck. A pedlar was standing a little way away at the foot of the stairs looking around him.

'Oh, there you are. Do you have some water for a weary traveller? I have some trinkets here that might be of interest to you,' he continued, rummaging in his sack.

'Go on your way. I don't need any of your trinkets, ' shouted Aaron. 'Help yourself to water from the stream there.'

'Thank you, but won't you spare me a few minutes of your time?'

Aaron had a brainwave. 'I don't think you should come any nearer. We've had plague here. Five deaths already.'

'I'm sorry to hear that,' shouted back the pedlar. 'I'll just have a drink and rest for a short while if that's alright with you?'

'You're welcome, but I don't know how long I can hold this dog back. He doesn't like strangers.'

King gave a loud bark as though on cue, and Aaron watched the pedlar scuttle off to the stream where he had a long drink of water, splashed his face and head, and then hurried away in the direction of the nearest village.

The close encounter made Aaron realise how vulnerable he was without Ulrich's strong presence, but felt he'd been quick witted with his response to the stranger who hadn't had a good look at him.

The time passed pleasantly enough and there was plenty of work to keep him occupied, but there were times when he succumbed to grief. One of those was when he was collecting water from the stream in a large jug, and noticed at the back of the house five marked graves. He felt a stab of pain in his heart as he realised that he didn't know where his parents and sisters were buried. He fell to his knees on the hard ground and wept bitterly. King came and lay down beside him as if understanding his distress.

He was also aware that he wasn't following his Jewish religion as he used to. His new life was so busy with all the routines necessary just to keep the small farm going. Ulrich lived by the movement of the sun, moon and the seasons and worked closely with the elements. The church bells rang on a Sunday in the next village and that gave Aaron a pang of guilt as he realised that he should have kept his Jewish Shabbat the day before. He decided to keep a tally stick with cuts in the wood to mark the passing days. Then he would know when it was a Saturday. He would at least try to say his prayers. He'd always like the Sanctification of the Moon ceremony which usually took place at the full moon immediately after Shabbat. It was a celebration to honour the moon which represented the waxing and waning of the Jewish tribes throughout history. There had always been good food and dancing afterwards, he recalled.

Tailoring was something he realised he was missing too. Perhaps he could alter some of the clothing that Ulrich kept in the chest into something wearable. They'd need extra warm clothes soon as the weather was turning colder by the day.

In the living room, he knelt down, opened the heavy lid of the chest and lifted out the garments on top. They were some of Ulrich's clothes which he laid aside. Underneath were smaller shirts and breeches, woollen hats, mittens and some knitted stockings. He felt saddened by the sight of them. Next he lifted out a girl's smock. There was enough material in that to make a simple shirt or tunic, so he laid it to one side. Next there was an assortment of rather worn, adult clothes; shirts, breeches, a dress, a patched skirt and apron, a hooded cloak, shoes. Aaron sorted through the pile and kept his selected garments to one side. He'd ask Ulrich's approval when he returned.

He didn't have long to wait. He could hear King's happy barking outside and ran to the door. Yes, it was Ulrich in the cart making his way towards the yard. Aaron hurried down the stairs to greet him.

Ulrich gave a wave and gestured to him to open the door to the stables. Once the horse and cart were inside and Janus was taken out of the shafts, Ulrich smiled and asked, 'Would you give the horse a rub down and see to his feed? I'm going to unload the cart.'

'Yes. It's good to have you back.' Ulrich looked so tired that Aaron didn't want to pester him with questions, but he was desperate to ask about his family. 'I've got some stew cooking. I thought you'd need a proper meal,' he said to Ulrich's back.

Ulrich gave a small laugh. 'You sound just like a wife.'

They both worked away in companionable silence. Ulrich stacked the sacks in the food store and put the meat in the pantry.

'Come, I have a surprise for you,' he shouted over to Aaron who'd finished tending to Janus.

Throwing back the sacks, he revealed the feather bed and mattress. Aaron grinned from ear to ear.

'Well, they won't get upstairs by themselves,' Ulrich grunted. 'Come on, take an end.' So they carried the light but bulky straw mattress and feather quilt up to the living area above. 'Choose a bed then,' directed Ulrich and Aaron selected the alcove on the opposite side of the fire to Ulrich. The bedding was installed and Aaron jumped on top of the quilt and flung himself on to his back in delight at the soft comfort.

'Oh, thanks so much, Ulrich. This will be even warmer than lying in front of the fire.'

'You're welcome,' came the reply with a laugh. Ulrich's face turned serious however when he saw the pile of clothes lying to the side of the chest. 'What's going on here?' he demanded, pointing to the bundle.

'Oh, I was going to tell you my idea,' answered Aaron jumping up sharply.

'I thought I could make us some extra clothes for the winter out of some of the material here.' He looked up at Ulrich anxiously to see if he was angry. 'I-I didn't mean to upset you. I just thought it was sensible to use what we...' he trailed off.

Ulrich patted him on the shoulder. 'It's all right my friend. That's a good idea. It was just a shock seeing my family's things lying there.' He sighed. 'But,' he said, brightening, 'if you go down to the cart, you'll find something else that I bought for you.'

Aaron didn't need to be told twice. He ran down the stairs with King at his heels and shouted with joy when he saw the bolt of cloth. 'I can make *new* things for us now!' He hurried up the stairs with his armful and thumped it down on the table.

'Hey, wait a bit,' said Ulrich with a laugh, 'I want that stew you promised before you start sewing.'

CHAPTER FOUR

Winter Celebrations

Aaron's first winter on the farm was long and hard. Snow started falling early and on many days Ulrich was unable to travel to the nearby village to sell his goat's milk and eggs. He bought bread, butter and cheese at the local market there when he could, and any other items which were needed. As there was nothing to be done in the fields, he took over the care of the animals to let Aaron have the time to cut and sew new clothes for them both. He was quietly proud of his young Jewish friend and admired his skilful tailoring. The days were dark and the shutters had to be kept closed to keep the house warm, so Aaron burned many candles while he stitched.

One day, Ulrich announced. 'It is time for the Midwinter celebrations. We shall have a feast and give thanks for our food and warmth.'

Aaron piped up, 'Oh, that reminds me, we always used to celebrate Hanukkah around this time too.'

'What's Hanukkah?'

'Well, it's a special Jewish festival that lasts for eight days. We have a particular candlestick called a menorah or hanukkiyah, which holds nine candles, and one is lit each day. We sing and give blessings, oh, and there's lots of food.' They both laughed,

Ulrich thought for a moment. 'How about joining the two celebrations? If you draw me a picture of your candlestick, I'll try to make one for you.'

Aaron nodded enthusiastically.

'Tomorrow, we'll go into the wood and choose a tree to cut down for our Yule Log. Then I'll slaughter one of the goats and we'll have the meat for our feast along with some pheasants.'

*

The next morning dawned crisp and cold with a pale, watery sun. Ulrich and Aaron set off with a sledge and the axe to the bordering woodland with King bounding alongside. Ulrich led them to where he had previously cut down a suitable tree and left it to season earlier in the year. They took turns at cutting off the branches with the axe and then selected part of the trunk as their Yule log. With much exertion, they chopped that off, then dragged it on to the sledge and pulled it all the way back to the yard over the snow.

'Now we've to get this up the stairs,' puffed Ulrich.

'Oh,' panted Aaron. 'How are we ever going to manage that?'

'Well, my father rigged up a pulley system to make it easier as we did this each year, so it won't be as bad as you expected,' and he laughed at the look of relief on Aaron's face. Going into the storeroom, he brought out a heavy rope and strong netting. With Aaron's help, he manhandled the netting around the log and tied the rope to it. He then walked up the stairs and fitted the rope around a pulley wheel above the doorway which Aaron had never noticed before. The long end of the rope then dangled down to the ground at the side of the stairs. Ulrich ran down and grabbed the rope.

'Right Aaron. You push and guide the log up the stairs while I pull from down here.'

It took some time amid much hilarity, but they finally pushed the log into the living room. The net was pulled off and snow brushed away.

'We'll drag it over nearer the fire to dry off, and tomorrow, we'll put it in the fireplace. It should burn for days,' said Ulrich, hands on hips and satisfied.

Starving after their exertions, the two enjoyed a meal of thickly sliced bread and cheese with some ale heated on the fire.

'Draw me a picture of your candlestick thing,' directed Ulrich afterwards, handing Aaron a twig and pointing to the floor.

Aaron smoothed over some dirt on the floorboards and drew a likeness of a menorah candlestick with the sharp twig.

'Hm... that looks complicated... but I'll think of something. Perhaps I could somehow bend some metal. I think we have some metal rails in the store room. Let's go and look.'

He found the thin metal rails but couldn't bend them very much; not enough to make the curves of the menorah.

'I'll take them into the village tomorrow and visit the blacksmith. Maybe he can heat the metal and beat it into shape for me.'

The candlestick was duly made, but the blacksmith was curious about it.

'I've never seen a candlestick like this before. Why did you want one like it?' he'd asked Ulrich.

'Oh, it's just like something I saw once in *Koln* and liked it,' he'd replied vaguely.

'Bit fancy if you ask me,' said the smith.

Aaron was delighted with the candlestick however, and immediately set it on the table. 'It should really be in a window, but we better not attract attention. We can celebrate Hanukkah starting tomorrow,' and he grinned.

'What does this Hanukkah mean?' asked Ulrich.

'Well, I remember my father telling me that at one time, people called Syrians had taken over the Temple in Jerusalem and Jewish revolutionaries won it back and wanted to rededicate it to God. The people needed eight days worth of oil for the purification rituals but could only find enough for one day. God granted them a miracle, and the oil lasted for eight days. That's why we have eight candles.'

'I can see nine candle holders.'

'Yes, the central one is called the Shamash and we use that one to light all the others. I'll show you tomorrow when we start our celebrations.'

*

Aaron was excited next morning as they both helped to set the Yule log alight. Ulrich told him that the tradition was to ensure that they'd always have fuel to see them through the winter. They sat back on their heels and stared as the flames leapt and crackled, giving out a welcome heat.

'After breaking our fast, we'll go out to the woods again. I'll show you another tradition that I follow,' said Ulrich.

'What is your religion called?' questioned Aaron.

'Religion?' Ulrich thought for a moment. ' I don't think it is a religion. Well, we don't worship a male God like you. We see the Divine in all the things around us. The sky, sun, moon and stars, the land, trees, birds and animals, the changing seasons; all are sacred. We honour the land and all it provides and give thanks for our food and homes. We give offerings of grain and fruits after the harvest to God and Goddess and light a bonfire at the winter solstice to ward off evil spirits and welcome the light so that the Spring will come again.'

Aaron took this in. 'Do you have a holy book like The Talmud?'

Ulrich laughed. 'No, I don't need a book to tell me to be grateful when the sun shines or the rain falls. I try to live in tune with the natural order of things.'

'Will we be building a bonfire today?'

'Yes, my friend. We'll light a big fire and dance and sing and give thanks for our lives. We are both very lucky, you and I,' Ulrich nodded, 'unlike our families.'

They both sat deep in thought until King gave them a nudge and whined to go out.

'Come on, let's get some food and then get on with our celebrations,' said Ulrich as he opened the door for King.

*

They spent the morning gathering wood and building a large bonfire.

'We'll light it later in the afternoon, when it's almost dark,' stated Ulrich. 'We need to get back to the house soon to start cooking our feast, but before that, we have something else to do. Follow me.'

Aaron followed, wondering what exciting thing was about to be revealed. Ulrich led him into the storeroom where he located some twine and dragged two wooden boxes over and sat down on one.

'Could you run up to the house and bring some bread down – stale if we have any,' directed Ulrich.

Aaron nodded and ran off, wondering what that was needed for. He came back with half of a small loaf.

'Perfect,' said Ulrich, smiling. 'Now, I'll cut chunks of bread and your job will be to thread it on to pieces of string. Tie a knot in the end, like this,' he said, showing Aaron what to do. 'We're going to hang these up for the birds as an offering. It's difficult for them to find enough food when the ground is frozen hard or covered in snow.'

Aaron thought this was a great plan and set about creating strings of bread and crusts for the birds.

'Next, we'll put out some fat as well,' said Ulrich.

'What about some apples? We have plenty, don't we?' suggested Aaron.

'Yes, that's a good idea,' and Ulrich smiled.

So they busied themselves creating the thoughtful offerings, which they placed in a basket and carried back to the wood beside the bonfire.

'Where shall we put the strings?' enquired Aaron.

'They get hung on the trees,' and Ulrich proceeded to show how to hang the strands for the birds around the lower branches.

*

The afternoon was spent preparing meat and vegetables and the aroma of cooking kept King hovering hopefully near the fireplace. Even the tomcat, who usually stayed in the storeroom, bolted inside when Aaron opened the door to go downstairs to fetch water. He was enticed by the smell of roasting meat and the heat from the Yule log burning in the grate. King gave a warning growl, but the cat ignored him and curled up near the fireplace quietly watching the goat fat dripping from the spit, and at the same time keeping an eye on the dog.

'Shall I light the Hanukkah candle now?' asked Aaron eagerly after checking that all the food was cooking nicely.

'Yes, that's a good idea,' answered Ulrich. 'And why don't we change into something new that you've made. It is a special occasion after all.'

In a short while, dressed in new breeches and tunics and looking suitably solemn, they approached the table where Aaron had placed the candlestick. He picked up a candle, put it in the central holder and lit it with a taper from the fire. He said a prayer in Yiddish and then took another candle and placed it in the rightmost position of the menorah.

Lifting the central Shamash, he used it to light the candle on the right. He then recited blessings which he translated for Ulrich to mean, '*Blessed are You, O Lord our God, Ruler of the Universe who has sanctified us with your commandments and commanded us to kindle the lights of Hanukkah. Blessed are You, O Lord our God, Ruler of the Universe, who made miracles for our forefathers in those days at this time. Blessed are you, O Lord our God, Ruler of the Universe, who has kept us alive, sustained us and brought us to this season.*'

'Thank you,' said Ulrich, giving a small bow.

'Now we can begin our feast,' replied Aaron, grinning at Ulrich. 'I'll get platters and you can pour us some ale.'

Ulrich genially did as he was bid. They both hacked some meat off the spit, then each took a roasted pheasant as well to the table, along with carrots and turnips and apples. Aaron asked if he could say a short prayer of thanks before they ate and Ulrich agreed. They bowed for a short grace, but were anxious to get stuck into the heaped platters before them.

After a few moments of silent eating enjoyment, Ulrich proposed a toast.

'To absent friends and family,' he announced and clinked his tankard with Aaron's.

'To absent friends and family,' repeated Aaron, his smile disappearing for a moment. Then he straightened and grinning stated, 'To new beginnings.'

'New beginnings,' affirmed Ulrich with a nod. They clinked tankards again and gulped down some ale.

They threw some bones and scraps to King who'd been patiently waiting, salivating and giving the occasional whine in case he was forgotten.

'It's all right. I wouldn't forget you, King,' said Ulrich ruffling his thick coat. 'And here's something for you too Cat,' he said and threw the pheasant carcasses onto the floor. They were pounced on instantly with much loud purring.

When the young men had eaten their fill, they both agreed that their feast had been a great success.

They rested by the fire for a while, quaffing more ale and dozing pleasantly until Ulrich stretched and announced that it was time he attended to the animals.

Aaron rose and cleared away the remains of the meat and took a covered plate of it down to the pantry. He carried a bucket of water upstairs from the stream to heat in the kettle on the fire, and when it was ready, washed up the dishes.

'Get your warm cloak on then. It's time to light our bonfire,' announced Ulrich when the chores were finished.

With a feeling of anticipation, they hurried down the steps carrying a branch each which they'd set alight in the fire. King accompanied them, barking excitedly. The evening air was icy with frost sparkling around them on the snow lit up by the torches. They scrunched their way through the white landscape to the wood and their prepared pile of dry branches which waited in the silence.

Upon reaching the clearing, Ulrich raised his lighted torch and declared,' I light this fire to drive away the evil spirits of darkness. I give thanks to God and Goddess for my bounty and ask that Spring may come again after the long sleep of Winter.' With that, he bent down and set alight the twigs at the base of the bonfire pile.

Aaron felt he should say something too and clearing his throat, he called out, 'Thank you that I have a home and a friend.' He turned smiling and red-faced towards Ulrich, feeling a bit embarrassed, but Ulrich gave him a playful shove and gestured that he throw his burning stick into the fire.

They stood watching the flames blaze up, crackling and sparking in the freezing air. 'The salamanders will work their magic and bring the light back next year,' said Ulrich, pursing his lips and nodding.

'Salamanders?'

'Yes. They are the purifying spirits in the fire,' he said quietly. 'They help those who respect the land and love nature.'

Aaron's brow furrowed but he said nothing. He admired Ulrich and although his beliefs were different from his own, he liked the idea of working with natural forces.

Suddenly, Ulrich stamped his feet then started to sing and dance his way around the bonfire. 'Come on, join in,' he shouted to his companion.

Aaron didn't know Ulrich's song, but he copied his dance with happy abandonment and they both laughed and rollicked around for a while as the fire burned merrily. King joined in the fun and capered about in the snow like a pup.

When the flames had diminished to a glow of red embers, they decided to return to the warmth of their Yule log fire in the house. As they climbed the stairs, Ulrich pointed into the distance. 'There's a fire over there... and there. Some other families are celebrating Midwinter. Brrr, let's get inside.'

CHAPTER FIVE

Marta

In *Koln*, Marta was finding life a struggle during the winter months. She took in washing and mending from some of the richer families in the city to give her a little income, but it didn't pay much. She needed lots of firewood to keep the fire burning in order to have hot water for washing as well as heat for herself and for cooking. Food was scarce as so many people had died of the plague that the trading had diminished considerably. She felt very lonely and fearful and longed for the weather to improve so that Ulrich could travel to visit her again.

One dark afternoon, she was returning after having delivered laundry to a house on the other side of town, when two dark-skinned men loomed out from a tavern doorway and lurched drunkenly towards her. Marta felt every nerve end tighten and quickly turned in order to escape down another street, but the men were tall and strong and one jumped ahead of her, barring her way with arms outstretched.

'No go run, pretty lady,' he growled, grinning and baring yellowed teeth.

'Let me past,' Marta shouted, dodging from side to side, trying to find a way around his menacing stance. His stinking breath was in her face.

The second man behind grabbed her waist and lifted her off the ground. Her basket fell from her grasp. She screamed and beat out with her fists but the men were much bigger and heavier than she was and the blows were useless. Laughing, they shoved her into an alleyway and forced her down to the freezing ground.

'Whore!' called one, as he knelt astride her and threw her skirts up over her head, while the other man pinned her arms.

Marta's muffled screams went unheeded as they took it in turn to use her in the cruellest manner.

When it was over, she heard them laugh and talk in some foreign tongue as they shuffled away, and then there was silence. She lay, shaking and sobbing. Pushing her skirts back into place she tried to stand up. Wet, cold, dirty and sore with lying on the ice covered cobbles, she staggered to her feet and stood against a wall until her breathing steadied. Terrified, she retrieved her basket and limped stiffly home, each step giving her pain. Once inside, she built up the fire and heated kettle after kettle of water to fill her bathtub then immersed herself in warm suds. The heat did little to ease the pain deep inside her. Her wrists were red from being held down and her back was bruised from the hard cobblestones. It seemed that no amount of scrubbing could get rid of the smell and feel of the loathsome men. Tears streamed down her cheeks at the memory of the indignity, pain and fear that she had endured.

'Holy Mary Mother of God,' she began to pray, but unable to continue, sobbed, 'Ulrich, oh Ulrich,' longing for him to be with her.

*

It was springtime before the roads were passable into *Koln*. Ulrich was desperate to see Marta again and was happily packing the cart ready for his journey. Aaron wished he could go with him. He was feeling very confined after spending the long winter months cooped up on the farm.

'I won't be away for long. There's so much to do in the fields now,' said Ulrich trying to comfort Aaron. 'You are a great help here. I know I can leave everything in your care.'

Aaron nodded but gave a sigh. 'I just miss my family so much and the hustle and bustle of city life – meeting people, the market, the synagogue, and... and Satis.' It was the first time he had mentioned her name to Ulrich who raised his eyebrows.

'Satis? You haven't mentioned her before. I take it, it's a 'her'? Was she your sweetheart?'

Aaron reddened. 'Um... not really. She... she was just a friend, but... I think in time, she could have been more.'

Ulrich moved to bring out the horse.

'Please don't think I'm ungrateful, Ulrich,' Aaron called after him. 'I like it here. I just felt a bit imprisoned during the winter and now that the weather is better, I'd love to be able to go into the village to have a look around or go with you to *Koln*, but I daren't.'

'I know. I know. I'm sorry,' replied Ulrich. 'Here am I getting all excited about seeing Marta again, and you are left here with only King and the goats for company. What can I bring you? I'm so sorry it won't be your Satis.'

Aaron shrugged and gave another sigh. 'Some new cloth would be good and sewing threads. I could do with new boots too. These ones are done.' He lifted up a foot to show Ulrich the worn-down sole.

'I'll see what I can do. It will depend what traders are at the market. Let's hope the plague has gone now and the merchants are bringing in their goods. There's sure to be a cobbler though and I need to stock up on foodstuffs and candles.'

He was soon ready to go and gave Aaron a swift hug then ruffled King's ears.

'Look after our friend, won't you, King,' he instructed the dog, who gave an answering bark as though in affirmation.

Ulrich had his usual two-day journey with overnight stop in the woodland to reach Cologne. He was anxious to meet with Marta again and pictured her lovely face as he trundled along in the cart. The market place was quiet for its size, much as before with only a few traders. The plague had obviously taken its toll of the population. He bought the household essentials and found a cobbler with boots and shoes for sale, so purchased new boots for himself and for Aaron. There was no sign of the colourful foreign mercer with all his materials so sadly Ulrich couldn't get any cloth this time for Aaron. He bought some dainty sweet cakes for Marta and headed off to the inn. Once the horse and cart were deposited with the stable lad, Ulrich gave his face and hands a sluice at the pump and made for Marta's house.

He knocked at the door, lifted the latch and tried to open the door, but it was stuck fast with something heavy.

'Marta, Marta are you inside? It's me, Ulrich,' he called.

'Oh, Ulrich, Ulrich. Thank heavens you're here at last,' came the answering cry as Marta ran towards the door.

There was the sound of something heavy being moved from behind it until it could open enough for Ulrich to squeeze through. 'Whatever has happened? What's the ma...' His question was cut off by Marta throwing herself into his arms and bursting into tears. He led her over to a chair and set her down. She clung on to his arm.

'Tell me what's happened,' Ulrich entreated.

Marta took a deep breath and wiped her eyes. 'I... I was attacked.'

'What! When was this?' shouted Ulrich standing up, ready to defend her.

'Oh, it was two or three moons ago now, I can't quite remember, but I'm frightened to go out. I am afraid that the men will find me and try to get me again.'

'Men! So there was more than one!'

'Yes, there were two of them. In their cups,' she added.

After a moment Ulrich enquired, 'Did they... you know... hurt you?'

Marta kept her head down, but gave an almost imperceptible nod.

'Oh, no! You poor thing!' Ulrich shouted and put his arms around her shoulders. 'What did they look like?' He stiffened. 'I'll sort the scum out for you.'

'No, no, my dear man. They'll be long gone. They were seafarers. It's just that the attack has left me so fearful, not having my father here anymore and you so far away. I hate living here on my own, almost unable to go outside for kindling or foodstuff.'

'Right, that's it decided. You're coming back to the farm with me. I'll be able to look after you properly there!'

'Marta stared at him open-mouthed. 'Oh, Ulrich. Are you sure? What will the priest say?'

'Priest? I don't answer to any priest. Has he offered you any assistance? Has your church helped you?'

'N... no, but then, I haven't been attending services since... you know... the burning.'

'All the more reason for him to come to visit you, to see if there's something wrong.'

'Oh no. I would likely be put in the stocks or worse, if it got out that I'd been ravaged.'

'What? When it wasn't your fault? That's it definitely decided then. You are coming with me. Get your things together, I'm going for the horse and cart.'

Ulrich soothed Marta and left her busily putting clothes into a bundle and gathering food and candles together. He stood with his eyes screwed shut and his fists clenching and unclenching. How dare anyone hurt his darling Marta in such a way! If only he could get his hands on them!

He soon returned with the cart having given the stable boy a shock at his sudden reappearance. Marta had her things ready.

'Can I bring my feather quilt and some of my dishes, and perhaps a chair?' she asked.

'Of course. You can bring whatever we can fit into the cart, even if it's piled high,' answered Ulrich kindly. He packed her bundles and belongings as neatly as he could.

'Is that everything you want to take?' he asked finally when Marta stopped bringing goods.

'Yes, there's nothing else here that I need.'

'Have one last look around the place in case, while I put out the fire,' instructed Ulrich as he kicked ashes into the embers. 'We'll go to your landlord and let him know that you won't be back. I'll pay any rent that's due.'

Marta nodded and had a last wander around with a heavy heart, but at the same time she was so relieved to be going. 'Farewell house, thank you for sheltering me over the years,' she whispered. 'I'm off to start a new life now.'

CHAPTER SIX

A New Life

Aaron was milking the goats when King began to bark and wag his tail, rushing backwards and forwards, trying to get Aaron to follow him.

'What is it boy? Surely it can't be Ulrich already.' He opened the shed door and King bounded out joyously to meet his master arriving with the horse and cart.

'What on earth...? Who is this?' muttered Aaron aloud, when he saw the piles of bundles and sacks in the cart. Then it dawned on him. It must be Marta he was seeing seated next to Ulrich. His stomach turned over and he felt his heart drop. Ulrich wouldn't need him now. He'd have a wife.

'Aaron, come and meet Marta,' Ulrich shouted as he jumped down from the seat of the cart. 'I'll explain later,' he said hurriedly into Aaron's ear. Stretching an arm up to help Marta to the ground, he put his arm around her shoulder and edged her towards Aaron. 'Marta, this is Aaron, the friend I told you about, who lives here on the farm.'

She put out her hand shyly and Aaron shook it and nodded to her.

'Let's get you inside. You just go up with Aaron and I'll bring in the things.'

Aaron was feeling a bit put out already. From the look of all the stuff in the cart, she was here to stay. Where would she sleep? Was she going to take over the running of the house? Could she cook? He stomped up the stairs without a word and Marta followed quietly behind. Opening the door he walked in first, rather rudely, and immediately regretted his actions. His father would have been appalled at his lack of manners to a lady. Turning quickly, he smiled to her and said, 'This is where we cook, eat and sleep.'

'It's a big room,' Marta answered, looking around. She was feeling awkward and knew that Aaron was feeling the same. 'I'm sorry to arrive unexpectedly like this. Ulrich will explain I'm sure. Something smells good. You must have been cooking?'

Aaron nodded. 'It's just some soup. There should be enough for three though.'

'That sounds good. I'm cold and tired after the journey so that will do for supper.'

Ulrich appeared in the doorway, struggling with the quilt and some bundles. 'Oh, good. You're getting to know each other. Sit by the fire and rest, Marta. Aaron, could you give me a hand to unpack the cart please?'

Aaron gave a tight-lipped nod and ran downstairs behind Ulrich. 'What's going on?' he hissed. 'You never mentioned that you were thinking of bringing her here!'

'I wasn't – at least not at that moment. However, when I got to her home she was in a terrible state. She'd been attacked and raped and was terrified living on her own.'

'Oh!' was all that Aaron could say. The hostility he'd been feeling was starting to drain away. 'How awful.'

'She'll live with me as my wife. I'm sure you'll like her,' said Ulrich, thrusting a chair into Aaron's arms.

'Well, if you care about her so much, she must be nice,' conceded Aaron with a grin. 'It will be good to have a woman to do the cooking and cleaning for a change.'

'Perhaps, but don't think you're going to be shirking, young friend. You can help me more in the fields now, ' he returned with a playful punch.

*

Aaron had to adjust quite a lot to having Marta live with them. From the start, she took over the cleaning, food preparation and cooking. It wasn't that she was bossy, but she had the womanly confidence of having looked after a household for years and seemed happy to look after the two men. Aaron struggled with his feelings over the first few weeks. He was pleased not to have to do these 'women's tasks' any more but at the same time was a bit jealous of her efficiency. She could do everything so much better than he ever did. He liked the way the house was always clean and tidy and it was good to have her new recipes to vary their diet instead of the same old soups and stews that he'd made.

Marta was quiet and hardworking and always had a smile. King allowed her to pet him and rolled over to have his tummy rubbed each time she tickled him. Aaron was annoyed with himself that he felt jealous of this. He felt betrayed by the dog. He knew it was stupid but couldn't help his emotions. He felt bad as Marta was always kind to him too.

'Ulrich has told me about what happened to your family,' she said quietly one day while she lightly kneaded dough for pastry on the table. 'I was there on that terrible night, so I know what took place. I am so sorry for what my people have done to your people.'

Aaron sat thoughtfully for a few moments. 'Do you think anyone else could have escaped? Apart from me, I mean.'

'Well, I don't know. I suppose it is quite possible. There are many roads out of *Koln* and there is the river Rhine of course. Was there someone in particular you were thinking of?'

'No, no,' he said hurriedly. 'I just wondered if you'd heard of any other Jews anywhere.'

'All I've heard is that Jews have been driven out of the towns now. Many fled to Poland and surrounding countries I believe. I've never been out of *Koln* until now, so I have no idea where Poland is.'

'Me neither,' said Aaron with a shrug. 'Well, I better go and attend to the animals. I have more time to clean their stalls now that I don't have to clean this room and clear out the ashes and set the fire.'

Marta laughed.

'Come on, King. Let's go,' and off he went feeling a bit unsettled.

*

Night times were awkward for Aaron. From the start, Marta shared Ulrich's bed. Aaron thought it was so that he could comfort her and keep her warm but from the sounds that issued from their corner of the room, it was soon evident that they were having more than just a cuddle. Aaron hid under the feather quilt covering his ears, trying to shut out the grunts and moans. It stirred up feelings in him that he didn't quite know how to deal with.

One day, a few weeks later, Marta quietly announced to them that she was with child. Ulrich was overjoyed and hugged her to him. 'Now we'll be like a real family.' He looked at Marta. 'You are my woman.' He looked over at Aaron, 'You are like a brother to me, and now we are to have a child.'

Aaron felt a glow inside. *'You are like a brother to me,'* Ulrich had said to him. That meant a lot.

'A strange family indeed,' said Marta, laughing. 'A Pagan, a lapsed Roman Catholic and a lapsed Jew.' They all joined in the laughter.

King barked happily as if to say, 'Don't forget me!'

'Oh, and a beautiful hound as well,' cooed Marta, holding King's face between her hands and planting a kiss upon his head.

*

As the days grew longer, Aaron spent more time helping Ulrich outside in the fields as well as doing his share of looking after the animals and chopping wood for the winter woodpile. The fire was still needed each day for cooking but it wasn't kept burning all night long.

Through conversation, Marta had discovered that Aaron was a tailor and expressed her own fondness for needlework. She had a supply of coloured cotton thread and a rag bag of mixed materials. Producing some lengths of lightweight cloth which she'd previously intended for turning into bedcovers, she asked Aaron if he'd make her a loose overdress to accommodate her expanding waistline. He willingly agreed and set to work cutting out the simple shapes. Marta meanwhile fashioned some soft baby nightdresses and bonnets and embroidered them prettily.

Ulrich was making a wooden cradle for the baby and worked on it in the lighter evenings. He chiselled and carved and finally produced a beautiful crib on rockers. Marta was thrilled.

'I'll make some soft covers for our baby,' she declared.

'I can give you some feathers and goats' wool to fill a small quilt,' added Aaron.

'Wonderful,' exclaimed Marta.

Everyone was delighted at the prospect of the forthcoming baby which Ulrich presumed would be arriving in the winter. When he asked

Marta when she thought she would be due to give birth, she just gave a vague reply indicating later in the year.

She often accompanied Ulrich on his trips into the next village to sell the milk and eggs. The villagers assumed they were married and accepted Marta who was always friendly and helpful. Ulrich asked her to find out which of the women assisted at births so he could contact her when required. This she did.

Aaron always felt envious whenever Marta went off in the cart with Ulrich. He so longed to be able to see what was outside the few acres of farmland which meanwhile imprisoned him.

One day, I'll leave here and travel the world. Perhaps I'll even find Poland, he thought.

*

The summer was long and hot that year and the crops ripened well. Ulrich and Aaron, who spent hours working outdoors, looked tanned and healthy. Marta became increasingly uncomfortable and liked to sit in the shade in the afternoons, easing her swollen feet in the stream.

'I think it would be a good idea to have a bed to yourself,' announced Ulrich one evening. 'It will give you more space and you can get up if you need to during the night without disturbing me.'

So from then on, Marta had her own bed.

One day, at the very end of the summer, Ulrich was out early in the fields forking the hay into stacks. Aaron had just milked the goats and put them out to graze and was leading the horse outside to his pasture when he heard Marta calling him frantically.

He rushed up the stairs, through the open door to find her doubled up in pain.

'What's the matter? Are you ill?' he blurted.

Marta straightened up and took some deep breaths. 'It must be the baby coming. The pains... they're really strong.'

'But I thought you weren't due to birth until the winter,' exclaimed Aaron, eyes wide. 'I'll go and fetch Ulrich.'

'No, no, don't leave me alone,' shouted Marta as she was gripped by another spasm. 'I'm so frightened.'

'I can't go into the village for the midwife. I wouldn't know where to go anyway.'

'You'll have to... stay... with me,' Marta panted. 'Oh, no, here's another pain. They're coming... so quickly,' and she doubled over in agony.

Aaron was panic stricken. It wasn't seemly for a man to be with a woman during childbirth. Marta was leaning over the end of the table now, groaning loudly. Then she called out as warm water spurted down her legs. 'Oh, something has happened... there's water... I'm all wet!'

'What can I do to help you?' asked Aaron shakily, handing her a drying cloth. He felt her embarrassment, but was terrified of the forthcoming birth. 'Should you be in bed or something?' He was desperately trying to remember what had happened during his mother's confinement, but had no memory of it as he'd been looked after by a family friend at the time.

'I... can't... move,' she yelled. 'I think it's coming NOW. I want to push it out.'

'Oh, God, please help us,' entreated Aaron. 'What'll I do, Marta?'

She was bent forward over the table, her knuckles white from gripping the sides. 'Lift up my skirts at the back,' she gasped. 'Is there something... to catch the baby?' She let out a long scream of agony which paralysed Aaron for a moment then he sprang into action, grabbing her shawl from the back of a chair. He lifted up her skirts tentatively, averting his eyes and trying not to look at her bare backside.

'Holy Mother Mary, help me,' screamed Marta as another contraction forced her to strain. 'Aaaaaaaah.'

Aaron looked in amazement as a baby's head appeared between her legs. 'It's coming out, it's coming out,' he shouted excitedly.

Marta was soaking with sweat and gasping from the exertion. Her knees buckled. 'Oh, no ... here it comes again, ' she wailed as her attention was focused once more upon the agonising pain which felt as though it would tear her in half. 'Aaaaaaaaaaah!' she roared as she summoned her strength and pushed with all her might.

With a suddenness which took Aaron by surprise, the baby slithered out in a purple mess and he just managed to catch it in the shawl before it hit the floor.

Marta sank to her knees, sobbing, and Aaron handed her the baby. It was a little boy with dark hair, covered all over in blood and a whitish slime.

'I'll get a clean cloth to wipe him... and I'll bring you a pillow,' he gushed. He was feeling dizzy with the excitement. *I've helped at a birth,* he thought. *I saw that little baby being born!*

He made Marta more comfortable on the floor with pillows and gave her a cloth to wipe the tiny baby clean. It was whimpering but when its mouth and nose were cleaned it gave a lusty yell.

Marta and Aaron however, were immobile with shock. The baby boy was black skinned.

*

While Aaron was recovering from the realisation that the baby couldn't possibly be Ulrich's, Marta suddenly doubled up in pain again.

'What's happening now?' she cried out. 'It can't be another baby!'

It soon became evident however that it was just a lump of flesh-like substance to which the cord was attached. Neither she nor Aaron knew anything about an afterbirth.

'Cut that cord Aaron, and tie a knot,' directed Marta. 'I think that's what to do.'

Aaron ran for his scissors and did as he was bid, feeling clumsy and inefficient.

'Now throw that mess on the fire please,' said Marta wrinkling up her nose in distaste. 'Could you heat up some more water please and I'll wash myself before Ulrich comes home?'

The baby was mewling and searching for food. 'I'll try to feed him,' she said turning aside and putting the baby to her breast. He did not latch on to her nipple at first, but she kept trying to lead him to the source of nourishment and finally, he succeeded with noisy suckling. He was soon satisfied and Marta swaddled him in a soft binder.

Aaron dragged the bathtub over in front of the fire and gradually filled it with hot then cold water to bring it to a comfortable temperature.

'I'll go outside while you undress and have your wash. Shall I take the baby for you just now?'

'Thank you, Aaron. I am so grateful to you. I don't know how I would have got through that without you. Put him into the cradle. He should sleep after his birth ordeal. Goodness knows, I could sleep right now.'

Aaron placed the already sleeping child tenderly into the cradle and laid a soft coverlet over him. He then left the house and went downstairs into the fresh air and sunshine. He felt elated and somehow connected to that tiny scrap of humanity indoors. What was going to happen when Ulrich returned? How come the baby was black? Was there something wrong with it or was the father a black man? He recalled the foreign mercer who sold the silks and satins at the market. His skin was dark too. Perhaps the father came from a far-off land like his merchant friend.

He walked around thinking and looking out for Ulrich until he felt he'd given Marta long enough to have her bath. He was just about to return upstairs when he saw Ulrich emerge from the woods and start towards the farmhouse.

'Ulrich, Ulrich,' he shouted. 'Hurry up,' and beckoned to his friend.

Ulrich tried to run but he was so tired he couldn't move fast. 'What is it?' he panted as he drew nearer. 'Has something happened?'

'Marta's had the baby.'

'What!'

'It's a boy.'

Ulrich stood with his mouth open for a few seconds then let out a yell of delight and with renewed vigour, took the stairs two at a time. 'A son, I have a son!' he shouted.

Aaron followed him up the stairs, anxious to see how he would react.

Ulrich looked around when he entered the room and saw that Marta was lying in her nightclothes on top of her bed covers. 'Marta, Marta are you alright?' He ran over and embraced her.

She gave him a weak smile and nodded in the direction of the cradle. Ulrich stepped over to peep inside and his face changed immediately. He gasped. 'What...what is this? How... how?' Then it dawned on him. 'So this blackamoor child is the result of you being ravaged! You never mentioned that the men were black!'

'Please Ulrich, it wasn't my fault,' pleaded Marta. 'And the little one can't help it.'

Ulrich was not to be pacified however. 'That... that blackamoor will never be called a son of mine. I want nothing to do with it – or *you* now for that matter.'

Aaron and Marta were both shocked. Marta burst into tears.

'Ulrich, you're just upset. It's not like you to be so angry,' said Aaron trying to soothe his friend. 'You know it isn't Marta who's to blame.'

Ulrich just stood for a moment, furious, then turned and marched out of the door and down the stairs. Aaron ran after him but Ulrich turned on him.

'Don't follow me! If you like the child so much, you can have him,' he flung back angrily, then his shoulders slumped and he staggered into the storeroom. 'Leave me be. Leave me. I'm going to blot out this day with ale.'

Aaron was bewildered. He'd never known Ulrich to be so angry. What would happen to Marta and the child now? He ran back upstairs and tried his best to comfort the distraught mother.

'Have a sup of this warmed goat's milk,' he said, offering a bowl to Marta when she had stopped sobbing. 'You should try to get some sleep. Your little one will be needing fed before long. I remember what it was like when my sisters were babies.'

Marta smiled to him. 'You are so kind, Aaron. Thank you for being there today.' She sipped the comforting milk. 'I had some pains on and off during the night but I didn't think the baby was coming yet. He's very small. I think he has come early.'

'Early or not, he's here and he seems strong. He yelled loud enough when he was born.'

'That's true... and he sucked his milk strongly enough too,' she answered as she remembered.

'He's beautiful,' said Aaron looking at the sleeping baby, 'even if he is bl... not like us,' he added hurriedly. 'I will be happy to help you look after him.'

Marta's eyes brimmed with tears again at his kindness.

CHAPTER SEVEN

The Visit

The autumn winds brought the rain and days became shorter. Ulrich and Aaron worked hard picking apples, plums and blackberries to store for the winter. The apples were laid out in shallow, wooden trays, not touching, and the blackberries were turned into a preserve, boiled with honey and tipped into large stone jars. Some of the berries were eaten of course as were the plums. The plums were mainly stewed and mixed with honey and also stored in stone jars and kept in the pantry. Marta often baked fruit pies while they had so much available.

'I must try to find some spices next time we go to the market,' she mentioned one evening. 'My mother used to add some to her apple pastries to give more flavour.'

'You won't be going to the market again,' declared Ulrich. 'At least, not with me.'

Marta was stunned. Ulrich hardly spoke to her these days, but he'd never voiced that she couldn't join him if she wanted. She'd stayed at home because of her son when Ulrich took the eggs and milk into the village to sell, but had assumed that when the child was weaned she would resume her trips.

'You can stay here over the winter months in exchange for cooking and cleaning the house, but I want you and that half-caste child out come the Spring.'

Aaron was shocked to hear Ulrich sound so cruel. He shook his head and looked sadly at the baby who was lying crooning happily on the rug. King curled beside him as a devoted minder.

'King, come here,' muttered Ulrich and the dog obediently went to his side. The two left the room and disappeared down the stairs.

'I don't know what's got into him these days,' said Aaron shaking his head again. 'I thought her cared about you.'

'So did I,' returned Marta. 'I'm sure he did, once. Somehow this baby being dark skinned has really upset him. I know he was so looking forward to having a son of his own to bring up on the farm. Do you think other men will hate little Moor too?'

Somehow the name, Moor, had been arrived at as that was how Ulrich referred to him on the rare occasions that he spoke about him. He was then either a blackamoor or just a moor.

'I don't know what others will think,' said Aaron truthfully, 'but I think he is fun. He grows and changes almost every day.'

He was indeed a beautiful baby with his mother's startling blue eyes but with dark curling hair. He seemed content and rarely cried and was adored by Marta and Aaron. Ulrich on the other hand ignored him. He had taken to walking into the village of an evening and sometimes stayed away overnight. When he came home again, he stank of drink and Marta knew he'd been with other women. He never invited her to sleep with him again and made sure she stayed in her own box bed with Moor who was fast outgrowing the cradle. Marta was heartbroken and worried about her future.

Once the snows came, Ulrich was forced to stay around the farm for weeks and became more introverted and surly, turning more to the bottle than ever before. Aaron worked hard as always and helped Marta as much as he could. He fashioned a wooden rattle and sewed a soft toy for

Moor and played with him to keep him quiet if Ulrich was around. It seemed a long, hard winter made worse by Ulrich's coldness towards them.

One day when the snows had melted and Ulrich had gone into the village to market, he came home with the news that the priest there had died. The cold weather had also taken a few of Ulrich's friends and he was saddened by their demise but dismissive of the priest's departure. 'I hope he will go to his Hell after the misery he's put others through in his time,' he said vehemently. 'Called himself a man of God! Huh! He made himself rich with the tithes from his 'flock' and locked himself in his house when the plague hit. He wouldn't even go out to give the last rites!'

Although understanding his anger in this instance, Aaron was again saddened by Ulrich's attitude. He was indeed a changed man.

*

Spring turned into summer but there was no further mention of Marta and Moor leaving. Marta didn't voice it and just kept herself busy looking after the house and keeping Moor occupied and out of sight when Ulrich was around. He seemed happier now that the weather had improved and had stopped going into the village so often. He found it tiring working in the fields and orchards all day and was glad just to rest before bed. He was friendlier towards Aaron again and civil towards Marta who hoped that eventually their love might be rekindled.

One afternoon, Marta was shelling peas out in the sunshine while Moor crawled around beside her, trying to pull himself up on his feet from time to time. He was being watched by King who was constantly at his side. Aaron was trying to bring in the goats for milking but they were being particularly obstinate and kept jumping away from him, wanting to stay out in the fields.

'Come on, you stubborn creatures,' shouted Aaron guiding them through the gate into the yard. 'You'll get out again once you're milked. You should know the routine by now.'

Marta laughed to see him so flustered. The goats eventually entered their barn with much bleating and kicking-up of dust. Peace settled once more and Marta smiled to hear the gentle rhythmic hiss-hiss of milk hitting the inside of the bucket as Aaron worked. She could see Ulrich in the distance scything hay.

Suddenly, King sat upright, his hackles slowly rising. A low growl rumbled deep in his chest.

'What is it, King?' asked Marta, looking in the direction of the dog's gaze. 'Is someone coming?'

After a moment or two she saw a man on foot, making his way towards the house from the road that came from the village. King growled louder and made to run off towards the man, but Marta grabbed his neck in time and held him near. 'Quiet boy, it's all right.'

Aaron appeared from the goat stalls. 'What's happening? Oh, I see someone coming.' He grabbed King. 'You pick up Moor, Marta. I'll hold the dog.'

She didn't need telling twice and lifting the child onto her hip she wrapped him in her shawl. They could see the man more clearly now. He had a staff to assist with walking and was dressed in a long robe. 'He looks like a priest,' said Marta, quietly.

'Shall I set the dog on him?' asked Aaron.

'I don't think that would be wise,' Marta answered.

King had started to bark now, frightening Moor who let out a wail. Ulrich heard the clamour down in his field and looked up to see what the noise was about. When he saw the priest approaching his home, he dropped the scythe and ran towards the house.

Catching up with the man as he opened the gate into the yard, he called out, 'Hello there. What brings you to my farm?'

The priest turned and smiled towards Ulrich who was bent over, hands on his knees, catching his breath. 'Greetings, my son. I am your new priest. You'll have heard that Father Braun died. I am his replacement, Father Becker. '

'Greetings to you, too,' panted Ulrich,' but you've had a wasted journey. I am not a follower of your faith.'

The priest frowned. 'Surely this cannot be. All peoples are required to adhere to the Mother Church. What is your name?'

Ulrich stood tall and answered, 'My Hofname is Ulrich Pauer. I inherited this farm from my father on his death.'

'I am sorry for your loss, my son,' said the priest with a perfunctory bow, and turning towards the yard, pointed towards the others. 'Is this your Frau and brother perhaps?'

Before Ulrich could prevent him, he strode forward towards Marta and Aaron.

'Keep the dog back, please. I just want to speak with you for a while and perhaps have some refreshment after my long wa...'

He stopped in his tracks mid speech. Moor had stopped crying and turned towards the newcomer, pulling down the shawl which Marta had wrapped around him.

Father Becker pointed his staff towards the baby. 'What is this? Is it *your* child?' he asked Marta. The contrast between her fair skin, light hair and blue eyes and the child's dark features were obvious.

'Yes, Father, ' answered Marta, stiffening. King kept up a low rumbling growl.

'Are... are you two legally wedded?' he asked her, indicating Ulrich.

'N-no Father.'

Ulrich interrupted. 'What does it matter to you how we run our lives here?'

The priest turned on him. 'It matters a lot how my parishioners run their lives,' he spluttered. 'You won't get away with this kind of thing now that I've taken over. I can see that Father Braun was much too lax!'

'Is that so?' Ulrich bristled. 'I must ask you to get off my land, now!'

'I'm going nowhere until I have full knowledge of this debacle. How did you come by that...' he was visibly shaking... ' black spawn of the Devil?' he spluttered at Marta.

'I... I was ravaged by two seafarers, Father.'

'Whore!' he spat at her. 'You call me Father. Do you belong to the Church?'

'I... I haven't been attending for a while,' she answered quietly, the tears starting to trickle down her cheeks. Aaron edged closer to her, protectively.

'And you,' the priest pointed to Aaron. 'Now that I look closer, you look like a Jew to me. Is that so? What is your name?' he thundered.

'Aaron Levey. Yes I am Jewish and proud of it. I'm also proud to call these people my friends. They're the only family I have.'

'That's enough of your questions,' shouted Ulrich stepping forward. 'I won't tell you again, leave this farm NOW!'

'I'm going, but I will be back with others to deal with you all.' He started to walk away but turned back and shook his staff at them. 'You will die for this! It's a hanging offence to be a non-believer, never mind that you are living with a whore who has a black bastard *and* you are giving a home to a murdering JEW!' He was puce with fury and spluttering with rage.

'Let King go,' shouted Ulrich and they watched as the priest galloped away in a most undignified manner with the dog snarling and snapping at his heels.

'Here boy,' shouted Ulrich calling King back, 'you don't want to get poisoned by biting him.'

I wish we had set King on him when he first arrived, Aaron thought.

They could hear the priest ranting as he waved his staff at them. 'You will all burn for this! Mark my words! I'll be back!'

'Unfortunately, I know he means it,' said Ulrich as he turned towards the stricken Marta and white-faced Aaron. 'We'll have to move on somewhere else. It will probably take him two or three days to summon some henchmen and return here.'

Aaron and Marta were too shocked by that announcement to respond.

CHAPTER EIGHT

Decision Time

They went indoors and sat down in stunned silence. After a few moments, Marta rose and heated some milk. 'We need some sustenance. Here drink this,' and she handed the men a beaker of milk each. 'I couldn't face any food but there's bread and cheese if you want it.'

Both men declined, but sipped at the milk.

'I'll feed Moor just now,' she said and turned away to nurse him. He was still fed from the breast each evening as her milk was plentiful. Once she had him settled down to sleep, Marta joined the men at the table.

'Are you serious about us having to leave?' she asked Ulrich.

'Yes. That priest meant what he said.'

Aaron had been quietly thinking. 'It is our fault, Marta's and mine, that you are under such threat. If you hadn't given us a home, you wouldn't be in this danger of perhaps losing everything.'

Marta nodded. 'It's true, Ulrich. Perhaps it should just be Aaron, Moor and me who leave.'

Ulrich frowned while mulling it over. He had been thinking that they would all leave, but this was a better solution. He didn't want to give up the hof which his parents had worked hard to keep going. 'Right,' he came to a decision. 'I've decided. I will stay here. It is my home and my living after all. However, you two must leave tomorrow. I know the priest was particularly horrified by the black child and by you, Aaron.'

Aaron gulped. 'I...I hear what you're saying, Ulrich, but shouldn't you move out too? That priest wanted you hanged.'

'I am strong and fit and I'll have King by my side. I'll put up a fight if necessary.'

Marta and Aaron were shaking their heads.

'It's too risky. There might be a gang of men. Please come away with us,' begged Marta.

'No, my mind's made up.' He got up and paced the floor. 'Perhaps he'll be more lenient with me as it was you two who angered him more.'

Although Aaron and Marta disagreed with Ulrich's decision, he was adamant that he was staying. 'You can take the horse and cart and fill it with what you need and make your way into *Koln*.'

Aaron's heart lurched at the prospect of being in that city again. Then he had a thought. 'Perhaps we might be able to get on a ship. Sail away to a new land.'

'That's as good a plan as any,' said Ulrich, 'but right now, I think we should pack up the cart and stow it in the woods.'

*

The three of them worked until after dark. They stuffed two sacks with clothes and carried them down the stairs into the shed where the cart was stowed. Ulrich picked out some bags of foodstuffs for them. 'That will keep you going for a little while until you find lodgings – or get on your ship.'

'That's very generous of you,' said Aaron. 'Would it be alright if we take our feather beds as well?'

Ulrich nodded. 'I will have no use for them. Take what you need.'

They packed the cart with a few essentials including cooking and eating utensils. Aaron picked out a spade that was spare and a large, sharp knife. If they were going through *Koln*, perhaps he'd be able to locate the items his father had buried at the back of their house. They decided to take Marta's rag bag in case her bits of cloth would be useful. Aaron had his scissors and needles in the leather pouch he'd arrived with. Ulrich covered the cart with a large piece of canvas and Aaron manoeuvred Janus between the shafts.

'Aaron and I will take this down to the woodland now,' Ulrich said when everything was ready. The two men couldn't look each other in the eye.

'I'll go and fix something for us to eat then,' said Marta and slowly climbed the stairs.

The men set off in silence for the short journey into the woods. They unhitched the horse and tethered him to a tree on a long rope. When they were ready to return, Aaron turned to Ulrich. 'I'll never be able to repay your kindness to me. I want you to know that I will always remember you. You... you once said that I was like a brother to you. I've never forgotten that.'

Ulrich nodded solemnly. 'I meant it.' They turned to walk back towards the house. 'I have to thank *you*. Without your help, I wouldn't have been able to keep the farm going. You came into my life when I had no family... when I needed someone.'

'We have helped each other to recover from our losses,' declared Aaron. They continued to walk in companionable silence. 'You know, the Jews are taught that God made them his Chosen People because they were given His commandments which they have to follow. I've often wondered why I was chosen to survive the burning in *Koln*,' mused Aaron.

'Well, your God chose to send you to help me and now he must have a new plan for you,' returned Ulrich.

Dear God, thought Aaron. *I hope your plan doesn't involve going through any more ordeals!*

When they returned to the house, Marta had a rabbit stew heated up and bread and fruit on the table.

They all ate the food placed before them as they knew their bodies needed it, but no-one felt any appetite for it.

'Thank you for that, Marta,' said Ulrich with an unusual turn of gratitude. 'I'm sorry things went sour between us. I don't know why I felt so repulsed by your black child. Perhaps it was because I had lost all of my family and so wanted to have a son of my own. I regret my bad reaction now.'

'I'm sorry that I ever went out on that dreadful day to deliver laundry,' said Marta with a sigh. 'We might have had a chance of a life together and our own children then.'

They sat in silence for a few minutes deep in their own thoughts.

'Well, we best get to bed. I think you two should make an early start,' said Ulrich, stretching and yawning. 'I'll be up with the larks to send you off to your new life.'

Those innocuous remarks belied the stone he felt in the pit of his stomach at what the morning might bring.

CHAPTER NINE

Departure and Desecration

No-one slept well that night. Ulrich rose and went outside just before dawn. The world was silent. He breathed in the sweet fresh air and looked around at the land that was his. A low mist hovered over the fields. He could see rabbits nibbling away at his young cabbages. *Let them eat*, he thought morosely. *I may not be here to pick them, so let them eat.* The sun rose gradually, spreading its warming, golden rays over the land. The birds carolled their joy at the new day. Ulrich walked around to the graves of his parents and siblings and stood there for a while deep in thought.

Aaron was up and dressed when Ulrich returned upstairs. Marta was also dressed and was making barley meal porridge at the fire. No-one spoke. Moor must have picked up on the tension as he was whimpering and clinging to his mother.

After a hurried breakfast, Ulrich urged Aaron and Marta to be on their way.

'We don't know when the priest will return. It may be soon or it may be days yet, but I want you all to be safe.'

'I wish we knew that *you* would be safe,' said Aaron.

Marta had Moor dressed and she pulled her shawl around them both and tied him in close to her hip. 'We're ready to go,' she said quietly.

Aaron knelt down and hugged King around his neck. 'I'll miss you dear friend,' he whispered, tears stinging his eyes.

King whined and licked his hand then nuzzled into is neck.

'Come on,' urged Ulrich, opening the door. Marta fondled King's ears but the lump in her throat prevented any words forming.

They all went quickly down the stairs and across the yard in the opposite direction from the gate.

'Take the back way to the woods. You know where the horse is,' Ulrich said without looking at either of them. 'Good luck. Do not return to this place.'

Aaron couldn't just walk away. He flung himself on Ulrich who returned his hug. Neither of them could speak. Marta gave a quivering smile through her tears. Ulrich patted her arm and nodded his head, his lips tightly pursed.

'I'm going to let the goats out now,' he muttered and turned away. 'Stay, King.'

Aaron, Marta and Moor made their way quietly through long grass to the edge of the wood. They looked back and could see King standing, watching. There was no sign of Ulrich.

Locating the cart, they hitched up the horse and were soon on their way, bumping over a stony path through the woodland to the drovers' road which would lead them eventually to *Koln*.

*

Ulrich came from the goats' stall with the small herd happily trotting in front of him; glad to be out in the fresh air. There were some recently born kids jumping and kicking up their hooves around their mothers, and he smiled, amused by their antics. As he let them into the field, he heard King give a low, warning growl. Following the dog's line of vision, he could see a bunch of perhaps eight or ten men – it was difficult to tell – approaching on foot in the distance. Three were carrying lit torches. As it was broad daylight it was obvious that they had some intention for them other than lighting their way. His stomach lurched. What could he do against so many?

Perhaps I can reason with them. Maybe if they know that the others have gone, they will spare me. Even as he thought this, Ulrich knew it was hopeless. The priest was going to be out for his blood.

He ran back to the shed and brought out his axe and pitchfork. Standing with feet apart at the foot of the stairs, he waited. He wasn't going to go without a fight. As he watched, the men gradually approached while King stood at his side, barking and growling.

The gang stopped in a huddle at the gate. They each carried rope or a sharp-pointed staff and had knives tucked into their belts. Ulrich eyed them up, and they him.

The priest pushed through to the front. King began to bark and snarl menacingly. 'Well, well look who's here waiting for us,' he called, his face twisted into a smirk.

'You didn't need to bring your henchmen. I'm alone now. The others no longer live here.'

'Is that so?' the priest replied. 'We'll soon see if that's true,' and he signalled for two of the men to go up the stairs. They barged through the gate and Ulrich urged King, 'Get them, boy.'

The wolfhound loped across to the two men in seconds and jumped for the throat of one of them who roared in pain as he tried to pull the dog off without success. His companion swung his knife and caught King in the side. The dog gave a yelping scream, dropping from his victim who fell to the ground with blood gushing from his throat. Ulrich leapt forward and plunged his pitchfork into the belly of the man still standing.

He stood, panting. He couldn't believe that he'd just killed a man, but was so incensed at the sight of his beloved hound lying dying before his eyes that he'd acted instinctively.

'Get him, men,' ordered the priest in low tones. 'Don't kill him... yet. We'll save that pleasure for a while.' A cruel smile played around his lips.

The remaining thugs surged through the gate into the yard and although Ulrich swung his axe round and around and plunged at them with his pitchfork, causing much injury, they soon managed to overpower him through sheer strength of numbers. Ulrich was fighting for his life and had the strength of a mad bear, but it was not enough. He was soon tied up and led to the priest with a rope knotted around his neck.

'So the ungodly heathen is not so mighty now,' snarled the priest, steepling his fingers piously and looking around at his followers. 'What shall we do with him then?'

'Hang him!'

'Chop him into bits!'

'Burn him, he befriended a Jew!' shouted another.

'Burn, burn, burn,' went the chant.

'He'll turn as black as the bastard he raised then,' shouted someone, and laughter broke out.

'Mm, well these are some very good suggestions,' the priest voiced and pretended to think it over. 'I think we'll do them all, just for good measure. God must be avenged for this heretic's behaviour.'

The men let out a roar of approval.

'Three of you, take him for a walk over to these nearby trees. Pick out one that will give him a view of his house and string him up by the hands meantime.'

Ulrich was dragged along by the neck with his hands tied behind him. Once they were in the field, he stumbled and fell down. The men laughed and ran, pulling him across the ground behind them. 'Here, boy! Woof, woof,' they mocked, whistling as though to a dog and laughing at his pain. When they reached the nearest big tree, one of them climbed up and looped another rope over a sturdy branch. The others meanwhile, dragged Ulrich's hands above his head and tied his wrists together with an end of the rope looped over the branch and pulled him up by his wrists until his feet were off the ground. He kicked out at his assailants to no avail. The men secured the rope overhead so that he could not wriggle free, then they tied his feet together.

'The Father wanted you to be able to see your farm. He must have some entertainment planned,' leered one of the assailants, nudging his companions. The laughter burst out once more.

*

Back at the farm, Father Becker ordered the remaining men to go through the house and storerooms to make sure that the Jew and the woman with the black child weren't hiding somewhere.

When it appeared that they had left after all, the priest told the men to take whatever they wanted from the house. 'You deserve recompense for your work this day, and for the injuries some of you have received. If you come across any money remember it comes to me... for the Church that is.'

'Yes, Father, Thank you Father,' they echoed and ran around gathering food and carrying chairs and anything else they fancied to place in piles outside the gate.

'What about the goats and hens, Father?' someone shouted.

'Oh, wring the necks of the fowls and share them around. We'll have meat for supper tonight. You can herd the goats into the village for me, and I'll sell them. For the Church funds, of course,' he added with a twisted grin.

'Very well, Father,' came the reply and a scurrying, bleating and squawking soon erupted, followed by silence.

Once the men had taken their fill of the spoils, and the priest had selected some items for himself, he ordered that the house be set alight. 'I'm just going for a stroll to see how our young heretic is enjoying the view. Follow me once you've set everything ablaze. Oh, and bring a torch for the next fire.' He grinned to himself. 'And bring that dead hound, one of you,' he added.

*

Ulrich was in great pain now. His own weight was causing the rope to cut into his wrists, and his hands were swelling as their blood supply was being cut off. He watched in horror as his beloved home was set alight. The flames quickly catching the dry wood and rising high, as black smoke belched upwards into the sky. He jerked about in fury at the sight of the priest strolling arrogantly towards him, smirking.

'Not so full of yourself now, eh,' remarked Father Becker with a grimace. 'We must make sure your punishment is suitably hard as befits your crime.'

'I ... committed... no... crime,' panted Ulrich, fighting for breath. 'Not... until today... that is.'

'Yes, now you've added murder to your list of ignominious offences. I thought heresy, whoring, harbouring a black bastard child, collaborating with a Jew, not paying your tithe to the Church and threatening a man of

God was quite bad enough, but you've surpassed yourself. Ah, look, here is your little friend. I thought you might like him at your side again.'

Ulrich looked on with a breaking heart as one of the men carelessly dragged King's lifeless body over the field towards them.

'Hang it up nearby where our captive can see it,' said the priest. 'We will demonstrate on the hound just what *he* is going to endure for his ungodly lifestyle,' he added, turning Ulrich's helpless body to face towards his dog's bloodied corpse. Two men tied King's large front paws together, then threw the rope over a branch and proceeded to heave the animal up until level with Ulrich.

'Now I believe that disembowelling would be in order as a punishment,' was the next pronouncement.

The men shouted in agreement. The priest nodded to one of them. A huge, strong-looking man who Ulrich recognised as the blacksmith, slowly took a large knife from his waistband and then with a yell, slashed across the dog's belly, spilling its entrails and blood onto the ground. It hung there, dripping and stinking with the smell of faeces.

Ulrich groaned and twisted around to no avail.

The priest covered his nose and mouth with his hand. 'You'll be smelling your own stench next,' he directed at Ulrich. 'It is about to be your turn.'

The blacksmith moved in front of the captive and leered up at him.

'You... you know me,' whispered Ulrich. 'The... candlestick.'

'Ha! I should have known then that it was a Jewish ornament,' and he spat on the ground.

'You... are... all... less than... human,' gasped out Ulrich. 'May... the... Gods... forgive you!'

'Enough!' thundered the priest and gave a nod to the knife bearer.

Ulrich felt a searing pain then screamed and roared in agony as the torturer scraped out his intestines. Mercifully, he lost consciousness, but not for long. He became aware of someone shaking and prodding him awake. He moaned and twisted, trying in vain to escape his suffering.

'Open your eyes, wretch. See what happens next,' came the order, along with a jab in the back from Father Becker.

Through half-closed eyes, misted with pain, Ulrich saw someone hold a torch to King's body. His fur was already singeing and smoking.

Oh, Father Mother God, please take me out of this! he begged in his head.

He heard the sound of branches being piled beneath him, then came the crackle of flames on dry twigs and he felt heat rising upwards.

'May the Lord have mercy upon your soul, ' shouted the priest making the sign of the cross and folding his hands as though in prayer.

Ulrich heard his mother's voice say, 'Come to us, darling son.' His mother and father, sister and brothers were holding out their arms to him. Leaving behind his earthly remains, he stepped forward into their embrace and walked with them into the Light ahead.

*

CHAPTER TEN

Flight to Koln

Aaron and Marta had covered a few miles when Marta turned around in the direction of the farm, to have one last look before they went around the final bend in the road that would put the farm out of sight altogether. She was shocked at what she saw.

'Aaron, stop, stop! Look,' she yelled, pointing to the smoke and flames rising above the woodland.

Aaron pulled up the reins and wrenched on the brake. His mouth opened in horror at what they were seeing.

'It... It must be the farm,' he stuttered.

That priest must have come back. We just got away in time!' replied Marta clutching his arm.

'We *have* to go back. Ulrich is all alone. He needs our help,' shouted Aaron, pulling on the reins again and trying to edge the horse and cart around.

'No, No, you mustn't!' screamed Marta hitting out at his arm. 'Please Aaron, don't make us go back there. You heard that priest, he said he was coming back to burn us all. For all we know, he may have had Ulrich killed already!'

Aaron sat staring at the fire beyond the trees. He was torn. What to do? He wanted to go to Ulrich's aid but perhaps Marta was right.

Moor started to cry, being awakened by all the shouting and commotion.

'What can we do? The priest has probably paid a gang of thugs to help him,' stated Marta. 'Shush Moor, it's going to be all right.' She rocked him gently and he quietened down. 'I'll never forget the way our priest behaved on that terrible night of the burning in *Koln*. Please don't make us return. *Please* give us the chance of a new life,' she pleaded.

Aaron knew that it was probably senseless to go back. She was right, they'd have captured Ulrich. He could even be hanged and dead by now. But what if he wasn't? This was the second time in his life that he found himself feeling like a coward.

'They'll kill us all too, if we go back there,' stated Marta with tears in her eyes.

Aaron was forced to agree. He was Jewish and Marta had a black baby. What chance would they have? Finally and reluctantly, he nodded, clicked his tongue and flicked the reins to move the horse on.

*

They trundled steadily onwards for the rest of the day and passed no-one on the road.

They only had short stops for some refreshment and to let Moor toddle around on the grass or splash his feet in a stream. Neither of them spoke much, both being deep in their own thoughts. Both felt responsible in a way for Ulrich's probable death.

At dusk, they pulled into a clearing off the road and made themselves as comfortable as possible for the night. Janus was tethered and his calico nosebag fitted, filled with sweet hay. They climbed into the back of the cart and lay down with the feather beds under and over them. The heavy canvas covering helped to keep the damp night air at bay. It was a dry but moonless night, with an overcast, cloudy sky which heralded rain for the following day.

And rain it did, but not until they were ready to set off on their journey again.

'Put on your heavy cloak, Marta. It will cover both you and the little one,' suggested Aaron. He threw on his own cloak and pulled the hood over his head. 'We can put some of these sacks over our head and shoulders as well. It'll help to keep us dry,' he said, pulling two sacks off the seat that they were about to sit on and handing one to Marta.

'Thank you.' She smiled at his kindness. Moor thought it was fun to sit on his mother's knee and peek out from the warm cloak.

It rained for the entire journey so they tried to keep moving as fast as Janus would allow, and thankfully, Moor either sat contentedly or slept without complaint.

It was only once the spires of *Koln* came into view that Aaron became uncomfortable. He looked around at the silent countryside, dotted here and there with small farmsteads. 'Whoa lad,' he said, pulling on the reins and bringing the cart to a halt. To his right was dense woodland. His stomach clenched and he must have involuntarily snatched at the reins as the horse tossed his head and chomped on his bit impatiently. 'Steady, Janus boy.'

'Why have we stopped?' asked Marta.

Aaron was staring at the trees. *Was that the wood? The same wood that intruded over and over into his dreams?*

'Aaron!' Marta's voice broke through his thoughts. 'What is it? Aaron!'

'A-yo,' echoed Moor, trying to copy his mother.

'Sorry, Marta. For a moment I was that young boy again, hiding high up above the ground in an old oak tree.' He paused. 'I could hear the screams of my mother and little sisters.' He shuddered and pulled his cloak more closely about him. 'I watched paralysed as my father fought with his captors. I watched as the lights of the torches bobbed all the way back to the city. That's all I did. I *watched*!' and he thumped his fist down on his knee.

'Stop it, stop it!' Marta cried. 'What could you have done? You were only a young boy against grown men.'

Aaron said nothing in reply. He was thinking that history had repeated itself the day before. He had watched as his home for the past two years had burned, and probably his best friend with it. Feeling a cold sweat break out on his face, he reached down for the earthenware jug of ale at his side. Unfastening the top, he heaved the jar up to his shoulder and took a long, gulping drink. 'That's better,' he said, roughly wiping his mouth with the back of his hand and passing the jug to Marta. 'My tongue was stuck to the roof of my mouth.'

Marta just nodded and took a mouthful herself from the jug.

A fine drizzle was persisting as they set off, so they were glad of the sacks over their heads and shoulders for extra protection. They arrived at the outskirts of the city within an hour, the cart rumbling and jolting over ruts and potholes past a few isolated homesteads. Entering through the gate in the city walls, Aaron could feel his heart thumping against his ribs as he recognised the area where he'd spent most of his life. The Jewish quarter was on the edge of the city so was among the first of the buildings to come into view.

'Something's different,' he murmured to Marta. Then it hit him. All of the houses and shops were empty. They were just standing there devoid of life. Some were burned out shells; some were boarded up; some were derelict with no roof. The window spaces were like black, sightless, accusing eyes.

'Please don't stop here,' whispered Marta. 'Someone might see us and wonder why we're here. You can come back later if you want to look for your house.'

84

Aaron nodded and kept Janus trotting on. They had previously discussed that they would attempt to stay at an inn. Marta knew of one which had been taken over by a young couple after the time when the Jews were exterminated. She directed Aaron to the street where it was located and he stopped at the door to allow her to go in and enquire about a room for the night. She left Moor with him.

A pleasant young woman greeted Marta. 'Yes, we have a room,' she answered to the enquiry. 'It's at the back, so shouldn't be too noisy. Would you like to see it?'

'Yes,' answered Marta and followed the woman up stone steps. 'My husband is waiting outside with our cart.'

'I'm Claudia, by the way, and this is the room,' she said, opening a door. It looked clean enough with a large wooden box bed and straw filled mattress. There were two pillows stuffed with feathers and two grey blankets. An old wooden chair stood beside a lattice window and a white chamber pot sat on the floorboards at the foot of the bed. There was a small washstand with a jug and basin on top. 'Your man can wash at the pump in the yard,' she pointed out of the window, 'and there's a gutter down there for doing your business and emptying your pot. If your husband gives the horse to our stable boy, he'll look after it, and he'll store the cart for you as well.'

'Thank you, we'll take the room,' decided Marta.

'Will you be wanting some food just now?' asked Claudia as they returned down stairs.

'That would be most welcome,' answered Marta, smiling.

'Well just come downstairs when you're ready. I'll dish up some stew for you and my husband, Jan, will bring you ale or brandy.'

'Thank you,' replied Marta and went outside to pass on the information to Aaron. She gathered Moor into her arms and as it was now raining heavily, it did not look odd that she was covered over in a blanket when she next hurried indoors and up the stairs. As it happened, no-one saw her as she entered carrying a bag and her child.

Aaron kept his hood well over his face when he spoke with the stable lad and likewise, when he later entered the inn. No-one was about so he quietly went upstairs to the room that Marta had indicated.

'We've made it, Marta,' he sighed and took off the damp, heavy cloak and hung it to drip from the hook on the back of the door. Marta's cloak was draped over the chair.

'The landlady, Claudia, is preparing stew for us. What will we do about eating?'

'How about if you go down and eat while I look after Moor? You can say that I have sore legs and would prefer to have a plate in my room. You could bring it up to me after you've finished your meal?' So that was the plan.

Marta rinsed her hands and face and then undressed Moor, changed his soiled napkin and washed him.

'Would you watch him please while I get rid of this smelly bundle, and I'll fill up the jug from the pump when I'm downstairs?'

'Of course,' replied Aaron, 'don't be long, he's hungry.'

Marta hurried downstairs and put the soiled napkin on the fire. She used soft rags for this purpose and they needed to be changed often to keep Moor dry. Running outside, she quickly washed her hands at the pump then filled the jug and returned to the room.

Producing some bread and cheese from her bag, she broke it into small pieces and fed it to the hungry child. He gurgled and chattered away in his own fashion as he ate. She then put him to the breast and he drank his fill. Sleepy now and satisfied, he allowed her to hold him over the chamber pot which he obligingly used. Clean and with a dry napkin on, Marta laid him in the big bed, where he lay looking around happily.

'You go down now and hopefully, I'll get fed later,' said Aaron and plopped down beside Moor on the bed. He sang a lullaby softly to him, in the way that his mother used to sing to him.

When Marta walked down the stairs she was met by the landlord, Jan.

'Would you like some refreshment, Frau, ' he asked with a smile.

Marta looked over to a table containing two beer barrels, two smaller kegs of port and brandy and a selection of tankards. 'I'd like some beer, please,' she replied. 'My husband has painful legs and would just like to rest. I'll take some food up to him and that will save him struggling down the stairs again.'

'Oh, Claudia will take it up.'

'There's no need. I'll be going back up straight away, as I'm tired and needing to sleep myself.'

'Very well. I'll let my wife know,' said Jan and left the room.

Marta sat down at a table near the fire, with her back to the other tables. The only other patrons were two old men sitting talking over their beers, and they paid no attention to her. Claudia came in bearing a large platter of stew.

'Here you are then, I hope you enjoy it. I'll bring you some bread to mop up the gravy.'

Marta gave her thanks and ate the food heartily. She was grateful for a hot meal after the long, harrowing journey. Jan brought her a tankard of light foaming beer which was also most welcome. Feeling warmed by the fire and satisfied after the food and drink, she asked Jan to let Claudia know that she'd now like some food to take up to her husband.

'Here you are then,' Claudia said cheerily as she handed Marta a tray. 'I hope he feels better in the morning. Goodnight to you.'

'Thank you, Claudia. Goodnight.' Marta walked upstairs with the supper for Aaron.

*

Neither of them slept well despite being warm and comfortable. The inn was quiet and there didn't appear to be any other travellers staying that night. They shared the bed and just lay down fully clothed with Moor lying between them. They talked in hushed tones over the events of the previous days until finally a fitful sleep overtook them.

Marta had mixed feelings about being back in *Koln*. She had been brought up in that city and although a large number of her friends and family had died from the plague, she was worried about bumping into someone she knew. What if someone recognised her and told the priest? What would happen if someone took against her because of her dark-skinned child? She fell into a restless sleep punctuated by part dreams and part memories. *One moment she was happily at her old home with her father, then he turned into Father Becker and called her a whore with the Devil's spawn. Then she was on a ship, and all of the men aboard had dark faces and they kept touching her pale skin and trying to pull at her clothes. She was back in the terror of being raped.*

She tossed around in the bed so much that Aaron wakened up. He had been having a troubled night himself. Being back in the city had dredged up the old memories that he tried to ignore. Some of his dreams were real memories and others were just hellish visions. He drifted in and out of a disturbed sleep.

He was lying somewhere, or was he floating? His hands were clenched over his ears but he could still hear screaming. Was it night or was it day? The sky was red and pink but there was thick black smoke everywhere. His limbs were painful as he tried to run. He couldn't run! He was going through the motions but couldn't get out of the flames. Then he was out in the mist, running. Abigail and Dorit were just ahead of him but he couldn't catch up with them. He just kept on running, running for days. Mustn't stop. Mustn't think. Lungs bursting. Mama, Papa, pain, head hurts, need water. Ulrich, it's burning, put out the flames, put out the flames! But the flames rose higher and higher.

Aaron wakened up in a sweat and for a moment couldn't think where he was. He rubbed his hands over his face, gradually letting the nightmares go and feeling his breathing settle down. Moor was sound asleep at his side, long dark eyelashes lying against his flushed cheeks. There was a soft dawn light outside, so he rose quietly and moved towards the door. Marta stirred from her light slumber.

'Where are you going?' she whispered anxiously.

'I can't sleep. I'm just going out for some air,' he whispered back. 'I won't be too long. Try to get some more rest.'

He went outside to relieve himself in the yard. He took a long drink of water from the pump and sluiced his face. Wide awake now, he made the decision to go to his old house while there was no-one about, to try to find the buried cache. A low mist lingered around the buildings and all was still. The only sounds were the soft thuds of his footsteps and a gentle whinnying from the stables as he walked past. He went inside and patted Janus, then walked around to where the cart was standing and reached inside under the canvas cover for the spade. He took one of the sacks from the seat at the front and headed for the former Jewish quarter.

Walking along deep in thought, he was brought abruptly to the present moment by a noisy gaggle of geese being driven from their hut nearby and chased onto the grassy piece of land ahead by a young boy. He stared at the slightly mounded field that had once been the green area in the city centre. 'That must be where the burning took place,' he gasped aloud. He could feel his flesh crawling as he thought of the amount of charred bones that must be buried deep beneath that calm exterior. *His own dear parents and pretty little sisters!* The geese were happily cropping the lush grass as he turned away quickly, breathing fast as tears spurted and strode onwards to his destination. When he reached the former Jewish ghetto, no-one was about. He walked towards his old home with trepidation. Would it still be there? Would it be burned down?

The house was still standing - at least the walls were. The roof had partly caved in. The door and windows were boarded up but the wood had been prised off one and was hanging loose. Aaron looked inside. The room was empty with only a broken lamp and dead leaves strewn on the floor; plundered long ago. He had no desire to enter.

Going around to the back of the building, he looked over to the boundary wall of the synagogue. The wall was still there but the synagogue was gone. There was just a heap of blackened rubble where the beautiful building had once stood. What used to be the centre of the Jewish way of life was now gone. Swallowing down the lump in his throat, he walked over to the wall opposite and counted back ten paces towards the house. The voice of his father rang in his head, 'Remember the Ten Commandments.'

'I'll remember, Papa,' whispered Aaron as he counted out the steps. Near to where he ended, there was a flat stone partly hidden by weeds. Aaron felt sure that this was the right place, so started to dig quickly and within a few moments, his spade hit something with a thud. He scraped away the earth with his hands to find his father's cash box wrapped in the now dirty and rotting muslin. Beneath that were the other treasures that he wanted so much – the menorah candlestick and the Torah and the other Jewish items which were so meaningful for him. He quickly packed them into his sack, shovelled earth back into the hole, heeled it in and set off back to the inn with the spade on his shoulder. *Will I be able to get back into Judaism?* His jumbled thoughts ran round in his head as he hurried along. *Oh Mama, Papa, I miss you so much.* He clutched the sack to him as though he was hugging them.

It was fully daylight by the time he'd walked back. A few market traders were already setting up their stalls as he hurried past. They nodded amiably towards him and he returned the nods but kept his head down.

Once back at the stables, he placed the sack beneath the canvas along with the spade. The stable boy was busy sweeping the yard unaware of his presence. He could hear someone working in the kitchen but no-one saw him enter, so he quickly crept up the stairs to the bedroom.

'Oh, thank goodness, you're back. Where have you been?' asked Marta. She was sitting on the bed dressing Moor.

'I went to see my former home,' he answered and leaned over to tickle Moor.

'Well, what was it like?' asked Marta when he didn't contribute any more information.

'Falling apart and wrecked,' he answered.

'I'm sorry. It must have been awful for you to see it like that.'

He nodded. 'However, I managed to locate some Jewish things that my father had buried in the ground, and a cash box, so we have plenty of money if we need to make purchases.'

Marta's face lit up. 'That's good news. If we want to journey by ship it will probably cost a lot.'

'I think we should leave soon and go to the *Altermarkt* to see if there are any merchants there who would perhaps allow us to travel with them on board their ship?'

'Very well,' replied Marta. 'We'll need to buy some fresh food when we're out. Moor will be hungry and we need to eat too.'

Wearing his still damp cloak, Aaron took a hat from their bag and put it on, pulling the brim well down.

'It's a pity that it's not still raining so I'd have my hood up, but we'll just take the chance that no-one will pick me out as a Jew,' he said. 'Let's go, then.'

Marta went quickly down the steps with Moor under her cloak and waited outside while Aaron paid their bill for the room, stabling and food. Claudia didn't seem to notice anything amiss. 'I hope you're feeling better today,' she directed at Aaron.

'I'm much better after the rest, thank you,' he answered.

'The damp weather brings on all the aches and pains, eh? Where are you off to now?' she asked.

'Oh, we're just in town to buy some supplies at the market,' answered Aaron. 'We must hurry before the fresh food is all gone. We will return later for the horse and cart. Thank you.' And he left as quickly as was polite.

'Do you think she was suspicious of anything?' asked Marta after they had set off in the cart again.

'No. I don't think so. She was just being friendly,' Aaron replied.

They made their way to the market place. Marta carried Moor on her hip. He had on a hat which partially covered his face and she had her shawl wrapped around him. Aaron kept his head down and hoped that they blended in with the crowd as there were many foreign merchants and their crews in the square, as well as mothers carrying their babies. He looked all about to see if there were any traders he recognised.

They purchased bread, cooked meat and apples so they could have something to eat, and sat down on the cathedral steps to partake of their light meal. They were just finishing when Aaron saw a familiar face by a stall. It was the mercer who wore a turban and sold the beautiful coloured fabrics.

'Marta, do you see that man over there with the cloth wrapped around his head?' He pointed across the square. 'Father used to buy materials from him. Perhaps he would let us travel on his ship.' He felt a glimmer of excitement.

'Oh, do you think so? What if he turns you in to the Council men?'

'I don't think he will. Ulrich saw him once and heard him say he was grieved to hear about my father's death. I'll just have to take the chance.'

They strolled over towards him and waited until no-one else was near, then Aaron stepped in front of the man and smiled. 'Do you remember me? I'm Aaron, Jerod Levey the tailor's son.'

The silk trader stared in amazement. 'Aaron – Aaron Levey! Is it really you?' He grabbed Aaron's hand and pumped it up and down, 'I am so pleased, so pleased,' he said nodding his head and grinning. 'I thought you dead.'

'Sh! Not so loud. Remember Jews are not supposed to be here,' Aaron cautioned.

'Yes, yes, I am so very sorry, so very sorry,' he said more quietly. 'How can I assist you sir, and you Frau Levey?'

Letting the misunderstanding go in the meantime, Aaron answered in hushed tones, 'Is it possible to buy a passage on your merchant ship, please? We need to leave this place immediately.'

'You come at very best moment,' he answered, nodding his head. 'Tonight we sail on high tide.' Two women moved in to look at the spread of silks and brocades. 'This silk is just made for you, Fraulein. Look how it lights up your eyes.' He held the soft, blue fabric close to her face and she and her companion fell into discussion about it. Turning to Aaron, he whispered, 'Be at South Port before dusk. My ship is called *Rashima*. I meet you there.'

'Thank you, oh, thank you friend,' Aaron said gripping his hand.

'My name is Raju,' he whispered then turned to his customers once more.

'What wonderful luck,' Aaron said to Marta with a grin.

She hugged his arm. 'What will we do with all our things and the horse and cart?'

Aaron thought about it. 'Well, we'll go and see if the stable boy knows of anyone who might want to buy the horse and cart. We can ride over to the South Port and dump our belongings outside the gate. Maybe you could stay with the bundles while I take the cart back to the inn, or the new owner? If we find one today,' he added.

'Well, luck has been with us so far, so let's trust that it will continue,' said Marta.

They made their way back to the inn and went round to the stable yard to look for the lad. He was grooming Janus as they entered his domain, which smelt of horses and sweet hay and leather.

'Everything is ready for you sir,' announced the stable boy. 'I'll get him hitched to the cart for you.'

When Aaron asked him about a possible buyer for his horse and cart, the young lad thought for a moment then said, 'I think Herr Muhler might be interested in your cart. I know he had problems with a broken wheel.'

'Does he live near here?' asked Aaron.

'Yes, he has the mill just outside the West Port sir,' the boy said.

'I'll pay you well if you'll run to him and ask if he is interested in doing business with me,' Aaron told him.

'Yes, sir, I will do that,' replied the boy eagerly and said he'd set off straight away.

'We shall wait here for you. Be as quick as you can.'

'I can run like the wind,' answered the stable boy.

Marta and Aaron sat down on some bales in the back of the stables and Moor was allowed down on the straw covered floor to play. Janus was the only horse in one of the stalls and all was quiet.

In a short while, the young lad returned, out of breath from running. 'Herr Muhler would like to see your cart,' he panted. 'He said... he might be interested in the horse too... so you've to go round to see him.'

'What good news. You've done well, boy,' said Aaron pushing some coins into his palm.

'You've to go after midday. He's working now, putting flour into sacks.'

'That suits us fine. Can you have the horse and cart ready for us at noon and we shall return then?'

'They'll be ready for you, sir,' replied the lad.

*

Aaron and Marta walked down to the South Port and wandered along the quayside. The air was fresh with a gentle breeze and they were both excited yet fearful at the prospect of boarding a ship.

'I've never been on a ship before,' voiced Marta.

'Neither have I,' confided Aaron. 'Let's have a look at those anchored along here. *Rashima* must be one of them.'

They wandered slowly past the massive, wooden ships berthed five deep in some places, and gazed at all the activity. The vessels were all so different. Some had a single mast and others had an additional mast at the back. They all had oars in some form as well as sails. There were beautiful carved figureheads on the prow of a few. Some had just pulled in and the crews were busy lowering sails or getting the gangplank ready for disembarking amid much shouting and clatter. Others were deserted and sat on the water, gently heaving up and down with the swell, their sails wrapped tightly and thick ropes securing the ships to great iron bollards on the quayside. There were unfamiliar accents and much to-ing and fro-ing. Moor seemed fascinated with these new surroundings.

'I wonder which one will be ours,' said Marta as she pointed out each vessel to Moor. 'Ships, sh, sh, ships,' she repeated as he tried to copy her words.

Just at that, they noticed dark-skinned men with bare chests wearing only loincloths and turbans busily loading supplies onto a ship up ahead. They were pushing handcarts piled with sacks of food up the gangplank to be loaded into the deep, shallow hold. As they drew nearer, Aaron approached one of the men and asked if this was Raju's ship.

The man shrugged and replied in a torrent of unintelligible language. He shouted over to another man, so Aaron repeated his question to him.

'Is this Raju's ship?'

'Raju, Raju,' he nodded, pointing to the ship and hurried about his business.

'I'm not sure if he really understood, but it looks like the word, *Rashima* carved up there,' said Aaron to Marta as he looked up at the prow with his hand shading his eyes.

'Well, I'm not sure what it says,' she answered. 'The writing is fancy and my reading ability is limited.'

'Well, we know where to come now. It looks strong enough and they seem to be taking on lots of cargo.'

Marta nodded.

'It's on its own too, so it will be easy to sail away when the time comes, unlike some which are blocked in,' he added.

'Where would we sleep?' asked Marta looking anxiously at the large, flat bottomed cog. 'There don't appear to be any rooms, just deck.'

'We'll find out later. I think there's a covered place at the front and the rear. Let's just be glad that we've found a way of escape,' Aaron answered. 'We'd better head back to the stables now.'

They turned and retraced their steps, enjoying the brisk breezy walk.

CHAPTER ELEVEN

Escape by Sea

Marta was waiting with their bundles at the South Port. Aaron had had a good afternoon as the miller was delighted with his cart, and bought the horse as well. He took part of his payment in sacks of flour and barley meal as he knew that his money would probably not be accepted wherever they would end up, so it was better to have some food to contribute to their upkeep while on the voyage. Herr Muhler offered to drive Aaron and the sacks down to the port and this was readily accepted. As Aaron spoke with the local accent and the miller was short-sighted, he did not notice Aaron's Jewish appearance.

They met Marta and Moor impatiently waiting and the miller heaved all their bundles onto the cart and drove it along with them to the *Rashima*. Raju was looking out for them and came hurrying forward at their arrival.

'Welcome, welcome, my friends,' he called to Aaron and Marta as he held out his hands to them in turn. 'How do you like my little ship? She is beautiful, yes?'

'She is indeed,' replied Aaron. 'Are you the captain?'

'Oh, no,' laughed Raju. 'I am no seaman. I am just rich merchant. You will meet my captain and crew soon, soon.' He beckoned to two men on board who ran over and started unloading the bundles and sacks from the cart.

Aaron bid Herr Muhler farewell and thanked him once more for helping them out. He stroked Janus fondly then giving him a final pat, he watched as the horse disappeared into the melee with the miller at the reins. He felt sad as he remembered his dear friend, Ulrich.

'Come aboard, come aboard. Sailing soon,' urged Raju, all smiles in colourful purple brocade tunic, gold pantaloons and turban.

Marta stepped up the gangplank first, carrying Moor. She waited anxiously for Aaron.

'We live simple here,' stated Raju. 'See raised forecastle there?' he pointed to the prow. 'Some sleep under, where me and captain and officers sleep. Others lie in the aftcastle.' He flapped a hand towards the back of the ship.

'Where shall we go?' Marta asked.

'Oh, you in beside mens in forecastle,' he replied. 'You will like squeeze up with Aaron,' he said, laughing and giving her a wink.

Marta looked uncomfortable.

Aaron appeared at her side. 'We'll manage fine. It's just good to be leaving this place full of bad memories,' he assured Raju.

They were shown to a small, dark space where their bundles had been piled.

'We'll put the feather bed down and at least we will have somewhere to sleep in comfort,' said Aaron, trying to reassure Marta who was looking less than delighted at the prospect of being crammed into the small place with just a piece of sail canvas separating them from the other men. 'We'll just have to make the best of it,' he whispered. 'It hopefully won't be for long.'

Marta managed a weak smile.

'Come, I show you *Rashima*,' beckoned Raju. 'The little one will like here. What his name?'

'We call him Moor,' replied Aaron.

'How did you get him? He's not yours,' Raju stated bluntly, looking at Aaron and Marta in turn.

'He's a foundling,' blurted out Marta, to Aaron's surprise. 'His parents must have died in the Great Death. I felt obliged to take him or he'd have died too,' she added.

'Well, that was good thing to do,' said Raju solemnly, then becoming brisk again, pointed to the mast in the centre of the ship, where the crewmen were heaving up the heavy square sail. 'We will move soon. We travelling with the current. No oars needed.' He pointed to where the rowing crew would usually sit at benches along the sides. 'Ah, here is captain. He has the grand name, Solomon.'

Captain Solomon came over and greeted Aaron and Marta with a gracious bow. He was not dressed as grandly as Raju but wore a turban and a lightweight tunic and pantaloons. He had a sash wound around his waist into which was thrust a curved sword. 'I am pleased to make your acquaintance,' he said and nodded to Aaron and Marta. 'I hope you will have a pleasant if cramped journey on *Rashima*. We are not equipped for passengers; we just ship materials from the traders on the Silk Route.'

'Thank you,' replied Aaron. 'You speak the language very well.'

The captain nodded and gave Aaron a smile.

'We are very grateful to have this opportunity to travel to a new life,' continued Aaron.

'Are you hoping to escape the Great Death?' the captain enquired.

'Yes,' answered Marta before Aaron could reply. 'We have both lost all family and friends.'

'My commiserations,' he said. 'Now, if you'll forgive me, I must get this ship underway. Food will be ready in an hour or so.' He took his leave and snapped out orders to the crewmen who worked together in an organised fashion to complete the raising of the main sail. Bowlines from the sides of the sail were then attached to the bowsprit at the forecastle to enable the sail to be manoeuvred. Raju pointed out various activities being performed and they walked over to the stern to watch as the ship pulled away from the quayside. The men responsible for raising the anchor, then the untying of the heavy hawsers around the bollards, leapt nimbly with bare feet from the land to the ship. They watched as orders were shouted down to a helmsman beneath the deck who worked a lever attached to the rudder. Slowly, the ship moved its bulk away from the quayside into the River Rhine. The sail billowed out as the following wind caught it and eased the ship forward with the current.

Raju took his leave while Aaron and Marta stood looking back at the city of their birth with mixed feelings. Both had happy childhood memories but death and persecution had darkened their recent years. Some children playing on the riverbank waved when they saw the sailing ship pass nearby. Marta raised her arm and waved back. 'Look Moor. Wave to the children,' she said and he held up his little starfish hand and giggled. 'We won't be coming back this way ever again,' she added with a sigh.

Aaron put an arm around her shoulders as they stood with the wind in their hair, looking back at the walled city of *Koln* with its spires and its memories.

*

Entranced by the unaccustomed views of the passing countryside and the other bustling ships and barges on the river, the three were unaware of time passing until there came a loud clanging which turned out to be the cook rattling on a metal pan to announce supper. They made their way towards the sound and joined a queue of men, who were curious to see the newcomers. They were each handed a large plate of a spiced stew and hard ship's biscuits. The cook laughed to see the child and indicated that he would give him something to eat. He produced a bowl of porridge-type soft food and a spoon. Everyone helped them to find somewhere to sit on the deck and were kind, particularly to Marta. They seemed intrigued by her fair colouring and blue eyes. Some of the men tried to stroke her long hair, but she recoiled from them with a glare.

Aaron and Marta sat down on a pile of ropes and ate heartily. Moor took his porridge without complaint, looking around at the other men all the time. He seemed to be enjoying himself and smiled readily to anyone who paid him any attention.

'I'll just go and give him his evening milk,' whispered Marta.

'Pull the canvas around so you have privacy,' replied Aaron. 'I'll come over in a while.'

Raju joined Aaron on deck and handed him a tankard of ale. 'You happy on my ship, Aaron?' he asked. 'We are good to you, yes?'

'Yes, thank you, Raju. Everything is fine. I must pay you for our keep. What do we owe you?'

'There no need for payment,' he answered, flapping his hand.

'But you must take something,' Aaron insisted. 'I have sacks of flour?'

'That good.' he nodded. 'Two will do. Take them to cook,' he pointed to the galley. 'Splendid, splendid.'

'Thank you so much, Raju,' said Aaron.

'I help you, you help me, that how the world should work.'

'Indeed,' Aaron agreed, nodding. 'If only everyone thought like that.' He took a draught of his ale and sighed with delight.

'We just have short journey this night,' said Raju.

'That's good,' replied Aaron.

'But, tomorrow will be busy. We travel up other bit of Rhine River, the Rotte, to Rotterdam. I go to market there to sell beautiful cloth. We stay there four days then we sail back on Rhine again. I do my best to find you ship to Denmark.'

'Oh, why Denmark?' questioned Aaron.

'That take you to Poland. That where Jews going.'

'Poland,' murmured Aaron. 'So you think there will be other Jews living in Poland?'

'Yes, yes,' affirmed Raju with nods of such certainty that Aaron did not doubt him.

'Where do you come from, Raju? It is not from around here.'

'I live Constantinople,' he answered proudly. 'Far country. Months of travel. I buy cloth from sellers coming on Silk Road from China and sell it all over countries.'

'I would like to buy some of your fine silks. I hope to make beautiful clothes for rich people some day and make my fortune,' and he laughed.

'And so you shall, friend,' said Raju. 'You pick what you want tomorrow, and I sell at good price to you.' They shook hands.

'I'll not go ashore at Rotterdam tomorrow. I am excited to visit new places, but I must be careful. Apparently Jews are not allowed to live in this area any more. I could be arrested and put to death,' Aaron said with a frown.

'It a worry indeed. We must take care you not in danger,' answered Raju. 'I going sleep now. I hope you have quiet night.'

He walked slowly around the deck on the way to his own quarters.

Marta appeared and hurried over to Aaron. 'I thought you were coming back to be with me,' she said anxiously. 'Moor is sound asleep.'

'Wait until I tell you what Raju has planned!' and Aaron related all that Raju had suggested. Marta was pleased but apprehensive.

'I wonder what Rotterdam will be like? Do you think they have had the plague there as well?' she voiced.

'Oh, I think it will have spread to all of the towns and cities. You can go ashore, if you like, but you must be careful. I will stay here on board where there's less chance of being discovered as a Jew. I'll look after Moor for you. I enjoy being with him.'

Marta gave him a light kiss on the cheek. 'You are kind, Aaron. You have been like a good brother to me. Thank you.'

*

Neither of them slept very peacefully that first night on board ship. They were cramped and slept in their clothes with Moor between them as they'd done at the inn. The sound of the water swishing was quite restful but the sails flapped and cracked in the wind and every so often a bell was rung. They decided it must be to tell the time, or perhaps it was for a changeover of crew. The snores and grunts of sleeping men nearby were also disturbing. There was no moon so it was particularly dark with only a few lanterns on the forecastle but nothing near their sleeping place. They were both glad when it was morning although they were feeling tired and crumpled. Moor woke up with his usual smiles, ready for fun.

'Let's go out and see where we are,' announced Aaron as he stretched and yawned. 'There's no chance of any sleep now.'

They rose and took Moor out to the deck. There was a low mist hanging over the water and they could just see a large town on their right hand side.

'That must be Rotterdam,' said Aaron, pointing. There didn't appear to be much movement ashore as yet. It was just after dawn.

Marta gave a little shiver and pulled her shawl tighter. 'How am I going to get freshened up with all these men around?' she whispered to Aaron.

'Mm. Perhaps we could ask Captain Solomon or Raju what you could do,' he answered.

She felt it was bad enough having to pee in a bucket in close proximity to Aaron but where did you empty it? Over the side? She decided to reorganise their bundles and unpack some of the things.

'Are you alright with Moor just now?' she asked. 'I'm going to look for a jug and basin that I think we brought with us, and I'll get a change of clothes for Moor. He'll be wet.'

'Yes, that's fine. I'll keep a lookout for Raju or the captain as well. I wonder if we get something to eat soon. I'm hungry from being awake most of the night.' He yawned again and Moor giggled, trying to copy him.

Marta set to sorting through the bundles and located a basin and pitcher, a rough towel and her hair comb. She pulled back the canvas door flap and signalled to a crewman passing nearby that she'd like the pitcher filled. He nodded vigorously and ran over to a large bucket on a rope, and threw it over the side of the ship. Pulling it up again immediately, he grinned and tipped some river water into the jug. It was surprisingly clean. Marta smiled nervously but thanked him and he nodded and bowed.

After closing the canvas over, Marta settled the basin on top of a sack, poured some water into it and stripped down to the waist. She took a rag and gave herself a wash, then dried off with her towel. Lifting her skirt, she wiped between her legs. She dressed and combed her long hair out, then pleated it into a braid which she coiled round her head and pinned neatly. She raked in one of the bundles and found her folded caps and bonnets. Choosing a white coif, she placed it firmly on her head, covering her fair hair. Feeling better, she lifted back the flap and signalled to Aaron further along the deck, to come back.

While Marta changed, washed and dressed Moor, Aaron looked out his cash box. He took some money and put it into his own pouch at his waist then took another pouch from the box and filled it with coins and handed it over to Marta.

'When you go ashore, take that to the money changer and see if he'll give you coins we can spend in Denmark.'

Marta nodded, then took the pouch and tucked it between her breasts inside her bodice

'We still have flour and barley meal in these sacks that we can barter with if necessary,' added Aaron. 'Do you think we should divide out some more of this money from the cashbox, just in case it gets stolen or something?'

'That's a good idea,' agreed Marta. 'I could sew some coins into my petticoat and put a pouch in the bag of Moor's clothes. It's best if we have it divided around as you say, in case of thieves.'

So Aaron took Moor out to watch the activity on board while Marta stayed behind the canvas flap sewing coins into her petticoat hem. She also sewed some into the lining of Aaron's thicker tunic. Just as she'd finished, the cook set up his metallic clamouring again, heralding breakfast.

*

After a short repast of stewed apples and plums, some kind of porridge, bread and a sweet white wine served hot and diluted, the crew busied themselves dragging back the cover over the hold and lifting out roll after roll of coloured materials. Aaron and Marta watched in fascination as part of the rainbow of hues before them was transported to the shore. Raju stood nearby overseeing the procedure, shouting out orders and pointing and gesticulating wildly. Moor clapped his hands with pleasure at the flurry of activity. Soon the rolls of cloth were transferred to a hand cart which was pushed and pulled along the quayside to the city gateway. Aaron sat on a bench along the side of the ship and he and Moor looked through one of the oar holes on deck, taking care to keep hidden. Inspectors from the Guilds of Trades were standing at the gate, waiting to examine goods being imported for sale at the market place. They poked, prodded, and fingered the materials and declared them suitable for sale. Raju was known to them and they spent a few minutes in animated conversation with much use of hands and facial expressions as they bypassed the language barrier. The cart was soon lost to sight as it was pushed into the market square and another one arrived at the gate filled with sacks, ready for inspection.

Marta appeared, ready to go ashore. 'I'll be glad to be on land again, with space around me,' she declared. 'I'm going to see if I can buy some goat's milk for Moor. He can eat the same as us now and it will be easier all round when he can drink from a beaker.'

'Don't forget to visit the moneychanger first,' reminded Aaron.

'I won't,' she answered with a nod. 'Goodbye, Moor.' She waved and blew a kiss to the child and made her way carefully down the gangplank. She was pleased to be away from the dark-skinned men for a while. They made her feel uneasy and reminded her too much of the attack she suffered in the past. Pulling her shawl firmly around her shoulders, she held up her head and strode purposefully through the gate into the market.

This city had obviously suffered from the effects of the plague as well. There were only about twenty stallholders scattered around the huge square. From the various accents unknown to her they were mainly foreign traders plying their wares. There was someone selling cheeses and handing out small sample pieces to tempt passers-by. Marta looked for milk and found a young girl standing beside two large milk cans. When she showed the girl a coin in her hand the youngster shook her head and pointed over to a man sitting against the wall with a small table in front of him.

Marta made her way over to the gentleman and handed him some coins. He didn't speak, but looked at them and picked up some others from various piles in front of him. He tipped them into Marta's open hand. She then took the pouch from inside her bodice and handed that over. 'I need money for Denmark,' she said.

The man looked at her then tipped out the coins. 'Denmark?'

'Yes.'

He nodded and selected coins from another two piles put them in the pouch and handed it over.

'I hope that is correct,' Marta said sternly.

The moneychanger shrugged and flicked his hand at her, shooing her away. She walked off hoping that he was honest, while he attended to neatening his piles of coins.

'Why did I not think to bring a pitcher for the milk,' said Marta to herself. She looked around for a suitable trader and noticed a potter's stall with bowls, beakers and pitchers of all sizes. She selected a jug and paid for it without any problem. Deciding to wander around the market for a while before buying the milk, she came to the area where Raju was displaying his cloth and stopped to pass some time with him. He had not had many interested customers. The population was so depleted by the Great Death that the few people who were there were mainly buying foodstuffs. However, it was still early in the day.

Marta walked on, looking at the stalls of fruit and vegetables and varied household goods such as pots and pans, lanterns, candlesticks, stools and chairs. Just setting up a stall in a corner were two blonde-haired people, a man and woman. Marta went over to see what they were selling and was delighted to find something beautiful. They had amber jewellery, furs sewn together to make coverlets of all sizes and intricately carved wooden furniture. The woman greeted her and Marta found that she could understand some of the language which was similar to her own tongue. They held a short, stilted conversation, then the stallholder pointed to the jug and Marta indicated through gestures that it was for milk for her baby. Eventually, she established that the couple came from Denmark. What a surprise! Her excitement must have shown as the man also stepped forward and listened to the conversation. Marta pointed to the river and then to the couple and asked, 'Will you take me,' she pointed to herself, 'my man,' and she indicated a taller person beside her, 'and my son?' she held her arms as though rocking a baby. 'We want to go to Denmark on a ship,' and she pointed to the ships then out to sea, making a wave motion with her hand.

The couple looked puzzled and spoke with one another.

'Wait,' said Marta, holding up her hand in a halting gesture. She hurried over to Raju's stall and hung around impatiently as he served a customer.

When the transaction had been completed, she tugged at his arm. 'Raju, Raju, please come over here with me. I've found people who come from Denmark. Could you explain and ask them if they can take us in their ship? I don't think they understand me.'

Raju nodded and turned with her towards the Danish couple's stall. 'I try for you. I know a little of the Danish.'

The young couple were surprised to be addressed by this dark-skinned man wearing extravagant clothes and a turban. Raju did his best to explain using his limited knowledge of the Danish language along with a mixture of other tongues, gestures and facial expressions. They appeared to understand however, and Raju was able to glean that they were leaving in three or four days, depending on business and the tides. They would take the three passengers if they could pay, he passed on to Marta.

She nodded vigorously and confirmed with signals and gestures that they understood there were two adults and one child and some baggage. They all nodded and smiled happily and Marta was anxious to return to the ship with the news for Aaron. She almost forgot to get the milk, but the Danish woman pointed to the jug as a reminder, and they both laughed.

Marta took her leave of the couple, walked back to Raju's stall with him, thanking him profusely for his help all the way, which he shrugged off. She then went over to the young girl with the milk for sale and bought a jug full and carried it carefully back to the ship.

Aaron was delighted at the prospect of a passage to Denmark but was apprehensive. What if the couple reported him to the authorities when they discovered he was a Jew?

'And I completely forgot to ask the name of their ship,' said Marta. 'I was so thrilled at the thought of getting well away from here.'

'Never mind. Let's go and see if we can discover which ship is theirs. I'll pull my hat well down,' said Aaron. 'My beard covers half my face anyway.'

They put a hat on Moor as well and bundled him up. Aaron carried him which helped to cover his face and they left the ship and wandered along the quayside as though out for a stroll. A number of barges had pulled in and men were unloading timber and sacks of grain as they passed. No-one gave them a second glance as they were so busy. There were another two cogs moored nearby and then they noticed a longer, wider ship. Could this be the Danish vessel? It had a single mast, oars along the sides and a rudder on one side. The prow had a carving of a ram's head but no name showing and there was a flag with a white cross on a red background slapping in the breeze.

'Is that the flag of the Danes, I wonder?' asked Aaron.

Marta shrugged. 'We can ask Raju tonight. He'll probably know as he's been here many times and knows the different seamen.'

The ship had a covered-in hold giving more deck space and looked as though there would be more room than on the *Rashima*.

'It will be a lot different, sailing on the ocean instead of on rivers,' mentioned Aaron.

'What do you mean?' queried Marta.

'Well, it will be a lot bigger for a start, and we probably won't see land for days. We might have stormy weather. That must be fearful.'

'Oh, I didn't think about storms!'

'Well we must be ready to accept whatever life throws at us. We want to start anew somewhere, don't we? Perhaps you will meet someone you want to settle down with.'

'That seems unlikely,' Marta said quietly. 'Moor is a lovely child, but he will stand out like a blackberry in a butter pat amongst all those blonde-headed, blue-eyed people. I don't think I'll be getting any marriage proposals.'

'We will just have to trust in God and look on it as a great adventure,' said Aaron. 'I hope to eventually meet up with other people of the Jewish faith. I miss the synagogue and the rituals.'

'I haven't heard you mention that before,' said Marta.

'Oh, I suppose retrieving the things my father buried at the back of our house has brought back memories of earlier years and happy family times. I look forward to being able to sit and hear the Torah scroll being read in freedom.'

'What is the Torah scroll?'

'It is a parchment written in Hebrew. I understand that its teachings were directly given to Moses by God. It's central to the Jewish religion.'

'You are so clever, Aaron. How wonderful to be able to read!' She walked on in silence for a few moments. 'I was not allowed to learn to read or write. Women are forbidden from learning. I heard that some of the wise women who worked with herbs and spells were burned to death because they'd tried to write down recipes which could be passed on to others.'

'They must have been witches, then,' said Aaron. 'Witches are evil are they not?'

'Perhaps some are, but the old women my mother knew were just trying to help people with their lotions and ointments to ease pains and rashes. Some helped at childbirth and gave the mothers potions to ease their labouring and painful, swollen breasts. They provided much needed tinctures for babies with the croup or sickness.'

'Was it your churchmen who accused them of witchcraft?'

'Yes, I think so. The priest was always preaching against women in general. However, I think men are far more evil. Women are homemakers and are peaceable but men are always looking for a battle!'

'I'm not!' retorted Aaron. 'But I know what you mean. Some men just look for trouble and if they are in a position of power that can be disastrous.'

'I like the way we can talk so openly about things, Aaron,' said Marta.

'Yes, me too. But we must be careful not to be overheard or we might end up like the witches,' declared Aaron. 'Shall we head back to *Rashima* now? Raju will hopefully be able to confirm our journey to Denmark.'

CHAPTER TWELVE

Celebrations

Raju had indeed spoken at length with the Danish couple. Their name was Andersen and the ship was named *Vaedder,* which they learned meant Ram. They knew to expect three new shipmates; one man, a woman and an infant. Whether or not Raju had mentioned Aaron's Jewish background or the black foundling was never discussed but he confirmed that the ships were both leaving Rotterdam on the same day. He to return on the Rhine, and the Norse ship to sail eventually back to Copenhagen.

Marta did not go ashore again but stayed on board for the remaining few days. Moor was a great favourite with the crew and received lots of attention. One of the men presented him with a toy boat which he'd carved out of wood. Moor clutched it to his chest and kept it with him constantly. No-one had behaved inappropriately towards Marta so she was feeling more comfortable and relaxed. She offered to help the cook to prepare food in the galley which he much appreciated.

The evening before they were due to leave for Denmark en-route to Poland, Aaron asked Raju if he could buy some of his silk and brocade.

'I have an idea that perhaps I could make beautiful clothes and sell them wherever we end up. I definitely want to take up tailoring for a living once I'm settled somewhere.'

'Of course. Buy whatever you want from my stock. We go look now.'

So the two men set off to the hold and with the help of three other crewmen to lift aside the long rolls of materials, Aaron chose many bolts of silk, brocade, sendal and perse in a variety of jewel colours. He and Raju shook hands on a price and Aaron settled the account in cash right away.

'I hope there will be room on the Danish ship for all this plus our other bundles,' said Aaron scratching his chin when he saw the pile he'd accumulated.

Raju just shrugged. 'It will all fit,' he stated.

Meanwhile Marta had been tidying their bundles in readiness for the move next morning to the other ship. She settled Moor for the night and came out on deck.

'I've made a kind of nest for Moor to sleep in on top of the sacks,' she told Aaron. 'It will give us a bit more room ourselves. I was very hot last night. It gets so stuffy behind that canvas.'

'Yes, you're right. That's a good idea.'

Just at that, Raju called over to them, 'Come, come. Join Solomon and myself for farewell drink.'

Marta was astonished to be invited, but they both thanked him. Aaron smiled and laid his hand on Raju's shoulder. They followed him into his tiny quarters in the forecastle where there was a wooden bed built against the wall, a table and four chairs and a large trunk. Two lanterns cast a warm glow around the cramped but clean cabin. On the table sat a tray with four pewter goblets and a bottle of brandy.

'Sit down, sit down. Ah, here is other guest. Come in Solomon.'

The captain nodded, smiled to the group and took a seat.

'Here,' Raju poured out the golden liquid and handed a goblet first to Marta, then Aaron, then Captain Solomon. Filling the final goblet for himself he stood and raised it in a toast. 'To good health, long life and friendship.' They all repeated his words, clinked their drinking vessels with each other and took a gulp of brandy.

Both Aaron and Marta coughed as the warmth of the liquor caught the back of their throats, but they tried not to make it obvious that it was the first time they'd tasted brandy.

The captain made kind enquiries about Aaron and Marta's plans and seemed to think it was a good idea to make for Poland. 'I heard through conversation with another captain today that King Casimir the Great of Poland is welcoming Jewish refugees from all the lands that have banished them. You should be safe there.'

'That is very good news indeed,' replied Aaron, smiling and turning towards Marta. 'Have you ever been to Poland sir?'

'No,' answered Solomon, 'but it should be a straightforward journey from Denmark, I believe. The crew on the Danish ship will be able to advise you, I'm sure.'

Aaron and Marta grinned to each other while Raju refilled the goblets. The evening was spent most pleasantly. Another bottle was opened and when it was time to retire, the couple found themselves staggering across the deck to their sleeping quarters, each leaning on the other for support, with much mirth.

They fell onto their feather bed and Marta, being greatly inebriated, lost her modesty and inhibition and started to remove her outer garments, but with difficulty.

'I'm too hot to sleep in my clothes tonight,' she complained, 'and I can't... get... these... laces... to budge!'

'Here, I'll help you,' said Aaron and with much giggling and fumbling, he managed to divest her of her clothes

'Now it's your turn. Come on, Aaron, don't be shy,' coaxed Marta and pulled at his shirt and breeches until they ended in a heap on the deck.

The inevitable happened.

They tumbled together on the quilt and Aaron whispered softly, 'Are you sure about this, Marta?'

'Yes, I'm sure,' came her reply.

Aaron hesitated.

'Is something the matter?'

'No... well... not exactly... it's just that I haven't been with anyone before.' He was glad of the darkness as his cheeks were burning.

'Oh, that's really sweet,' Marta whispered, gently kissing his soft beard. 'Come here and I'll teach you.' She pulled his face to her lips and then down to her breast. 'I don't think you'll need much help,' she added laughing, as she felt his hardness against her thigh.

*

Next morning, they were awakened by the cook clanging the triangle for breakfast.

'Oh, oh my head,' groaned Aaron, covering his eyes from the daylight penetrating the edge of the canvas flap.

Marta said nothing. She rose very slowly. Her head was thumping and her mouth was too dry for speech. Moor stirred and raised himself up, holding out his arms to her. 'Mm,' was all she could muster.

'Mama,' Moor said clearly. 'Ayon, Ayon,' he called over to Aaron who gave an answering groan.

Marta was gradually recalling the events of the previous evening as she looked at the rumpled clothes strewn around. Pulling a petticoat over her head, she shrugged it down to hide her nakedness. Lifting Moor, she held him over the bucket which served as a chamber pot, her stomach heaving.

Aaron moaned again but rose from the bed and pulled on his breeches. He went out onto the deck to relieve himself through one of the openings in the side of the ship. There was a grey dawn light and the mist was still clinging to the surface of the river. He shuddered in the chill dampness, and then slung a bucket overboard to haul up some water. After sluicing his face and head, he felt only slightly better.

The canvas flap was lifted back and a white-faced Marta signalled to him to bring her some water too. He obliged, hardly daring to look her in the eye, and she closed the flap again to have her ablutions. Soon after, she and Moor emerged, washed and wearing clean clothes.

They joined the rest of the crew for food but Marta and Aaron could scarcely stomach anything. They both struggled with a little bread and cheese washed down with hot, diluted ale. However, having solid food inside them seemed to ease the queasiness. They had something else to bear too. Word had got around about their night-time activities and there were many knowing grins and winks from the men. Nothing was private with the close-knit sleeping arrangements on board the *Rashima*.

Aaron excused himself and hauled up more water to have a thorough wash. He put on a clean shirt and made himself presentable, ready to leave this ship and move on to the next stage of their journey.

CHAPTER THIRTEEN

Anya's Kindness

The quayside was beginning to fill with people to-ing and fro-ing between ships and shore. Raju commandeered a hand cart and had his men carry all of Aaron's and Marta's goods down to it at the harbour's edge. When it was filled, two of his crew pulled it along to the *Vaedder* and hailed Jen. He was expecting them and gestured to them to bring the bundles and sacks aboard. The merchant couple, and their son and daughter, were waiting to meet their new passengers.

Raju bid farewell to Aaron and Marta. 'I wish wellness to you all. Good luck go with you. We meet again someday,' he said with glistening eyes. Then he grabbed Aaron and hugged him closely. 'Be strong. You chosen for a great tailor one day.'

'Thank you... thank you for everything, Raju,' Aaron gulped.

Raju kissed Marta's hand and held it lovingly for a moment then turned his attention to Moor. 'Goodbye little one. Be good.'

They parted company and Raju stood and watched as they walked along the quay to the Danish vessel. Moor was calling, 'Bye bye,' and waving his hand happily.

When they reached the *Vaedder* Aaron raised his hand in a final wave of farewell to this kind man who had done so much for him.

The Andersen family were waiting at the top of the gangplank to welcome their new passengers. A family of blonde heads, they greeted Aaron and Marta with smiles.

The tall man pointed to himself and announced, 'Jen. Jen Andersen.' His wife gave a similar gesture and said, 'I Sigrid,' and smiled. A boy who looked about fourteen stepped forward and shook Aaron's hand. 'Tomas Jensen,' he nodded. A pretty girl of around twelve years of age, smiled shyly and said, 'Alina Jensdatter.'

'Oh, I see, Jen's son and Jen's daughter,' Aaron said aside to Marta. Smiling to Jen, he said pointing to his chest, 'I am Aaron Levey and this is my friend, Marta Adler,' he said, as he touched Marta's arm, 'and this is Moor,' as he uncovered the wriggling bundle of smiles.

'Oh,' they all said in unison. There was some chatter among them which indicated their surprise.

Jen pointed at both the adults in turn and then at the black baby boy, raised his eyebrows, lifted his shoulders and spread both hands out facing upwards that suggested, how did that happen?

Aaron and Marta laughed. Aaron shook his head and his hand, indicating that the baby wasn't theirs. The Andersens still looked puzzled but invited them on to the ship.

It was certainly bigger than the *Rashima* with a wide deck which had hatches which led down to the hold. At the front there was a forecastle underneath the prow with the ram's head carving, which Jen led them towards. He showed Aaron into a small cabin with two hammocks. Tomas pointed to one and indicated that it was his. Aaron was to have the other one. There were two stools fastened to the deck, a porthole giving light and a lantern hanging from the ceiling. Aaron thumped down his bag containing his treasures and various pieces of clothing. He smiled and nodded to Tomas.

Meanwhile, Sigrid and Alina took Marta and Moor to a similar cabin with two hammocks, on the other side of the forecastle. Marta was to share with Alina. They had fastened a beautiful, carved crib to the floor for Moor. It was big enough for him and Marta was thrilled that they'd gone to such trouble. She smiled and voiced her gratitude. Sigrid showed her a closet where she could keep clothes and a chamber pot for her own use.

Just at that, they saw their bundles and sacks being loaded aboard. Aaron ran forward to help and offered the Andersens two sacks of flour, bags of barley and some dried fruits. They were delighted and accepted graciously. Marta retrieved her water jug and basin and some bedding. Moor clamoured for his toy boat. Their belongings were stacked in the hold in an easy to retrieve position. Jen pointed to the bolts of fine material and raised his eyebrows questioningly.

'Oh, they are for me,' said Aaron, pointing to himself. 'I am a tailor. A tailor,' he said again, mimicking sewing with a needle and pointing to clothing.

'Ah,' replied Jen nodding with understanding. 'Tailor.'

*

Soon after, the main sail was raised and the ship pulled away from the harbour at Rotterdam. Aaron and Marta were fascinated watching all the bustle on deck and Moor's big eyes took in everything. Jen and Tomas had helped raise the sail and Aaron thought that he would offer to assist them in the future. Sigrid came and stood by Marta and Moor and pointed to what she thought might be things of interest. Marta pointed out to sea and asked, 'Where are we going?'

'Bremerhaven... Bremerhaven,' answered Sigrid, hoping that she'd understood what Marta was asking.

There was a high wind so the ship sailed briskly along with the current. It wasn't long before they left all signs of habitation behind as the river opened out into the North Sea. The change there was evident.

The waves were much larger than before and the vessel heaved up and down as it forged its way along the western German coast towards Denmark. Marta started to feel queasy before they had been out in the ocean for an hour. Aaron was the same. To his embarrassment, he had to rush to the side of the ship where he threw up. When Marta saw him being sick, she thrust Moor into Sigrid's arms and just made it to the edge of the deck herself. The pair of them spent the rest of the morning lying in their cabins, when they weren't rushing to the deck side to vomit. Marta was particularly ill and ended up lying low for the rest of the day. She was glad that Sigrid was happy to care for Moor, who seemed none the worse for the journey.

Jen popped his head in to Aaron's cabin to check that he was all right. Aaron was hunched in his hammock with a hand over his eyes. 'Vand?' Jen asked, offering him a cup of water.

Aaron could barely lift his head, he felt so vilely nauseous, but he tried to sip some of the water. He nodded his thanks, unable to speak more or to sit up. His skin had taken on a greenish tinge. Jen gave him a friendly pat on the arm and said something which Aaron didn't comprehend but knew that he was being kind and understanding.

The journey continued to be an ordeal for both Aaron and Marta. It would be at least three or four days before they reached Bremerhaven, the next stop for trading for the Andersens. Moor was happy to be with Alina or Sigrid during the day, and Alina put him in his crib beside Marta when darkness came. Marta seemed much worse than Aaron and could not even keep a sip of water down. She lay, moaning, becoming very weak by the second day. By evening on the third day, Aaron was starting to feel better and made the effort to rise from his hammock and come out for some air on deck. Although he felt shaky, he knew he was over the worst of the sea-sickness.

Sigrid gave him a little light soup which he managed to keep down. He nodded in the direction of Marta's cabin and asked how she was. Sigrid shook her head and looked concerned. She beckoned to him to come with her to see Marta. Alina had been playing with Moor on the deck but it was growing colder so she took him into the cabin at the same time as the others. Moor called out, 'Mama, Mama,' when he saw her lying in her hammock, and reached out in her direction, but Marta could barely open her eyes for a second. Aaron was shocked to see her so ill. He took Moor from Alina and held him close.

'Come and have some supper, then we'll get you into bed,' he said to Moor giving him a happy smile which belied how he really felt. 'Mama is sleeping just now.'

Jen and Sigrid were looking very serious when they came into the galley where Aaron was feeding Moor some bread and milk sops. They tried to explain what they were thinking about Marta's condition, but Aaron didn't understand their words. He could see that they were very worried. Sigrid kept shaking her head and pointing towards Marta's cabin and patting her chest in the heart area.

'Do you think there is something wrong with her heart?' Aaron asked them. But of course, they couldn't understand what he was saying. 'Ooooh, this is an impossible situation,' Aaron forced from the back of his throat, holding back a scream of frustration. Feeling desperate, yet not wanting to upset Moor or the kind people who were helping them all they could, he took a deep breath, put a smile on his face and finished feeding Moor. He indicated that he would settle him in bed and made his way over to the cabin which Marta shared. Her condition had deteriorated in the short while since Aaron had last seen her. She was deathly pale with a sweat glistening on her forehead and top lip. Her breathing seemed laboured.

'Mama, Mama, kissy,' said Moor, reaching out to her.

Aaron leaned over her and let Moor kiss her cheek. 'Sleeping... Sh,' the child whispered.

'Yes, she's sleeping. You be good and go to sleep now too. Here is your boat,' he said quietly as he handed Moor his toy and tucked him into his little bed. Alina was with her mother, away from the suffering Marta.

Aaron spent the night sitting beside his dear friend, watching her struggling to breathe. He bathed her face with damp cloths, wiped her parched lips and tried to squeeze a little water between them. He propped more clothes behind her back to try to raise her a bit to ease her breathing, but she did not improve. Managing to open her eyes one time, she whispered, 'Moor.'

'He's all right, he's sleeping beside you,' Aaron assured her. 'We should be reaching Bremerhaven in the morning. You'll feel better once we are in calm water.'

She gave him a tremulous smile and shook her head. 'I feel... my heart beating... oddly, ' she gasped. 'Aaron,' she tried to reach for his hand, 'Aaron, will you look after Moor... when I'm gone.'

'You are not going anywhere. We'll get you medicines tomorrow in Bremerhaven.'

Her eyes closed again. 'Moor,' she whispered.

'Yes, I will look after him,' Aaron reassured her, and she relaxed a little but her breath was rasping.

Sigrid looked in from time to time and signalled that she would sit with Marta, but Aaron shook his head. He patted Sigrid's hand and smiled his gratitude but he couldn't leave his friend's side. Sigrid nodded her understanding and for the remaining time, just came in to bring him some hot ale or to replace the bathing water.

Just after dawn, they pulled into the harbour at Bremerhaven. It was a cold morning with a sharp wind. Aaron went out on deck to look at the land. There was just a small settlement there as far as he could see. Would there be a woman who had herbs to cure Marta? How could he get her to someone who could help? He paced around, thinking.

Sigrid came and found him. 'Moor?' she asked, indicating that she would see to him. Aaron nodded, and they both went into the cabin where Moor was awake and in the process of climbing out of the crib.

'Ayon, Sigid,' he called up to them, laughing. Sigrid picked him up. 'Mama sleeping,' he whispered and put a finger to his lips as he looked over at his mother.

Sigrid took him out and saw to his needs.

*

The crew were busying about, striking the sail and tying ropes around the bollards on the harbour. Aaron became aware of men ashore who were speaking in the Germanic tongue with which he was familiar. His spirits lifted. Were they still in the Empire? If so, he could speak with people and be understood. But what if they captured him? Oh, what to do? He decided to wrap himself up in his cloak, which would not look odd as the weather was so cold and windy. He'd go ashore and ask for help.

Hurrying back to his cabin, he searched for his cloak and flung it around his shoulders, pulling the hood well forward over his head. Tomas was already out on deck with his father, opening the hatches to the hold in readiness for bringing up some cargo to take to market. Aaron ran over to them and did his best to sign what he intended. He gathered covers and Marta's cloak and beckoned to them to help him lift her. He pointed to a board which was used to extend the gangplank when required, and signalled that they could carry her on that. Marta was barely conscious and gave shuddering breaths as Aaron lifted her with Jen's assistance on to the board. They wrapped her warmly against the wind. Jen held up a hand to stop Aaron, and ran over to the hold where he shouted something to Tomas who handed up a fur rug large enough to cover Marta. He placed it gently over her and the two men then carried her carefully down the gangplank to the level ground of the harbour. A few people were watching and one of them shouted over, 'Come no further if she has the plague.'

'It's not the plague,' Aaron assured him. 'I think it's her heart. Is there someone who can give her a physic or potion?'

'Well, there's a woman nearby in the forest who might help her,' came the answer.

Aaron asked urgently, 'Please can you show us where she is?'

'Just follow that track away from the harbour,' the man pointed the way. 'It leads into the woods. Keep to the track. You'll come to her house.'

'Here, my lad will show you,' offered another.

'Thank you, thank you,' shouted Aaron, and nodded to Jen to follow the boy who was waving to them just ahead.

It was difficult to keep the board level as they made their way along the path as directed, but they finally saw the lad pointing to a small house of wattle and daub, its thatched roof partly covered by the branches of a large tree. Aaron was relieved that they had made it. Oh, how he hoped that this woman might have herbs or something to help Marta who now looked deathly pale and oblivious to what was happening. Aaron noticed that her laboured breathing had lessened. The young lad ran and knocked at the door of the small building and called out, 'Anya, Anya, someone needs your help.'

A woman immediately opened the door. She looked as though she was wearing all the clothes she possessed as there appeared to be a patched kirtle over layers of skirts then two shawls which she pulled tightly around herself, tying the top one in a knot at her chest as she moved quickly towards the men. Her hair was white and loose and fell down to her waist. Her kind-looking face was serious as she came forward and looked at the girl on the board. 'Bring her inside,' she ordered and Jen and Aaron followed her into her cottage. She cleared some utensils from the bare, scrubbed-top table in the centre of the room and they laid the board down on it.

Aaron spoke up. 'My name is Aaron and this is my friend, Marta. She became very sick when we first sailed out into the sea, and has grown weaker each day. Can you do anything to help her?'

Anya looked closely at Marta who did not now appear to be breathing. She bent her head down to listen to Marta's chest. She felt her forehead and the side of her neck then lifted back Marta's eyelids, one at a time. She looked up at Aaron. 'I'm afraid it is too late. There is nothing I can do for your friend. She has already gone.'

'No, no, she can't be!' exclaimed Aaron, throwing himself over Marta, patting her face and rubbing her hands. 'Marta, Marta. She is warm. She was breathing when we brought her off the ship!'

Jen pulled him gently back then stood with an arm around Aaron's shoulders.

'I'm sorry,' said Anya. 'Perhaps she had a weakness of the heart that was made worse by the sickness.'

'What shall we do?' Aaron implored Jen, who could see what had happened although he couldn't make out the conversation.

'I think you need a little time to think about this,' said the woman quietly. 'Sit yourselves down and I'll give you a calming drink,' She

126

pointed to two wooden chairs and Aaron promptly flopped down on one as though his legs had given way. 'Jasper, run and bring your father, there's a good lad,' she called over to the boy who was still hanging around the doorway. He ran off obediently right away. Jen sat down beside Aaron, feeling shocked himself at this turn of events made harder for him by his lack of the language.

Anya handed them both hot drinks. 'That will do you good. They are an infusion of herbs which will help to calm your grief and clear your mind.'

Both men nodded their thanks and sipped the strange-tasting liquid which certainly felt soothing. Aaron could feel his own breathing slowing down as he relaxed slightly and was able to refocus. Anya stood quietly beside them also sipping a cup of the tea. The sound of running steps came within minutes and a man appeared, breathless at the door. 'Jasper told me... what happened... to your young lady,' he panted. 'Can I be of help?' He stepped forward and shook Aaron's hand then Jen's. 'I'm Sven. I am sorry for your loss.'

Aaron became aware that he must keep his face shielded, just in case... 'Thank you. How kind of you,' he answered. 'My name is Aaron and this is Jen. He is Danish... doesn't have this tongue. I... I suppose we will have to think about burying her.' He kept his head down with his hood pulled forward. Sven didn't think this was odd, just that the man was grieving.

'Where were you heading? Do you want to take her body with you on the ship?' the man asked.

'Eh, no, I think Marta would prefer to be buried here. She is from *Koln* so at least she will be laid to rest in her home country,' Aaron decided, deliberately avoiding mentioning that he was making his way to Poland.

'Why don't you leave the young lady here and go back to your ship just now. You can come back later with others to help dig a grave in the woods if you like?' suggested Anya.

Aaron was moved by her kindness. 'Thank you, thank you so much. Yes that is the best thing to do, I suppose.'

'Would you like me to attend to her? 'Anya enquired.

'I could get a priest,' suggested Sven.

'No! No priest,' said Aaron sharply. 'I think she'd be happier going to her Maker with just kind friends around.' Anya and Sven nodded. 'Thank you for your offer to take care of the necessary offices for her,' he said to Anya. 'I'd be most grateful if you would do that.' He shook her hand. 'I... I'll come back in the late afternoon... to bury her.' His voice broke. It all seemed so sudden and talking of burying her seemed unreal when she wasn't yet cold.

Aaron moved towards the door and Jen followed behind him. Sven accompanied them back down the track to the harbour area. 'I don't want to speak out of turn, but I'm a carpenter, and I have some, um, coffins in my wood store. Would you be er, wanting one for this afternoon, or do you have some other arrangement in mind?' he broached tentatively to Aaron.

'I haven't given it a thought yet, but yes, if you have a suitable coffin, I will be happy to purchase it,' he answered.

'Then I'll get it taken to Anya's home today and it will be there for you later.'

'Thank you. Everyone is being so kind,' said Aaron.

Sven gave a nod and turned away to walk into the town, while Aaron and Jen climbed back on board the *Vaedder*. Sigrid hurried forward to meet them when she saw them approaching. Jen explained what had happened to Marta, as far as he knew. Sigrid burst into tears and turning to Aaron, flung her arms around him, saying words in Danish which Aaron could only suppose were expressions of sympathy. Then she called out, 'Moor?' looking from her husband to Aaron.

'Oh, no! I hadn't given him a thought,' groaned Aaron.

Alina appeared carrying the little boy who was clutching his boat and smiling as usual. He held out his arms to Aaron who hugged him tightly as tears flowed down his cheeks.

*

For Aaron, the rest of that day went by in a blur. He brought a bolt of white silk up from the hold and cut off a length to be used as a shroud. When Tomas saw what he was doing, he offered to take it ashore for him. Aaron pointed out the young boy, Jasper, who was busy pushing laden carts around on the pier. Tomas nodded and ran down the gangplank to give the silken bundle to the boy. He pointed to Aaron on deck then to the woods. Nodding, Jasper waved to Aaron, went over to an older man who was probably his boss, had a quick conversation which received a nod from the man, then ran up the track and was soon out of sight among the trees.

Aaron sat about in a daze until late afternoon. Jen, Sigrid and the family came to his cabin where he was sitting holding Moor. Jen beckoned to him and pointed over to the woodland. He had left three spades leaning against the deck side which Tomas lifted as they walked past. Moor clapped his hands with pleasure at being carried off the ship.

They walked in silence along the path to Anya's cottage. Sven was waiting at the open door and when he saw them approaching, he pulled off his cap and bowed his head. Anya came to the doorway and beckoned them inside. Marta was laid out on the table wrapped in the white silk. Wild flowers had been placed in a little coronet on her head and formed into a posy in her hands. A plain wooden coffin lay to one side of the room. Moor called out, 'Mama, Mama,' holding out his arms when he saw her.

It tore at Aaron's heart to hear him. 'Give Mama a kiss, Moor,' he said and bent down so that the little boy could touch his lips to her cheek. He himself kissed her forehead and turned away holding the child close. Taking Moor outside, he gave a nod to Sven who entered the room. He could hear the rustling as the men lifted Marta and placed her in the coffin. He winced as he heard the nails being hammered into the lid. Anya came forward and touched his arm. 'Come and see where I thought your friend could lie in peace,' she said, leading him into the wood. She pointed to a small clearing where the sun shone through the trees. A stream bubbled lazily nearby over pebbles smoothed by years of washing. 'This is a lovely spot. The bluebells grow all around like a blue carpet in the spring and the birds love to drink and bathe in the water. I often come here just to enjoy the peace or to gather herbs and fungi.'

'I think Marta would like it here very much,' Aaron said quietly. 'Thank you, Anya. You have been so very kind to us – especially as we are strangers to you.'

'I could see into your heart,' she answered, 'and I knew you were an honest man.'

Aaron smiled and they turned and walked back towards the cottage where the group were awaiting his instruction.

'Follow me please,' he said, beckoning them towards the clearing.

Sven and Jen carried the coffin while Tomas brought the spades. Aaron chose a place beneath a large beech tree and handing Moor over to Sigrid, he commenced to dig, along with the other two men. They managed to make a sizeable hole despite the tree roots, and when it was completed, they laid down their implements. Aaron took Moor by the hand. 'Moor, you are too young to understand what has happened, but I will explain when you are older. Your Mama is asleep and will not wake up now. We are going to place her in the ground here, where she will be safe and at peace.'

He helped Jen and Sven to lower the coffin into the grave. Not knowing what to say, he stood with the little boy and said some words in Yiddish that he felt were appropriate. Then, remembering Marta's Catholic upbringing, he said, 'May your God receive you into Heaven with the Blessed Virgin. Thank you for being my friend. I will miss you. I promise to look after Moor.' His throat constricted with held-back tears as he squeezed Moor's hand.

'Mama,' wailed Moor, picking up on the solemnity of the occasion. 'Mama.'

Alina came over with a bunch of wild flowers. 'Moor,' she coaxed and showed him how to throw the flowers upon the coffin.

The child took the flowers from her hands and threw them one by one into the grave.

'Say bye-bye to Mama now, Moor,' Aaron whispered. Everyone shed a tear at the sight of the sad little black boy saying goodbye to his mother. Lifting him into his arms, Aaron stood back as the others filled in the grave. Anya had tied two sticks together in the shape of a cross which she pushed into the earth, and then stood to the side reverently. Aaron looked around for a suitable stone and finding one, he pointed it out to Jen who carried it over to him. He scratched the word MARTA on the smooth surface and laid it at the base of the cross. Heaving a long sigh, Aaron turned away and they all straggled sadly back to the cottage.

Aaron paid Sven for providing the coffin and assisting at the burial. He handed Anya a small pouch containing money as well. 'No, no,' she said, shaking her head but Aaron insisted that she take it.

'You have been so kind. Please take it. I have nothing else to give you and I'm sure you will need money over the winter to buy food.' She nodded and accepted the money graciously.

Aaron suddenly remembered something. 'The fur wrap! Please keep it. It will remind you of us and will keep you warm when the snow comes.'

'Thank you. Thank you. I will indeed be grateful for its comfort,' she replied.

They all took their leave and walked slowly back to the ship. Moor was distressed and cried against Aaron's shoulder all the way back.

'It's alright little man. You still have me,' Aaron said patting him and trying to bring him some comfort.

CHAPTER FOURTEEN

Aaron and Moor

Aaron kept Moor close to him over the next few days while the ship was in Bremerhaven. Jen and Sigrid took their goods to the market each day for sale or barter, and Tomas often helped them with the loading and unloading. Alina assisted in keeping Moor occupied when she could but he was tearful and clung to Aaron. Trying to divert the child, Aaron decided to go ashore with him. He wouldn't risk going into the town itself, but thought he'd visit Anya again.

'Let's go for a walk in the woods,' he suggested to Moor. 'You can play with the leaves that have fallen from the trees.'

'Yes. Play with leaves,' he answered, not knowing what they were. His face lit up at the prospect of something different.

They wrapped up against the chill wind and Moor insisted on walking down the gangplank himself, refusing to be carried this time. 'You must hold my hand tightly,' ordered Aaron, 'otherwise you could end up in that deep water, and we don't want that.'

Moor peered down into the dark depths and shook his head. 'No,' he declared and clutched Aaron's hand. They hurried as fast as Moor could toddle along the quayside and made for the track which led through the wood to Anya's cottage. Once in among the trees, the little boy let go of Aaron's hand and ran through the deep piles of fallen leaves. They both spent a happy time kicking and throwing around the colourful dried leaves. Aaron felt like a young boy himself again, He could remember playing with Abigail and Dorit. They used to try to catch a leaf in mid-air as it fell from the tree. If they caught one, they could have a wish. The wind was blowing off many of the leaves that morning. Moor was laughing and enjoying the rustling sounds as he ran between the trees. Aaron stood for a moment and watched as the multi-coloured leaves swirled down in the dappled sunlight. He reached out and caught one - from a beautiful copper beech. Clutching it to his heart he whispered, 'Marta, please help me to look after Moor. Bring us to a safe place to live.'

'Here,' came the excited voice below him. He looked down and Moor was offering him a bunch of leaves. 'Leaves for Aayon.'

'Why thank you. They are lovely.' He tucked his beech leaf into his belt and took the leaf bouquet from the little boy. 'Why don't we take some to Anya?'

'Yes, more leaves,' cried Moor happily, and took his time to select the best ones for his present.

When they arrived at Anya's cottage, she was just returning from the opposite direction with a basket on her arm. 'What a lovely surprise. I didn't expect to see you again.' Her face lit up. 'Oh, thank you so much!' she exclaimed when Moor ran forward, holding out his posy of leaves to her.

'Leaves,' he said.

'Yes, and such lovely colours. This is red,'

'Wed,' he repeated.

'And this one is yellow.'

'Wellow,' he tried.

'Well done.'

They all went inside the small cottage and Anya offered them a chair while she pulled the kettle on to the fire. 'I've just been gathering mushrooms. Would you like to join me for something to eat?'

'Well, if you have enough to go round, that would be good,' answered Aaron.

'That's it settled then,' and she put a large skillet onto the fire and threw a knob of butter on it. Moor was fascinated as he watched the butter sizzle and melt.

'You can sit on this little stool and watch, but don't go any closer to the fire,' Anya instructed him as she lifted over a small three legged stool.

Moor nodded vigorously, delighted to be doing something new. Aaron sat at the table watching the proceedings as Anya trimmed the mushrooms and plopped them onto the skillet. She brought bread and butter to the table and three plates. He couldn't get out of his mind that the last time he'd been here just a few short days ago, his dear Marta had been laid out on the very same table.

'Ssss,' called Moor, pointing to the mushrooms, sizzling appetisingly in the melted butter.

'Yes, sssss, they are saying,' laughed Anya. She gave the mushrooms a shake and they tumbled over, starting to turn golden. 'Would you like some of my herb tea or just water from the stream?' she asked Aaron.

'Oh, I would be happy to have some of your tea again, thank you. Moor will just have water. I could go for it?'

'No need, I filled that big jug there earlier,' she answered pointing to a pitcher. Aaron lifted it over to the table for her. 'Well I think our meal will be ready now,' she announced, and Moor watched with interest as she tipped the mushrooms out on the plates. 'Come little one. Sit up at the table like a big boy.' She lifted him onto a chair where he knelt, and she handed him a spoon. 'I'll spread some butter on a piece of bread for you.'

Moor nodded and tried his best to shovel a mushroom onto his spoon then into his mouth.

'Do you like that, Moor?' Aaron asked, smiling.

'Mm, hm. Squishy,' he replied with his mouth full, nodding.

'It's good to see you again, Aaron,' Anya said once they'd enjoyed their repast. 'It must be hard being in this house after your last visit.'

'I-It is a little disconcerting, but I'm glad we came. We leave for Denmark tomorrow, so I wanted to say goodbye to you and visit Marta's grave. I don't expect we shall ever be back here again.'

Anya nodded. 'I will look after the grave for you. It is an honour.'

'You are a very unusual person indeed,' declared Aaron. 'As a Jew, I have only received such kindness once before.' His thoughts turned to Ulrich. He continued after a pause, 'Moor and I are outcasts in our home town, but although you live in the same country, you have shown us nothing but compassion.'

'You too are a very special person. You have been chosen as guardian to this wonderful child. It will not be an easy life but you will be well rewarded. You have a good heart, as I've told you before, and you will be protected.'

'How do you know these things, Anya?'

'Oh, I have the sight. I can foresee a busy, profitable life for you, working as a tailor. You will have a willing assistant in the child.'

'How did you know I was a tailor?' Aaron gasped.

'I told you. I have been gifted with foresight, although not everyone thinks on it as a gift. The Church for one. That's why I live quietly in the woods, out of the way. The locals seem to trust me and come to me for potions. I have heard of others like me who have been burned as witches, so I live each day as it comes in thankfulness for my simple life close to nature and hope for the best.'

'Your attitude reminds me of a dear friend who had similar beliefs.' He didn't mention that the friend he was thinking of had probably been murdered by a so-called priest of the Church. 'Well, we'd better be getting on our way. Come along, Moor. Say thank you to Anya for the mushrooms and bread.'

Moor clambered down from the chair and hugged Anya's legs. 'Thank you,' he said. 'I liked you mush-ooms.'

Aaron and Anya both laughed.

'Thank you for coming to visit me,' Anya replied hugging him back.

'I'll take him along to his mother's resting place and then head back to the ship. Thank you once again,' said Aaron, giving Anya a firm handshake.

'May you have a long and happy life,' she answered.

'Bye-bye,' called Moor giving her a wave and she blew him a kiss.

As they turned to walk into the woods, she called, 'You have a mighty guardian walking with you.'

Aaron was puzzled. Was she calling to Moor? Did she mean that he, Aaron, was a mighty guardian to Moor? But she was looking at me, he thought. Did she see someone walking beside me? Who? He felt a little shiver run through is body.

Moor was happily rustling through the dried leaves again. Soon they came to the clearing where the fresh grave lay beneath the beech tree. Some golden leaves had blown down upon the turned earth. Moor hesitated and held back against Aaron. He seemed to remember what had taken place there.

'Mama, mama,' he said with a quivering bottom lip.

Aaron knelt down beside him. 'Yes, Moor, this is where your Mama lies. She's sleeping under this tree. Let's gather more leaves and put them over her for a quilt.'

Moor nodded and solemnly gathered armfuls of beech leaves and laid them gently on the soft earth over the grave. 'Mama sleeping. Cosy now.'

They sat for a while by the stream whose gentle gurgles were the only sounds to break the silence. Aaron felt as though the very trees were in mourning along with him. Even Moor stayed quiet, sensing the sadness in his dear friend. Shortly afterwards, Aaron rose to go. 'Say goodbye to Mama, Moor.'

'Bye-bye,' said the child and blew a kiss towards the grave.

Aaron sighed. 'Goodbye, dear friend. He beckoned to Moor, 'Come little one,' and they returned along the track. Moor gathered a bunch of leaves to take to Alina. There was no sign of Anya at the cottage and the two continued on to the path leading back to the water.

It was turning colder and they were glad to be back on board ship. Moor called for Alina and proudly presented her with the handful of autumn leaves he'd collected.

'Thank you, Moor.' She smiled and gave him a kiss and said other things which Aaron didn't yet understand although he was picking up some of the Danish language each day. Moor was tired after all the walking and was happy to go for a rest in the afternoon, so Aaron settled him into his crib where he fell asleep in minutes.

Alina indicated that her parents would soon be back from the market and would want to get the ship ready for sailing the next day. The small number of crewmen were already packing food into the hold and checking the sails. Aaron made himself a hot drink and went into the cabin which he shared with Tomas and Moor, to rest and wait for Jen and Sigrid to return. He dozed off in his hammock but awoke to the sound of things being dragged across the deck and went outside to find Jen and Tomas loading cargo into the hold.

Jen hailed him. 'How are you, friend?'

'I am well. I have been ashore to visit Anya, and I took Moor to Marta's grave.'

Jen nodded and seemed to understand. 'You like to help me?' he indicated.

'Of course,' Aaron answered and helped the others as they carried supplies of cheese and meat, flour and dry goods into the hold. Then there were barrels of fresh water to roll across the deck. 'Did you sell your furs and carved wood?' he asked Jen with some pointing and hand signals.

'Ya, ya. Yes, we had busy day. We have many towns to visit now,' Jen answered.

They worked on until everything was loaded and secured, by which time Moor was awake and looking for food and company. It was becoming darker earlier in the evenings and much colder. *I might have to make some warmer clothing for Moor,* thought Aaron. I'll have a look in the bags Marta brought. Perhaps there are things there that will fit him.

They enjoyed their supper sitting all together with the lanterns lit, casting a soft light on the wooden table. Moor became upset again at bedtime, crying for his mother, so Aaron sat with him, singing and talking to him until he dropped off. He decided to retire for the night himself and was surprised when the beech leaf he'd caught earlier popped out from his waistband. He'd forgotten about it and fingered it lovingly as he placed it inside his holy book. Yawning, he lay down and promptly fell asleep. He didn't hear Tomas come to bed later. His dreams were full of happy times with Marta and Ulrich and even Anya appeared to him, smiling.

*

They cast off early in the morning, before first light. Jen explained that their next port of call would be Esbjerg. Depending upon weather conditions, the voyage would take a number of days. It was raining heavily and unpleasant to be out on deck. Alina offered to stay in the cabin playing with Moor to allow Aaron to assist the men on deck for a while. Naturally, she spoke to Moor in Danish and he was soon picking up many of her words as they played together. Tomas worked hard alongside his father, learning seamanship as well as how to trade goods.

Once they were well underway, Aaron returned to his cabin to find dry clothes. He decided to search through Moor's clothing bag for suitable warm items and found a number of little shifts in a heavier material than the ones he'd been wearing, as well as a hooded cape and soft boots. It reminded him that there was also a bag somewhere containing Marta's clothes. Should he offer them to Sigrid? He decided that he'd mention it at supper. Perhaps some of the clothes would be suitable or could be altered for Alina. That's if they'd like them.

After supper that evening, Aaron mentioned the matter of Marta's clothes to Sigrid and asked if she'd like to have a look at them.

She nodded. 'Ya, I will look.'

She brought Marta's bags from her cabin and went with Aaron into his cabin to check through the bags. She selected a number of items. 'I try,' she said, holding some kirtles and skirts against her, and went off to her own cabin.

A short while later, she came to Aaron with a smile and nodded, 'Thank you, I keep all.' She pointed towards the bundles containing the remainder of Marta's clothing. 'I take market?' she asked.

'Yes, that would be good,' replied Aaron. Sigrid smiled and left. Aaron decided to sort through the clothing to see if any of the material might be useful to make jackets or breeches for Moor. He selected a few pieces and laid them aside. Rummaging in the bottom of a bag, he came upon a small pouch. He tipped out the contents into his hand and found the string of blue beads which Ulrich had given Marta. She'd worn them a lot. Next there was a gold ring which he knew had belonged to her mother, and a small gold brooch in the shape of a flying bird. He held the brooch in the palm of his hand and admired the delicate workmanship. He'd keep them all and maybe find someone to wear them someday or keep them safe for Moor. Putting the jewellery back into the pouch, he placed it with his own treasures.

*

The journey to Esbjerg took four days in cold, wet weather. Aaron spent a lot of his time keeping Moor occupied. The child was finding it hard and was now asking for his mother throughout the day, not able to understand that she was gone for good. He was particularly fond of Alina so was happy enough to be left in her care for short times while Aaron helped Jen.

When they arrived at the port, Aaron assisted with unloading goods for Jen and Sigrid to take to the market place, but declined to go ashore. He had an idea. If Alina would play with Moor during daylight hours, he could get back to tailoring and cut out and sew garments. These could be for the Andersen family and, if he could make enough, some could be sold at the markets. Jen would have to agree to this of course.

He spent the day planning. He'd start with the material from Marta's clothing and create warm winter clothes for Moor. He'd find out who, if any of the Andersen's was in need of a new garment, and make that next. The problem was, where could he work? He really needed a table. The only one he could think of was in the galley where they ate, and the cook needed that on which to prepare and serve the meals. The cook was becoming a good friend as he adored Moor and happily mashed foods down for his meals. He'd handed over wooden spoons and bowls for the child to play with and Tomas had parted with a set of wooden bricks and a pull-along box on wheels which he had long outgrown. Moor loved to bang the spoons on the bowls and anything else that would make a noise. He pulled the box around containing the things he'd acquired along with his little boat.

'Let's go and talk to Hans, the cook,' Aaron suggested to Moor. They made their way slowly to the galley, Moor trailing his box on wheels behind him. Hans was delighted to see them and offered Aaron a welcome hot drink.

'Thank you, Hans,' said Aaron, pulling out a chair to sit at the table. Moor clambered up on his knee. When they both had drinks in front of them, Hans sat down too and had a short rest from chopping vegetables.

Aaron pointed to the table. 'I would like a table,' he said, pointing to himself and again to the table. 'I sew,' he said, mimicking stitching. Hans looked puzzled and shrugged his shoulders. Aaron picked up an oven cloth lying nearby and mimed cutting cloth and sewing, pointing to the table again and to himself. Hans seemed to understand.

'Jonas,' he said, pointing towards the forecastle. He tapped the table and spoke away in Danish but seemed to be miming cutting and sewing, just as Aaron had done. 'Jonas.'

'Thank you, Hans. I think you are telling me to go and find Jonas,' Aaron said with a smile to the cook.

'Jonas,' said Moor, and both men laughed at the young mimic. When their drinks were finished, Aaron took his leave and he and Moor made their way over the deck to where two crewmen were mending a sail. They greeted him gruffly, a little unsure of the bearded young man with the black child.

'Jonas?' queried Aaron.

One of the men turned around and shouted to someone inside the cabins under the forecastle. A strong looking man came to the doorway holding a hammer and wearing a sackcloth apron. 'Ya?' he queried.

Aaron beckoned him to follow over to the cook's domain. Jonas obediently walked behind Aaron and Moor who was chanting, 'Jonas, Jonas,' as he toddled along. Aaron smiled apologetically to the man who seemed to be the ship's carpenter. Now Aaron understood! Perhaps this man would be able to make him a table.

Hans explained to Jonas what he understood to be the request from Aaron. There was much miming and laughter among them all but Jonas finally nodded. He stood rubbing his chin, deep in thought. Then, walking towards Aaron's cabin, he went inside and looked at the walls. He signalled to Aaron to enter and again with much miming, indicated that he could attach a piece of wood to a wall which could then be folded up when not in use. He reached into his apron pocket and bringing out a measuring stick, proceeded to take some measurements. Aaron and Moor again followed Jonas back over to his workplace where he selected a thick piece of wood which was as wide as Aaron's open arms. Aaron grinned in amazement. It would make a perfect table. Jonas mimed that he would smooth it down and put hinges on one side and a fixture for holding it against the wall when folded up. The cabin would be cramped when it was pulled down, but it would be flat against the wall when he and Tomas needed to go to their hammocks. Some rearranging of their belongings was all that was required. Aaron shook the carpenter's hand vigorously to show his appreciation of the plan and Jonas responded with a large grin, waved them off and returned to whatever he'd been doing in his cabin workroom.

Delighted that he'd managed to make himself understood with so little knowledge of the Danish language, Aaron decided that from now on he would make an effort to learn some new words or phrases each day.

When Jen and Sigrid arrived back at the ship at dusk, Aaron was bursting to explain his plans for a table so that he could get back into tailoring. They were both intrigued by his explanations and after consulting with Hans and Jonas, they seemed to understand what he was about. Thankfully, Jen was quite happy about Aaron's plans and consented to the addition of the fold-up table in the cabin without any fuss. Aaron had completely forgotten that his plan to cut and sew materials depended largely upon Alina's willingness to look after Moor, but he needn't have worried, she was thrilled at the prospect of caring for him.

So began another new phase in Aaron's life. While the ship was anchored in a harbour and Jen and Sigrid were conducting their business in the towns they visited, Aaron was busy making garments. He found it impossible to work while they were at sea as the rolling movement of the ship made it difficult to keep his material on the table, let alone cut it. However, it was easy when they were sitting calmly at anchor in a harbour. Alina took charge of Moor on these sewing days and kept him occupied away from sharp scissors and pins. Sometimes she took him ashore for a short walk but kept away from the busy markets where someone might challenge her having a dark-skinned child in tow. On the days when they were out at sea, she would come to Aaron's cabin at some point each day and they would teach each other words from their own language as they played and taught Moor. Over the course of the voyage, Alina learned much from Aaron in both the Germanic tongue and some Yiddish. Aaron picked up the Danish language well and soon became able to understand the conversations at suppertime. Moor was like a little sponge and took in all of the learning from both sides. He was developing as multi-lingual and understood everyone.

The journey around the coastline of Denmark took them to Thyboran, then up the Skaggerak to Hirtshals, round The Skaw to Skagen and then on to Frederikshavn.

Autumn had turned into winter and the seas were becoming very rough and dangerous. Jen was glad to anchor in Frederikshavn as his brother lived there with his wife and family. The Andersens always visited Rolf when they reached that port and it was a most welcome visit this time as the weather was so bitterly cold. Jen went first to his brother's place as soon as they berthed and returned within the hour to pass on the news that Aaron and Moor were invited to go with the family to Rolf Andersen's home.

Aaron dressed Moor warmly then wrapped his thick cloak around himself, pulled up the hood and the two set off on foot with the others. It was just a short walk to Rolf's home and his wife, two daughters and two sons made them all very welcome. Deta was the woman's name and she had venison roasting for them over a spit in the large, open fireplace. A delightful smell of spiced apples came from the ovens to the side of the fire.

Alina and Tomas were pleased to reacquaint themselves with their cousins and disappeared into another room. Aaron was warmly welcomed as a friend of Jen and Sigrid's and Moor became the centre of attention, much to his delight. It was a bit overwhelming for him to meet so many new people at once, but his shyness did not last for long. He was intrigued by their large, golden coloured dog, Guld, who allowed him to stroke and ruffle his coat. Soon they were lying together in front of the fire.

Rolf offered ale to Jen and Aaron and they sat by the fire talking and enjoying the warmth while the womenfolk caught up with their news whilst preparing the meal. Rolf asked Aaron about his life and how he'd come by Moor. Aaron gave him a summarised version, wary of saying too much about his Jewish background and repeated Marta's story that Moor was a foundling child. However, he needn't have worried, Rolf had no animosity towards Jews and had never known any in that area.

He was sympathetic when told of Marta's recent death and held admiration for Aaron in taking on guardianship of the little half-caste child.

Aaron felt that he could relax with this charming family and thoroughly enjoyed the day spent with them. The meal with the whole group was challenging and he had to have his wits about him to pick up the conversations, but managed well and was congratulated on his pronunciation of the Danish words. Alina helped the others out with translation from time to time and her parents were proud of her new skills with language.

It transpired that Rolf was a merchant trader in wood and furniture.

'Aaron is a tailor,' Jen announced to the group after dinner. 'He has been making clothes for us all during the times when the ship is in port and Sigrid and I are at the market, trading.' There was a murmur of interest from everyone.

'Where did you learn your trade?' asked Rolf.

'From my father,' answered Aaron, feeling his cheeks redden as everyone's eyes were upon him. 'He was a fine tailor in *Koln* and taught me well.'

'He did at that,' said Rolf eyeing Aaron's clothes approvingly.

'He made this kirtle for me,' said Sigrid, posing for the others to admire, then pointing to her husband's new clothes, 'and Jen's tunic.'

Deta lifted the material of Sigrid's dress to look at the needlework. 'Your stitching is so tiny and neat. You can sew much better than I. Very skilled work indeed,' she said approvingly.

Aaron felt proud and pleased that he had their approval. 'I would really like to make beautiful clothes in silks, velvets and brocades with beads and ribbon adornments, but there wasn't much call for such work where I lived before. I am hoping to travel to Poland eventually so perhaps I'll get the opportunity to do good quality tailoring work there.' They all nodded in agreement.

Rolf had been thinking quietly, then said, 'I don't know about Poland, but I happen to have a friend in the aristocracy in Copenhagen. He is the Count of Holstein. He has purchased much of his fine furniture from me. I could write you a letter of introduction to give to him. Would you like that?'

'Why, that would be wonderful, thank you,' answered Aaron. 'I would like that very much.'

So it was arranged.

'You must all come back again tomorrow for supper. I'll have the letter ready for you then, Aaron.'

The rest of the day was spent most amiably with everyone enjoying each other's company and Moor being lavished with attention. They had another light repast at dusk then set off back to the ship with orders to return after the close of market next day. Moor had acquired some new playthings from the family and was asleep as soon as he was laid in his crib after all the excitement of the visit.

*

The next few weeks were busy for Aaron. The weather was too stormy to take to the seas, so the Andersens stayed harboured in Frederikshavn and frequently visited with their relatives. Aaron received the letter of introduction to the Count of Holstein, as promised by Rolf. He kept it safely in his cabin, away from little fingers. He took advantage of the time aboard on calm water in the harbour, and created many garments. He'd decided to make gowns secretly for Sigrid and Alina as presents for Jule, or Yule as he'd known the winter celebration with Ulrich, and had to do this when the women were otherwise occupied. He chose a rich claret coloured material for the dress for Sigrid and a rose pink silk for Alina's gown. He was good at guessing sizes but already knew their measurements from doing alterations to some of Marta's clothes for them. He kept the gowns folded and hidden and worked on them when he could. At his request, Deta had purchased beads and ribbons for him and was in on the surprise.

'Tomorrow is Saint Lucy's Day,' announced Sigrid one evening at supper. 'We are all invited to go to the procession with Rolf and Deta and the children.'

'Oh, that will be fun,' cried Alina. 'We've been to the procession before with them, Aaron.'

'What happens on Saint Lucy's Day then?' he asked.

'Well, it comes on the shortest day in winter, and in the past, the story was that Saint Lucy was supposed to bring back the light,' answered Sigrid. 'There is a lovely procession with girls from the town carrying lanterns. Then we eat and drink and make merry of course,' she laughed.

'It sounds similar to the pagan celebration that my friend Ulrich shared with me. He cut down a tree to provide a Yule log for the fire. We decorated a tree in the woods and lit a bonfire and danced and sang around it. There was also a great feast as I recall.'

'Ah, the Yule sounds like our Jule,' declared Jen. 'Do you have a Jewish celebration around the solstice?'

'Yes, we have something called Hanukkah,' answered Aaron. It seemed so long since he had been involved with any Jewish tradition. He could feel a sadness creeping upon him.

Sigrid was quick to notice this. 'Tell me about your Hanukkah. Perhaps we could have a joint celebration tomorrow.'

Aaron's face lit up. 'That would be wonderful. I did that once before when I lived with Ulrich. I must get into the hold in the morning to find my special menorah candlestick.'

'Oh, tell us all about it,' exclaimed Alina.

Aaron spent a happy time explaining all about the Hanukkah tradition and Sigrid promised to look out suitable candles. There would definitely be a feast at Rolf and Deta's house to chase away the darkness of winter. They all looked forward to the following day, Aaron in particular. He and Tomas went down into the hold and found the bundle containing not only his own treasured family menorah candlestick, but also the one which Ulrich had had made by the blacksmith. He brought both up on deck.

'Why don't we have one lit here, on the ship, and keep one at Uncle Rolf's house too?' suggested Tomas.

'Well, if everyone is agreeable with that, then I will be happy too,' answered Aaron.

So that was what happened. Aaron lit his own hanukkiyah and set it on the table in the galley. Everyone in the crew and the family gathered round while he said the blessings. He translated them into Danish and they all thanked him and seemed pleased. Later in the afternoon, they went ashore and joined the other Andersens to watch the Saint Lucy procession. It was delightful and full of joy and light.

'Now it's time for feasting and merrymaking,' announced Rolf, laughing. 'Have you brought your special candlestick, Aaron?'

'Yes, I have the one which my friend, Ulrich had made for me,' he answered.

'We have candles for you,' said Deta. 'Hopefully they'll be the right size,' she added.

'Oh, we'll make them fit,' said Jen, with a laugh.

They returned to the house which was filled with the aroma of roasting meat. Lanterns and candles were lit and placed in all the windows and around the rooms. They all gathered around Aaron as he lit the menorah reverently and proceeded with the blessings once more. As previously, he translated into Danish for them which they appreciated and reciprocated with some traditional songs. Moor danced in the centre of the floor and clapped his hands to everyone's delight. Rolf produced spiced hot home-made wine which helped along the singing and merrymaking, and soon it was time to sit down for their delicious feast. The festivities carried on well into the night.

*

'We'll be doing it all again soon, at Jule,' groaned Jen next morning, holding his head in his hands.

'When do you think we'll be able to set sail again?' asked Aaron, who was similarly suffering the after effects of Rolf's home-made wine.

'Probably not for at least another month, depending on the ice,' came the answer. 'But as soon as possible in the New Year.'

Aaron was quite happy with that. He could make many garments while they were in port and perhaps Jen and Sigrid would be able to sell some. He had finished the dresses for Alina and Sigrid and was now making long waistcoat-type garments in heavy lined brocade as gifts for Jen and Tomas, Rolf and his two sons, Ben and Reinhard. He still had to make something suitable for Deta and her daughters Anna and Catharin.

He planned to make them cloaks, each with a different coloured lining. The collars would be beaded, so it would need a lot of candle hours. Hopefully, he'd get the work finished for the Jule celebrations and could spend the remaining days on board making clothes for Jen and Sigrid to take to market.

*

The snow fell thickly that winter, creating a beautiful sparkling white quilt over Frederikshavn, blotting out all imperfections. The townsfolk stayed mainly indoors, used to the severe weather each year and only ventured out to buy fresh food when it was available.

Whenever the snow fall ceased, Jen, Tomas and Aaron were to be found busily knocking snow from the tops of the folded sails and rigging on the ship. Then they shovelled and swept it from the decks.

'We've got to try to move as much snow as possible to avoid damage,' explained Jen. 'We want to be able to get on our way without wasting time on repairs when the weather clears.'

The Jule celebrations were enjoyed by all. Moor had a wonderful time and was showered with presents. He had new wooden toys, a fur hat and boots, bells to jingle and lots of sweet treats. The clothes which Aaron had made with such thoughtfulness were received with much exclamation and warm thanks. Everyone wore their new garments to the Jule party and felt very special indeed. Aaron was not left out when presents were exchanged and he was thrilled to receive a sewing box containing a myriad of coloured silks with needles and scissors from Rolf and his family, but Jen and Sigrid's present touched him the most.

'We feel that you are much more than just a passenger on our ship,' announced Jen. 'We feel that you and Moor are part of our family.' There was much clapping and whooping at this point. 'As our present to you, we would like to take you to Copenhagen at no further cost to you and... you can stay at our home there for as long as you want!'

Aaron gasped. 'I ... I don't know what to say. I am so blessed to have found such good people. Such mitzvah... er, kindness. Thank you. Thank you so much.' He sat shaking his head in amazement.

'Let's have a toast,' shouted Rolf, topping up everyone's drinks. 'To friendship!'

They all clinked drinking vessels and echoed, 'To friendship.'

It was very late when Aaron and the others waved their goodbyes and scrunched through the snow on a crisp, moonlit night back to the ship. Moor was sound asleep against Aaron's shoulder, snug in his new fur hat and boots and clutching his favourite new toy: a little reindeer, carved by Reinhard and painted red.

CHAPTER FIFTEEN

Copenhagen

It was nearly two months after the Jule celebrations before the weather improved enough for the ship to safely set sail again. Everyone was sad to be saying goodbye. Aaron would probably never see them again, and Moor would certainly miss their company and that of his canine friend, Guld. Jen, Sigrid, Alina and Tomas would return during the summer months for a short visit to collect furniture and carvings from Rolf to sell around the markets. Aaron had made a number of simple warm garments for sale at the ports of call, and was now spending time mastering how to work with the fine silks and satins. His dream to design and make beautiful cloaks, dresses and tunics in rich materials with the addition of beading and fancy stitching was becoming a reality. He was quickly learning how to handle the fine fabrics which slipped and slid around his table.

After leaving Frederikshavn, the Andersens' next stop was round the coast and into an inlet to Alborg. Sigrid took a load of Aaron's newly made clothes for sale along with their own goods and sold them all during the four day visit. Aaron was thrilled and handed over a third of the takings to Sigrid and Jen, which had been previously decided upon. Aaron had wanted them to keep half of the money, but Jen insisted that he had the major proportion as he'd have to buy more material in future and keep building up a stock.

'Why don't you make some sample garments of your own design, ready to show to the Count of Holstein when we reach Copenhagen?'

suggested Sigrid. 'I'm sure he'll have some wealthy friends who would love to have your individually made dresses and coats, as well as his wife and himself.'

'Mm, yes, that's an idea,' mused Aaron. 'I have some tunics in brocade already but I'd like to try some heavily beaded additions to the collars of cloaks. I just haven't had the time yet to perfect any fancy sewing.'

'Perhaps Alina could help you with the beading when we reach home?'

' 'But she's already helping by looking after Moor. If she'll carry on, that is.'

'I'm sure she will. Maybe she could sew with you in the evenings, when Moor is asleep?'

'Oh, I don't like to encroach on her family time with you and Jen.'

'Nonsense, she talks about you and Moor all the time anyway. I'm sure she'd be happy to sit and sew with you. It will do no harm to improve her own needlework skills and take her mind of her cousins. She's been missing them, particularly Reinhard. They've always been close.'

So it was decided that once they reached Copenhagen, Alina would assist Aaron when she had the time. She agreed to continue looking after Moor during the day and would be happy to do some beading or embroidery to help him on some evenings.

The *Vaedder* sailed over the Kattegat to its destination in Copenhagen. The weary travellers were so glad to disembark and head for the Andersen family home. Jen's mother lived in their large, typical wooden house and acted as housekeeper while they went on their trading voyages. She spied the ship as it sailed into the harbour and hurried down to meet them. Amid much hugging and kissing and exclaiming, she was introduced to Aaron and baby Moor. She was called Berta and was a widow of indeterminate age. Plump and cheerful, she helped as they pushed a handcart piled with some of their belongings up the road from the quay to their front door.

'Aaron and Moor are going to be living in the house with us for some time, mother. Is the old storeroom empty? I thought we could turn it into a bedroom and workroom for Aaron. He is a wonderful tailor, you know,' gabbled Jen as he walked.

'Oh, I haven't been in that room for a while. I think there are some bags and boxes but they could be cleared out easily,' Berta answered. 'We don't have any spare beds though.'

'That's alright. I have a feather bed in the hold,' said Aaron. 'I could just lay it on the floor for now. It would be wonderful to have a room for Moor and myself. We will manage, whatever you come up with.'

*

The first few days were taken up with making the storeroom habitable. Jen and Aaron cleared the stored boxes to another outdoor shed and with Sigrid's help, swept and scrubbed the wooden floor clean. They then laid down Aaron's feather bed and installed the boxes and bundles which had been stored in the ship's hold.

'This is perfect! There's even a window, so I can open the shutters once the weather is brighter, and sew by daylight,' Aaron exclaimed once everything was in.

'All you need is a table and stool and you'll be able to start working straight away,' said Sigrid. 'Perhaps one of our friends or neighbours nearby will have something suitable that they no longer need. We'll ask around.'

'I can't thank you all enough for this kindness. You've given me a home and the opportunity to earn a living,' Aaron said, feeling a lump rise in his throat.

'You are both considered our family now,' said Jen 'and we look after our own.' He gave Aaron a pat on the shoulder.

Moor meanwhile was jumping around on the feather bed. 'Can I sleep here too?' he asked excitedly.

'Yes, but only if you can behave,' answered Aaron putting on a mock stern face.

A suitable table and two chairs were donated by a neighbour and soon Aaron had his materials stacked on shelves on one side of the room and the table and chairs beneath the window. Moor had a small chest for his clothes and a box where he kept his treasures. They both slept comfortably on the feather bed on the floor, but Jen promised to make a wooden base for it so that it would be warmer in the winter months. They settled down well in their new home in Copenhagen and Moor was a great favourite with Berta, who he called, *Bedstemor*, meaning grandmother, along with Alina and Tomas.

There were many different nationalities frequenting the busy city of Copenhagen and no-one questioned the young Jew. Whenever anyone asked about Moor's parentage, they were told that he was a foundling whose mother had died and he was being looked after by Aaron and the Andersen family. Most people assumed it had something to do with the plague. As far as Jen knew there was not actually a Jewish community in Copenhagen, but neither was there a push to persecute them. Aaron however kept mainly to the house and the nearby neighbourhood to avoid any confrontation with the church or authorities.

*

After a few weeks had passed, Aaron had sewn a number of beautiful garments for both men and women, with Alina's help. He decided it was time to approach the Count of Holstein with his letter from Rolf. Prior to the actual visit, Jen walked with him to show him the way to the Count's home. It was a large, stone built house, rather like a small castle and Aaron sucked in his breath when he saw it. 'I... I feel a bit inferior when I look at this huge house,' he said. 'Perhaps the Count won't even see me.'

'Nonsense,' replied Jen. 'If you just hand in the letter from my brother, I'm sure he will give you an appointment.'

The next morning, Aaron set off wearing his best clothes and pushing a small handcart containing his clothing samples. When he arrived at the Count's abode, he knocked at the front door which was opened by a servant girl. She took his letter and asked him to wait.

He hovered near the door feeling very nervous and not at all sure that the Count would value his handiwork, but he didn't have long to wait. The servant girl returned straight away and invited him to enter. He lifted the garments out of the cart and struggled through the doorway into a large square hallway. The floor was colourfully tiled and a staircase curved upwards to another level. Many doors led off from the hall and the servant ushered him through one of them. He found himself in a comfortable room with beautiful rugs on the floor and heavy drapes at the windows. The Count rose from where he'd been sitting writing with a quill at a wide desk and welcomed Aaron. He was a tall man with dark hair greying at the temples and a ready smile.

'Greetings to you. I understand from Rolf Andersen that you are an accomplished tailor and have some garments to show me that might be of interest?'

'That is correct, sir. Thank you for seeing me,' he said, struggling to stick out his hand to the Count.

'Put your bundles down on the armchair there, Levey, and you can show me what you have.'

'Yes, thank you, sir,' answered Aaron and gratefully laid down the heavy armful.

While the Count sat down in an easy chair by the fireplace, Aaron lifted the garments one at a time and allowed him to study them closely. He examined the coats, tunics and dresses and exclaimed favourably about the workmanship.

'The materials are exquisite and your beading and finishing touches are beyond anything I have seen before. You are indeed a very skilled tailor.'

'Thank you, sir. I am glad that they meet with your approval,' replied Aaron.

'I will most certainly have a surcote made to start with and we'll see how that turns out.'

'Shall I take some measurements now, sir?' asked Aaron.

'Yes, yes, Levey,' answered the Count standing up for him. 'Measure away.'

Aaron worked quickly and quietly. 'Perhaps your wife might also like to see the garments? I could make whatever she desired.'

'Oh, I'm sure she will want a whole new wardrobe once she sees these silk dresses.' He laughed as he tugged at a bell pull at the side of the fireplace. The servant girl opened the door moments later. 'Ask the Countess to come down to my study, if she will.'

'Yes, sir,' answered the girl, bobbing a curtsey and disappearing to run upstairs.

Within a few minutes, the study door opened and a pleasant-looking middle aged woman entered and smiled towards the men. 'You sent for me, dear?' she enquired.

'Yes, yes,' said the Count, holding out his hand to take hers. 'I think you will be interested to see what this young man has created. Come and have a look at the quality of these garments.'

He gestured towards the clothes on the chair. Aaron bowed and lifted one of the silk dresses for her to handle.

'Oh this is beautiful,' she exclaimed. 'And such delicious colours,' she murmured as her eyes lit upon the other dresses. 'Oh, I must try on that cloak.'

Aaron lifted the one she was admiring and fastened it around her shoulders.

'It feels so rich and warm, and I love the collar,' she declared.

'I told you she'd like your things,' said the Count in an aside to Aaron. 'Take an order for whatever she wants. I will give you a little money now and I'll settle with you on delivery.'

Aaron couldn't believe his luck and his heart leapt in his chest. 'Yes, sir. Thank you, sir.'

'What other colours could you do dresses in?' the Countess enquired. 'I would love something special for the Spring ball that we are hosting next month.

'I have most colours but perhaps I could bring you some pieces of material to select from. And... er... I would need to take some measurements from you as well.'

'How wonderful! Could you come back tomorrow? I am free around midday.'

'I will certainly be happy to come back then, Countess,' answered Aaron.

'I just love this,' the Countess said, whirling around the moss green velvet cloak that she hadn't yet taken off. 'Is it for sale?'

'Why yes, of course, Countess,' replied Aaron.

The Count nodded his head and going to his desk drawer, opened a box from which he drew out some money. 'Tell me your price then, Levey. This is going to cost me a lot of ducats I can see.'

Aaron told him the cost and the Count did not question it.

'Seems reasonable to me, considering the workmanship. Good man.'

Aaron was offered some refreshment, but declined graciously, anxious to return home to tell the others his news. He practically ran along the road, unaware of the weight of the cart he was pushing, so overjoyed at his good fortune. After breathlessly sharing his news and receiving handshakes and hugs, he immediately set about cutting short lengths from his bolts of material to show as samples the next day.

The Countess was ecstatic when she saw the beautiful array of sumptuous materials in the glorious assortment of colours. 'For the ball, I must have this golden raw silk,' she exclaimed. 'Can you design something exciting and new for me? Oh, and this ruby satin... and oh, this beautiful shade, the colour of the sea! However am I going to choose? I'll just have to have lots!'

Aaron could hardly get a word in and found it difficult to keep calm himself, so exciting was the prospect of all this work.

The Countess summoned her maid and suggested that Aaron take the measurements he needed. This he did deftly and made notes on a scrap piece of cotton to aid his memory. He also noted the garments the Countess ordered by putting scraps of her chosen materials alongside his notes. She wanted three ball gowns, two kirtles, two skirts, a long cloak and a short cape. They spent a long time discussing styles and linings and decoration. Finally, the order was decided upon and Aaron took his leave with the promise to return as soon as he had garments ready for trying on before the final finishing.

He couldn't believe how fortunate he'd been. If the Count and Countess were satisfied with their clothes, then hopefully this could lead to much more business from their acquaintances. His dream was certainly coming true.

*

Aaron tried to organise his working days to fit in with Moor's needs. He spent time each morning with the child. They had breakfast together and then Aaron would take him for a walk. Moor loved to go down to the waterside to watch the ships and they would discuss everything around them as they frequently stopped and started on their stroll along the cobbles. Moor was interested in each flower or tiny insect, each boat or barge, the people walking by and the houses, big or small. The local folk got to know him and greeted him warmly when they passed. Later in the morning, when Alina had finished her chores for Sigrid, she took over the care of the little boy and played with him and taught him new words while Aaron worked in his sewing room/ bedroom.

The new clothes for the Countess were sewn meticulously and once she had had a fitting, Aaron finished them off perfectly. Alina helped sew the beading on the collar of the cape. It was in a gold raw silk to match the ball gown. Aaron added beads around the low neckline of the gown and on the hem of the train at the back. The Countess had decided that she'd like fur trimming on her cloak, with a long liripipe on the back of the hood, so Aaron purchased suitable strips of fur from Jen and spent hours stitching it around the hood and the hem of the rich ruby velvet garment, lined with brocade. The Countess couldn't wait until all of the clothes were ready but asked if Aaron would bring each garment to her as he completed it. Her husband was true to his word and paid Aaron well each time he made a delivery. He was delighted with his new surcote and ordered another with a fashionable fitchet slit in the front, to access his purse. Everything was satisfactory and the Countess was eager to show off her new apparel at the ball.

On the day of the event, the elegant gown was greatly admired and the Countess, though reluctant to divulge the source of her beautiful clothing, soon had the name of her exceptional tailor wormed out of her. When he visited her to hand over her two skirts, she gave him a small pile of cards with the names of other members of the gentry who wished him to call upon them. Aaron was overwhelmed with gratitude and the prospect of so much good business.

'You deserve the recommendations, Levey. Your tailoring is outstanding. We have not had such quality here before. You have real skill,' declared the Lady.

'Thank you, Countess Holstein. I am grateful to you and hope to be asked to make more clothing for you and your husband in future,' replied Aaron.

'Oh, that goes without saying. I will be requiring a summer wardrobe soon so will be back in touch.'

I only hope I can cope with all of this work, thought Aaron. *How am I going to manage on my own?*

*

Jen had been acquiring new stock for his trading missions and had been filling the *Vaedder* hold with furs, wooden furniture, carvings and amber jewellery. He was keen to be back to sea and announced one spring day that the family would be leaving in two days.

Alina was excited. She would soon be seeing Reinhard again when they called in to her uncle's home to visit and collect more wooden furniture.

'I'm sorry, Aaron, but I won't be here to help for a few months with little Moor or with the sewing. What will you do?'

Aaron had been so busy that he hadn't given any thought to what would happen when the Andersens left on their ship again. 'I will have to find someone to look after Moor if I am to fulfil my orders for tailoring,' he declared. Then with a sudden thought, 'I wonder if Berta would oblige, or would he be too much for her?'

'Oh, I'm sure *Bedstemor* would love to have him for a few hours a day. She could teach him more words and he could help her to bake and cook meals.'

'I'll go and speak with her right away,' Aaron decided and marched through to the kitchen where Berta was busy chopping vegetables. 'Berta, I have a favour to ask of you,' he began. 'I realise it is an imposition, but would you be willing to look after Moor for a little time each day so that I can have peace to do my sewing? If it's too much, just say and I...'

'Aaron, Aaron, hush. Of course I will be delighted to have Moor's company each day. He is a dear child and it is lovely to have the two of you living here instead of being alone for months when the others are at sea.'

'I cannot thank you enough, Berta. You are so kind to sacrifice your time for me.'

'I don't feel that it's a sacrifice,' she answered. 'I think that you are doing *me* the favour, giving me a reason to get up each day. I always feel so bereft when the family go off, but this time I'll have the chatter of your little boy in the house, helping to keep the sadness away.'

*

So it was that when the family were finally ready to go, Berta, Aaron and Moor waved them off from the quayside. Jen intended being away until the autumn this time and had promised to purchase more materials for Aaron if he saw anything suitable at the markets he visited.

'I know it's unlikely, but if you should meet Raju, let him know how we are, and pass on my good wishes,' shouted Aaron as the ropes were being unravelled from the bollards.

'We will,' shouted back Sigrid, waving. 'Take care and we will see you after the summer.'

Berta and Aaron turned away once the ship had sailed out of sight. They didn't speak. Both of them had lumps in their throats. Even Moor was subdued.

'I want Alina, ' he whimpered.

Aaron picked him up and sat him on his shoulders for the walk back to the house. 'She'll be back soon,' he said without conviction. He felt somehow that she would stay with Rolf's family and perhaps marry her cousin, Reinhard. She was nearly fifteen after all.

Aaron soon got into a routine with Berta and worked hard each day cutting and sewing. 'I could do with someone to help me do simple cutting and stitching,' he announced at supper one evening. Do you know of anyone nearby who might want the job?' he asked Berta. 'I'd pay them of course.'

'I wish I could help you myself, but my eyesight isn't what it used to be,' answered Berta.

'I wasn't meaning you,' Aaron quickly asserted. 'You have enough to do with looking after the house and Moor and feeding us all.'

'There are some youngsters around here without work and the families are always in need of money. I'll ask about and see if there is a willing apprentice for you,' she replied. 'Do you want a boy or a girl?'

'It doesn't matter, but I suppose a boy could go on to have a proper trade if he took to tailoring,' Aaron answered. 'Just as I have done under my father's tutoring. '

Within a few days, Aaron had a willing helper. He was a boy of twelve who lived a street away. His name was Rik, short for Frederik and he was quiet and diligent, doing everything Aaron asked but was obviously slow to begin with. They both rubbed along well however, and Rik soon fitted in as though he'd been working there for years. He was quick to learn and had a keen eye so Aaron could trust him to do a good job of cutting out a pattern or tacking hems or counting out beads, all tasks which saved Aaron precious time. The summer months passed quickly and Aaron's reputation continued to grow by word of mouth. He was very busy and had to make time to sew clothes for Rik and himself so that they always dressed smartly, giving a good example of his tailoring skills. Moor continued to thrive under Berta and Aaron's care and chattered fluently in Danish as well as understanding Aaron if he spoke in the German tongue or in Hebrew. Aaron was instructing him in the basics of the Jewish faith. Berta did not interfere in this area, leaving his religious upbringing to his guardian.

How I wish there was a synagogue and Jewish community here, thought Aaron more than once. His own memory of his faith could be unreliable as so much had happened in his young life. He still followed a lot of the pagan way of life instilled in him by Ulrich, but yearned for his Jewish roots.

*

One afternoon, when Aaron and Rik were busy in their workroom, Berta shouted through, 'The *Vaedder* in coming in! Quickly Aaron! The family are back.'

Aaron ran to the kitchen window beside her and sure enough, he could see the ship coming in to the harbour. Moor was so excited he was jumping up and down.

'Rik, come with us to the harbour,' called Aaron. 'The family are back. Come and meet them.'

'I already know them,' said Rik as he sauntered through beside them. 'I'll just stay here and get on with cutting out that surcote.'

'Oh, of course. I forget you live nearby and will have always known them,' answered Aaron. 'Well, we shall head down to meet them, won't we Moor,' he said grabbing the boisterous child by a hand and opening the door for Berta who had hurriedly removed her apron and pulled a shawl around her shoulders. 'We won't be long. Just go home when you've done the cutting out and I'll see you in the morning.'

It was wonderful to meet up with the Andersens again. Jen was looking tanned and strong as ever and Tomas had grown taller. Sigrid waved happily as they approached but there was no sign of Alina. Aaron's thoughts had been right. She had decided to stay on in Frederikshavn with her parents' blessing in Rolf and Deta's care. She sent her love to Moor and Aaron.

'We didn't see any sign of Raju, but we did manage to buy you some fine woollen material, some linen and muslins,' Sigrid told Aaron later that evening when they gathered at their meal.

'That is good. I am needing warmer cloth for winter surcotes and kirtles. I have a new apprentice now, you know.'

'Oh?'

'Yes, his name is Frederik Hanssen, you will know him, a young lad, and he is turning out well. A quick learner. I needed someone to help as I have so much business, I can hardly keep up with it. '

'How wonderful. I'm pleased that you have a helper.'

'Hanssen? I think I know the name,' commented Jen. 'The man I know isn't well liked but if it's the same person, obviously he must have a good son or you wouldn't have taken him on.'

'Yes, I'm pleased with Rik and it's thanks to Rolf's letter of introduction to Count Holstein that business is so good. I've never looked back.'

'Well, the letter will have helped, but it is really down to your skilled workmanship that you have all the orders,' Sigrid assured him.

The others murmured their agreement.

'You'll soon need bigger premises at this rate, ' said Jen and they all laughed.

*

And so it transpired that Aaron settled into a busy routine, working long hours to keep up with the orders for rich clothes for the Holsteins and their friends. Rik was gradually introduced to stitching and proved to be a fine needle worker. Aaron was satisfied with his apprentice tailor.

The years passed happily while the Andersens continued with their trading voyages around Denmark, Holland and Germany. Sometimes they were away for almost nine months and at others, just three moons would pass. Alina married Reinhard as Aaron had predicted and they lived in Frederikshavn in a small house gifted by Rolf and Deta. Tomas wanted to keep on travelling with his parents and enjoyed working on the ship and trading with the merchants. It was always a happy time when everyone was at home and Berta was then in her element, cooking for her family.

'I am thinking about having new premises built,' announced Aaron one day when the family were all together.

'Oh, we don't want you to move away,' said Sigrid looking at him with a serious expression.

'Where were you thinking about?' asked Jen.

'Well, there is a small piece of land just behind you, next to the dry goods store and the butcher's place at the edge of the market square. It might be useful to be near where the people congregate to buy food. I've been thinking about taking on another boy as we still have plenty of work, but Rik could be making simple garments that the local people can afford while I concentrate on the fancier clothing.'

'That's a good point,' said Sigrid, nodding. 'I don't think many people know what you do as you are always working indoors. You could open a shop offering simple tailor-made clothes at affordable prices. Not all mothers have the time or expertise with a needle to clothe their families.'

'And you would still be living close by,' added Jen. 'That will please Mother, won't it?' he said, looking over at Berta.

'Oh, yes. I'd still keep an eye on Moor for you,' she answered quickly, anxious to be included in Aaron's plans. 'He's just like one of my own grandchildren to me. He's good too, always wanting to help me with the chores.'

'I'll come to see the landowner with you, if you like?' suggested Jen. 'I'm sure there shouldn't be any problem. Then we can visit some other friends of mine who are timber merchants and carpenters who may be interested in building you a house and shop front.'

Everything went ahead as planned. Aaron continued to live with the Andersens while his new property was being constructed. He took on another apprentice, Rik's younger brother, Peter, who proved to be a good enough worker, but slow. He spent a lot of time chattering making it necessary for Aaron to reprove him and constantly ask him to concentrate on his work.

When the house was ready, Jen helped Aaron and the boys to carry over the bolts of material along with Aaron's and Moor's belongings. On the ground floor there was a large living room with fireplace and cooking ovens. Off that was a work room with shelving and three tables leading into a small front shop. Aaron had asked for a wooden floor to be laid in the workroom and shop to prevent the materials from being soiled. Straw was scattered on the dirt floor of the living area. Up a wooden stair from there was a small gallery which contained two wooden box beds. A privy was erected at the back of the building. Water could be collected from the village well in the centre of the market area.

Sigrid and Berta brought over some cooking utensils, dishes and cutlery but Berta insisted that Aaron and Moor come for supper each evening in the meantime.

'You'll be too tired to cook after working all day, and that child needs good food, so you must just come to us,' she ordered.

'I won't argue with that,' answered Aaron. 'It's been a while since I did any cooking anyway. I'll be fine during the day and can send one of the boys to buy fresh bread and whatever we need from the market.

The arrangement worked well and Moor ran over to spend the mornings with Berta after he'd eaten breakfast with Aaron. Rik and Peter arrived early each day and had their tasks assigned to them. The local people welcomed the tailoring business in their midst and Rik was now in charge of making skirts, kirtles, cloaks, shifts and undershirts for men and women. Peter was still learning pattern cutting and basic stitching so he assisted both Rik and Aaron. Aaron now preferred to work all day while there was good light and spend his evenings with Moor after supper at the Andersens'. His business was thriving and he was making a good profit after paying his apprentices. Berta wouldn't accept any money for looking after Moor, so Aaron kept her attired in good quality garments for which she was grateful.

Moor had many friends in the neighbourhood and Berta was happy that the little boy was accepted. No-one ever mentioned his dark skin and the other children never seemed to notice. After doing any chores that his *Bedstemor* required of him, he was free to play out in the streets or go down to the water to fish with his young friends. Berta knew that, like all boys, he'd return when his stomach demanded it. She could usually see him from her windows and kept an eye on his activities.

CHAPTER SIXTEEN

Betrayal and Flight

1359

The years had passed pleasantly enough for Aaron who built up his business by hard work over long hours. Rik now assisted him with the sewing of the finer fabrics and Peter was in charge of sewing the coarser materials for the local people. Moor had expressed an interest in learning the tailoring trade, which surprised Aaron at first, but then he remembered that Marta had been an excellent needlewoman, so he realised Moor must have inherited his mother's skills. He spent some time each afternoon sitting beside Aaron, watching and helping by handing him pins or beads. He was soon assisting Peter and proving to be a good helpmate. Aaron was proud of the way the lad was turning out. He himself had worked beside his father from an early age and didn't regret it.

One day, the news came to Copenhagen that plague had caused deaths in the nearby towns.

Oh, no, thought Aaron. *I thought that nightmare was behind me.* He ordered Moor to stay indoors and work with him, and hoped the illness would bypass their town. It was not to be however. Within days, word spread that the Great Death had arrived. Peter was always ready each morning with the latest gossip, and news of any tragedies he'd heard his parents discuss.

He burst in with the latest word one morning. 'A ship arrived in the harbour at dawn with the whole crew dead on board,' he told Aaron and Rik breathlessly. Moor was listening unnoticed at the side of the room. 'The wind must have brought it in. Some men went out in a small boat when they saw it just drifting there with no-one on deck. Father said that the Council think it must be something to do with the water.'

'That's what happened in *Koln*,' Aaron said quietly. 'Unfortunately, they decided that the Jews had poisoned the well, so they killed them all; hundreds of them... my family included.'

Rik and Peter sat in stunned silence.

'Are you a Jew, then?' asked Peter.

'Yes, I am... and I have never poisoned anyone,' answered Aaron. 'Get on with your work, please.'

The brothers worked in silence with heads down, but looked at one another and at Aaron from under their eyebrows from time to time.

At midday, it had become customary for Moor to fetch some bread and meat from the pantry and they all had a short break for their meal. 'I'll need to go out for bread,' he announced. 'I won't be long.'

'Don't hang about,' shouted Aaron after him.

Moor was intrigued by the news which Peter had brought, and quickly ran down to the shore to see this ship for himself. There was plenty of bread in the pantry, he'd just made up an excuse to go out.

There was indeed a new sailing ship in the harbour and men were standing about in groups looking at it. On the ground lay two long rows of what he surmised must be dead bodies wrapped in calico. The boy was fascinated and walked over to them to have a closer look.

'Hey! Get back from there, you!' yelled someone. 'What are you doing?'

'J-just looking,' stammered Moor and took to his heels.

Some men turned to stare at him. 'Didn't like the look of that boy,' said one.

'Me neither,' said another. 'Isn't he the half-caste boy that Jewish tailor Levey keeps?'

'Jewish? Then it's likely that that boy has put a curse on the town! I've heard that's what happened in other countries. They had to burn all the Jews to stop the plague!'

'Oh, think straight, man,' shouted another. 'The plague hasn't stopped, has it, so killing Jews hasn't helped.'

The discussion continued for some time, leaving a few of the men disgruntled and fearful.

*

Peter couldn't wait to tell his father and mother what Aaron had said earlier that day.

'So Aaron Levey is a Jew,' mused his father. 'I suppose I should have known that from his name, but I never thought about it before.'

'He has always been good to us,' said Rik glowering at Peter. 'All his family were murdered by the Council in *Koln*. That must have been terrible.'

'Oh, his family were murdered by the Council were they?' the father said, nodding. 'Well, the Council must have thought there was good reason! I think I'll be having a word with my brother, who as you know is Lord High Constable.'

'Yes, father,' said Rik adding under his breath, 'and you never let us forget it!'

'I've always thought it was odd, him having a black child living with him,' said the mother. 'What's that about? Who's the mother and where is she?'

'Aaron told me that Moor was a foundling baby and a woman friend took him in. She became ill and before she died, she asked Aaron to look after the child. That's all. I like Moor. He is a kind boy and works hard,' Rik added.

'Well, I think it is our duty to investigate this business,' the father announced.

*

That night as Peter lay snoring, Rik lay awake worrying about what might happen to Aaron. His parents came to their bed on the other side of the same room and he listened as they talked in hushed tones.

'I've been thinking,' said his mother. 'If you go to your brother about Aaron Levey now, it's going to look bad for you.'

'What do you mean, woman?'

'Well, you've sent our sons to be his apprentices.'

Exactly, thought Rik. *I've been working with him for nigh on seven years, for goodness' sake!*

'Hmm. You're right, I suppose. We'll have to come up with some other plan to get rid of him. We don't want to risk getting the plague if he puts a curse on us or something.'

Oh for heaven's sake, Father, thought Rik, barely able to keep quiet.

'You could talk to your other friends on the Council and just happen to mention that you'd heard that Jews have caused the plague in other countries.'

'Yes, that's what I'll do.'

'And it won't hurt to mention that black child who lives with him,' she whispered.

'Yes, maybe he has been cursed. That's why his skin is black.'

'Of course! That's what it'll be. You must do something quickly, husband.'

'I'll speak to someone tomorrow. Meanwhile,' he yawned, 'let's get some sleep.'

*

Nothing was mentioned in the morning and Rik hoped that his father would be too busy to do anything, until at least later in the day. He told his parents he was going out early for a walk by the sea as it was a bright morning and he'd be cooped up inside sewing all day. They didn't think there was anything odd about that.

Rik hurried round to Aaron's house and knocking first on the door, entered quickly.

'Oh, hello, Rik, what's the rush this morning?' said Aaron, startled as he cleaned out the fireplace.

'Aaron, I've got to talk to you.'

Putting down his brush and shovel, Aaron went over and sat at the table. 'Sit down. What is it?'

'My father is going to speak to someone on the Council to try to get you sent away... or worse,' he added. 'I heard him talking with Mother last night. He is going to mention Moor too. It's because his skin is dark. He thinks you must have cursed him.' He bowed his head apologetically. 'I'm so sorry, Aaron. It was Peter. He told Father what you told us yesterday about the Jews.'

Aaron sat, still and white faced, staring straight ahead. *So it is all happening again,* he thought. *Just when I had my business going so well... and good friends... I have to leave again.*

'Aaron,' Rik almost shouted. 'What are you going to do?'

Aaron slowly responded. 'It looks like I will have to move away from here –from my business, my home and my friends if I want to save Moor and myself from persecution yet again.' He sighed and his shoulders slumped. He looked up at Rik. 'Thank you for telling me.'

Rik gave a perfunctory nod of the head.

'Where is your father now?' Aaron asked.

'He will be down at the harbour helping unload a ship. He's unlikely to be able to meet up with any of his friends on the Council until late afternoon or even tomorrow.'

'Will you carry on as usual in the shop? Just tell Peter that I'm delivering orders. I'll be back later.'

'Yes, of course,' Rik replied and giving Aaron a weak smile, left the room and went through to the workshop.

Aaron jumped up immediately, washed his hands and face and changed into his best clothes. Moor was already over at the Andersens' with Berta, so, setting his hat firmly on his head, he left the house quietly and walked to Count Holstein's home without delay. He knocked on the door and when the maid answered he quickly doffed his hat. 'I need to see Count Holstein urgently,' he stated.

'He... He's not dressed yet, sir,' replied the girl.

'That doesn't matter. Take me to him,' Aaron said with unusual directness and pushed past the maid into the hall.

'He is still at the table... in here,' said the girl, pointing to one of the doors.

'Thank you.'

'What's going on?' queried the Count who was sitting with a breakfast plate in front of him, still wearing his nightshirt, night cap and dressing gown. 'Oh, it's you, Levey. What's the matter?'

'I need to speak with you sir, on a matter of great urgency.' He looked over at the maid, still hovering at the door.

'That will be all,' signalled the Count, waving her out of the room. 'Now, what is so urgent at this time of the morning?'

'You are aware that the plague is spreading throughout Denmark, I'm sure, sir?'

'Yes. What has happened?'

'It appears that I am to be handed over to the Council because I am Jewish. The Jews were wrongly blamed for causing the plague in Koln, or Cologne as you know the city. Hundreds were exterminated, my own family included, and now it looks like it is going to happen all over again.' The Count said nothing. Aaron stared at him. 'I am appealing to you to speak for me, sir. You must know I would never do anything wrong. I am honest and hardworking and a good guardian to my ward.'

The Count sighed. 'I'm afraid, Levey, that I will not become involved. I have to think of my own reputation. If the authorities decide to legislate in some way against Jews and I am seen to be going against that, then I and my wife will be in danger.'

Aaron was appalled. 'But you and your wife and friends have been wearing the clothes I have made you for years. You cannot deny my existence!'

'Perhaps, but I can deny that I knew you were Jewish. I'm sorry, Levey. I will not speak *for* you, but I give you my word that I will not speak against you.'

Speechless with hurt and anger, Aaron turned from the Count and left the room, startling the maid who was pretending to dust in the hall as he barged past her and out through the door.

He marched down the road in a fury at the injustice of life, and made his way to see Jen and Sigrid. He'd calmed down a little by the time he reached their house and Berta gave him a wave as he approached.

'Jen, here's Aaron coming to the door. He looks very serious and all dressed up,' she called.

Berta ushered Aaron into the kitchen where they were joined by Jen and Sigrid.

'Hello my friends,' began Aaron, then his voice broke.

'Whatever has happened!' exclaimed Jen, pushing him onto a chair.

As Aaron related his conversations with Rik and the Count, Jen and Sigrid grew more horrified with each moment. Berta was soon dabbing at her eyes with a corner of her apron.

'I don't have any right to ask more of you,' carried on Aaron, 'You have given me so much already.' He hesitated.

'Ask away, Aaron,' urged Jen.

'Will you take Moor and me to Poland on your ship?'

Without a moment's hesitation Jen answered, 'Of course we will. We were about to leave again in a few days anyway, so most of our necessities are already aboard. We'll just be going to a different destination, that's all.'

Sigrid and Berta were nodding in affirmation.

'This is terrible. You *must* go to Poland. It's where you wanted to go eventually anyway, wasn't it?' said Sigrid. 'Berta, would you wake Tomas and tell him what's happening? We will make plans to sail tonight. Is that what you were thinking Jen?'

'Yes, my dear,' said Jen. Turning to Aaron he took his hands and said quietly, 'We must get you both away before that ass brings the Council to your door bearing flaming torches and cudgels.'

At that moment, Moor came in carrying bread from the bakehouse. 'Aaron, what are you doing here all dressed up? Are you going somewhere special?'

'Well, yes, you could say that. In fact we are all going somewhere special. I want you to stay here today and not go outside.'

'Is it in case I get the plague?' asked the child.

'That's as good a reason as any,' answered Aaron.

Tomas appeared with Berta. He smiled to Moor and Aaron. '*Bedstemor* has told me what's happening,' he said. 'I'll help you move your things.'

'Move?' queried Moor. 'Are we moving?'

'Yes, I'm afraid we have to go on a sea journey again. It is very important, Moor, so please just be a good boy for me,' said Aaron.

Moor picked up on the tension in the air and just nodded his head. Aaron gave him a hug. 'We'll be fine. Jen, Sigrid and Tomas are coming on the ship too.'

'Come with me just now and we'll play a game,' said Tomas, and they went into another room.

'How much can you take with you?' asked Jen.

'I'll go home just now and pack up our clothes. I hope I can take my Jewish things too. I'll leave the bundles together and you and Tomas could come in for them at some point and take them to the ship, Jen. Would that be all right?'

'So long as no-one sees us leaving your house, it won't be at all suspicious to see us carrying bundles to our ship. We do that all the time,' he answered.

'It breaks my heart to leave all that I've built up behind. All my lovely materials,' Aaron said, shaking his head. 'I must get my money away safely.'

'Go back to the house now and pack your things. Tomas and I will be over in an hour or so,' said Jen. 'You better get back to the shop too so that the boys don't get suspicious. You don't want that Peter to go blabbing to his stupid father.'

Berta gave Aaron a hug. 'I'll send Moor over to fix your midday food so that everything looks the same as usual,' she said.

'Thank you. That's a good idea,' Aaron answered then he said his goodbyes and left in a leisurely fashion as though he'd just been visiting for breakfast.

*

Back at his house, Aaron hurried quietly around, packing up clothes and treasured belongings which he left in sacks to one side of the room. Having changed into his usual work clothes, he entered the shop and took his place at his table. Looking over at his two apprentices, he smiled and said, 'Good morning. Deliveries done. I must get on with this cloak,' and picked up the heavy velvet he was working on.

Rik and Peter just nodded in acknowledgement and carried on with their allotted tasks, Peter prattling on inanely as usual.

At midday Moor arrived with plates of bread, meat and fruit for them all and gave his apologies but said that *Bedstemor* needed him to help with some cleaning, so could he be excused for the afternoon.

Aaron pretended to be a bit cross, but agreed that Moor could help Berta. When he went into his living room later on, he was relieved to find that the bundles had all been removed. Jen must have them safely on board the *Vaedder*. He could hardly wait for the end of the working day, but couldn't rush anything or Peter might be suspicious. When finally it was time for the boys to finish, Peter was the first to go out of the door. Rik hung behind and said in hushed tones, 'Have you managed to sort something out, Aaron?'

'Yes, and it is best that you know nothing, Rik. That way you cannot be implicated. Thank you for warning me about your father's intentions.'

Rik couldn't speak. He just pursed his lips tightly, nodded and shook Aaron's hand firmly. Turning quickly, he marched out of the door and ran up the road.

Aaron collected all his money and separated it into four pouches, then took a small piece of parchment and wrote upon it. *I leave this house and workshop to Frederik Hanssen to carry on a tailoring business for which he is now fully qualified. Signed Aaron Levey*

On other pieces of parchment he wrote, *Wages due for Rik* and *Wages due for Peter.* He placed the appropriate amounts due to the boys in two piles on top of the parchment notes.

Looking around the workshop for the last time, he ran his hands tenderly over the few remaining pieces of silk, picked up his scissors and needle case, closed the door and made his way to the Andersen house.

*

Once it was dark, Jen and Sigrid said their goodbyes to Berta.

'Stay indoors as much as possible, Mother,' urged Jen. 'I don't want you getting the plague. Don't drink the water, just have ale and we'll be back in a few weeks. If we have the chance to do any trading in Poland, we'll take it, otherwise we shall return soon.' He and Sigrid both hugged her and left quietly to walk down to the ship.

A few minutes later, they saw a lantern being swung from side to side. That was the signal for Aaron and Moor to go.

Berta couldn't speak, she was so choked with emotion.

'Thank you, thank you for everything. We couldn't have managed without you,' said Aaron, holding her tightly.

She hugged him back, then released him to bend down to crush Moor to her bosom. Crying openly now, she kissed and hugged him. 'Goodbye my darling, boy. May God go with you. Take care of each other.' She released Moor who was also in tears and he and Aaron left quickly and disappeared into the darkness.

'Why do we have... to go?' sobbed Moor.

'I'll explain it all once we are on board the ship. I don't want to go either, but we must. Hush now.'

They walked quietly along the road. All of the houses they passed had their shutters closed and they saw no-one.

'There you both are,' said Jen when they boarded the *Vaedder*. We will set sail straight away.'

And true to his word, he caught the hawser that Tomas threw from the quayside, his son jumped on board and the wind billowed the sails with a great slapping. They moved swiftly out into the Baltic Sea with only Berta as onlooker from her window.

*

Aaron and Moor didn't have much sleep that first night. The sea was rough and it had been a long time since they'd slept on board. Moor was particularly upset by parting from Berta and he knew that he'd be leaving Jen, Sigrid and Tomas next. He lay in his hammock sobbing. 'Why did you have to do this? I don't want to go somewhere new. I won't know anybody. It's not fair.'

'I know it isn't fair,' said Aaron in gentle tones. 'Life isn't fair.'

'You said you'd explain it all once we were on the ship, so why do we have to go?'

'I think you are old enough now to be told the truth about our backgrounds,' said Aaron gravely, and proceeded to tell Moor about the holocaust from which he'd escaped in Cologne, his life with Ulrich and about meeting Moor's mother, Marta.

'So you knew my mother. Why have you never told me this before, Aaron?' asked Moor, incredulous.

'Marta always told people who asked that you were a foundling, an orphan, as she herself would have been branded as a bad woman for having a child out of wedlock. It would have been even worse to have a black child as she was white. For your own safety, I thought it best that you knew little.'

Moor didn't really understand. 'So did you know my father as well?'

Aaron shook his head. 'Your mother didn't know him either. He came from a country far away. He was drunk and attacked her, then you came along.'

Moor sat for a while, taking it all in.

'Was my mother pretty?' he asked.

'Yes, very,' came the answer. 'You look like her. You have her blue eyes and kind and generous nature. Oh, and of course, you inherited her skill with a needle,' he added with a smile.

Moor seemed happier after that news.

'But why do we have to keep moving? You haven't explained that,' he demanded after a few more minutes.

Aaron told him a diluted version of the happenings at Ulrich's farm when Marta and he had fled. He explained how the Jewish people were constantly being banished from their homes or worse because of ignorance and fear. He went on to tenderly talk of Marta's death and how Moor had seen her at Anya's house and visited her grave.

Moor shed more quiet tears then and sat holding Aaron's hands. 'I wish I had something of my mother's,' he whispered.

Aaron suddenly remembered. 'I have some jewellery which belonged to your mother. There is a string of pretty blue beads that she loved to wear, a small brooch and a gold ring. They are in my treasure box in the hold. We'll get them as soon as we are settled on land. Maybe the ring would fit you.'

Moor's face brightened considerably. 'That would be good,' he said, smiling.

'We are on our way to Poland now where I understand that the Jews who have had to flee from their homelands are welcomed. Maybe at last we can settle and make a home there,' said Aaron returning the smile. He squeezed Moor's hand. 'Let's try to get some sleep now.'

*

In Copenhagen early next morning, Hans Reigerssen forbade his sons to go to work at the tailoring workshop. He had arranged with two of his friends on the Municipal Council to meet outside the front door of the Levey house at daybreak, with the intention of evicting Aaron and driving him and his ward out of town. On their arrival they were surprised to find that no-one answered their loud rapping on the door. Lifting the latch, they entered, and discovering the place cold and empty, they strode through to the workshop where they found the notes left by Aaron. Reigerssen was furious. Why would they have left? Someone must have warned them. He would question the boys, maybe one of them would have an idea. The Councillors agreed that the letter was legal and as Reigerssen's son was now owner of a house and business, they suggested he should just keep quiet and be grateful.

When questioned by their father later, the boys denied all knowledge of Aaron's disappearance. Peter suggested that Count Holstein may have assisted in some way as he had helped Aaron from the start.

Reigerssen and his Council friends went around to the Count's residence and demanded to see him.

'I believe you know Levey the tailor well, sir?' Reigerssen suggested curtly when the Count received them.

'Levey? Yes, I believe he has made a few garments for my wife and me,' he answered. 'Why?'

'Well, he is a Jew and we believe that he has put a curse on the town. That black boy of his is not natural either.'

'They escaped from *Koln* when all the other Jews were burned for starting the plague. If you are harbouring him, you will be in deep trouble, Count,' threatened one of the others.

The Count turned pale. 'I am most certainly not *harbouring* him. Look around for yourselves if you don't believe me. I never liked the man, I just allowed him to do some tailoring for my wife as she loved the silks and velvet that he used. I have no time for Jews,' he lied.

They searched the house and surrounding area but nothing relating to Aaron or Moor was ever found.

*

The seas were rough and the weather was cold. After an arduous journey of many days, the ship pulled into the harbour at the small township of Gdansk. Aaron and Moor were sad and apprehensive about stepping ashore. Would they be made welcome in this strange new land with yet another different language? They were also sad for another reason; they would finally have to say goodbye to people they loved and regarded as family.

Once the ship was secured, Jen and Tomas gathered Aaron's bundles together and found a handcart on the quayside. Sigrid was standing with her arms around Moor, unwilling to let him go. Moor was equally unwilling to leave her and looked pale and tearful as they stood there in the drizzle.

'We'll come with you and make sure you are allowed to enter the country,' said Jen. 'Have you separated your money into different places?' he added in a whisper. 'We don't know that the officials here will be honest.'

Aaron nodded and smiled his appreciation to Jen. 'I'll be glad of your company. Especially as I don't know the language.'

'I won't be much help there,' Jen said with a wry laugh, 'Neither do I. We'll have to rely on sign language.'

The five of them made their way through a stone arch and were directed to a wooden hut. A stern man indicated that the cart must be left outside and they all followed as Aaron and Moor stepped inside the doorway. A bearded man in uniform sitting at a desk looked them up and down and barked something at them. Aaron shrugged and shook his head trying to show that he didn't understand. The man threw up his eyes, heaved a sigh and thrusting a piece of parchment and quill in front of Aaron, pointed at Aaron with his finger and then at the paper. Presuming that he was to write his name, Aaron wrote, *Aaron Levey*. The man nodded then pointed outside and held up his hands as though questioning.

'I think he wants to know where you come from,' suggested Jen.

Aaron wrote, *Koln and Copenhagen*. The man seemed satisfied. He looked at the group and circled them all with his finger as though asking if they were all immigrants.

'No... just us,' said Aaron, pulling Moor to his side.

The man looked closely at Moor then indicated that Aaron write down his name also.

'Jew?' the man asked.

Aaron nodded, 'Yes.'

More words were written down and the paper handed to another uniformed person who pointed to a door behind the desk leading to the outside. When Sigrid, Jen and Tomas made to go with Aaron and Moor, their way was immediately barred.

Aaron turned back and looking intensely at each one in turn he said,' I cannot thank you all enough for what you have done for us. If I never see you again, know that you will always be in my thoughts and prayers.'

The seated official rapped on his desk and the man at the door pulled Moor's arm.

'Goodbye dear friends, goodbye, good luck,' said Jen, huskily. Sigrid couldn't speak. Moor broke away from the man and ran back to give Tomas and Sigrid a last hug.

'We must go now,' said Aaron pulling him gently away, and they followed the official through the doorway.

Their handcart had been brought around to the back and the bundles had obviously been searched. Aaron tried not to look anxious, but prayed that his money and his treasures had not been stolen. The official indicated that he should push his cart and follow him. Moor helped and they made their way to a row of wooden huts with smoke rising from the chimney holes. The man led them to one of the huts and opening the door, ushered them inside. He held out his hand in the manner of asking for money and glared at them. Aaron pulled out his leather pouch and handed the man some coins. He looked at them with disdain, shook his head and grabbed the pouch away from Aaron.

'No, stop, that's my money,' shouted Aaron, but the man just turned and marched away.

'You won't see that again,' said a voice from inside the hut. Aaron looked round to see the kindly face of an elderly gentleman who was sitting by the fire. With a relieved smile, Aaron recognised that he was Jewish. He had a thick white beard and wore the little cap called a kippah on his balding head. 'It's good to hear a language I can understand,' stated the old man. 'Welcome to Poland.'

It transpired that the gentleman was from southern Denmark and he had been appointed to oversee the Jewish immigration. Inside the long hut was a dormitory with straw filled palliasses lying in a row along the ground, each separated by a rough curtain. Some had people lying on them but others were vacant.

'Take your bundles and go to the nearest beds. The others will show you where to wash. Kosher food will be served on the trestle table here at mealtimes when you will hear a bell. Prayer meetings and other services will be held on the usual days. Tomorrow is Shabbat so you are lucky to have your day of rest. You are free to go outside to wander, but not beyond the fence.'

'Thank you,' said Aaron, feeling rather dazed. Ushering Moor over to where there were two free beds, he nodded to the other people, some of whom were looking over at the newcomers and they gave him a smile or small wave in return.

*

Over the course of the next few days, Aaron and Moor settled into their temporary accommodation and managed to cope with the strange new routines. Aaron was happy to find that all their belongings were intact, including his box of treasured possessions. He told Moor that he wouldn't open it in the hut but would wait until they were in a more private place.

They learned from the others that they were all waiting to be transported to the Duchy of Mazovia, further inland. They would travel by boat on a river to their destination where there was a large Jewish settlement. It was a great relief to Aaron to be able to communicate with most of the other inhabitants of the hut. They were either from Denmark or from Germanic states. They all had tragic tales to tell of being extricated from their homes and of their flight to this country of refuge. Moor sat wide-eyed listening to some of the stories and knew then why Aaron had had to escape. He clung to Aaron's side each day and they did not close the curtain between them at night.

Four weeks passed tediously before the old Jew in charge told them to prepare to move the following day. Aaron's spirits lifted as he packed up his bundles again. 'We are going to start a new life now, Moor. We'll be happy, you'll see. We'll be with other Jewish families and you'll make good friends, just like before.'

Moor didn't share his enthusiasm.

*

CHAPTER SEVENTEEN

Poland

Next day, the weather was bitter and the Jewish immigrants wrapped up warmly against the icy wind. They were each given a parcel of food for the journey and were packed closely together into a river boat. Everyone had their bundles with them and had to make themselves as comfortable as they could. Aaron was glad that Moor was old enough to look after his own things. Looking around at the other families, some with infants, he was reminded of his previous journey with Marta.

The elderly gentleman who had initially welcomed them into the hut explained that they were travelling to *Lviv* and that some of them would be taken on further to beautiful *Warszawa*. It would take all day and perhaps night as well, depending upon the wind.

'It won't be long now, Moor, until we have a new home. At least we can watch the land as we pass by instead of being stuck in that hut and compound eh?' said Aaron, trying to cheer the boy.

Moor looked up at him and nodded, giving a strained smile. Aaron squeezed his shoulder and pulled him close to his side.

The atmosphere on board the boat was one of anticipation. People were smiling and talking animatedly and soon, Moor started to feel his spirits lift a little. 'Can I go and sit with Jakob?' he asked when he spied one of the boys from their hut nearby.

'Yes, of course, but stay where I can see you. I can't leave our belongings,' answered Aaron.

Moor moved happily over beside his new acquaintance and they stood watching the passing scene from the side of the boat. He glanced frequently over to Aaron and they exchanged waves of reassurance.

It was very late that night when the boat pulled in to *Lviv*. Names were called out in turn and some of the people were ushered off into the darkness. The group who were left, which included Aaron and Moor, were then allowed to leave. Aaron rose stiffly and gathered up his bundles. Moor, who had previously been sleeping, shivered as he lifted his sacks, yawned and followed Aaron from the boat. They were directed into yet another hut where they rested for the night on pallets like before. Apparently they were the group who were travelling onwards to *Warszawa*. There was a fire burning in the hut and the weary travellers were soon having hot soup to warm them. Aaron and Moor managed to catch a few hours of sleep before it was time to be on the move again.

*

Warszawa was not as beautiful a place at first sight as Aaron had imagined it would be. The streets were muddy and churned up with the passage of carts and feet and the houses looked dark and forbidding. The Jewish group from the boat lost some of their excitement as they trudged along the path in wind and sleet. They were directed to a building where an official gave each family or individual an address and directions on how to reach it.

'You will be living with another Jewish family meantime, until you can buy or rent a home of your own. Those of you who have a trade should find that your business will be welcomed in the community,' they were told.

Reluctantly setting off into the icy wetness of the murky streets again, Aaron made a mental note to purchase pattens as soon as possible, to help keep their feet dry.

Any hardships the pair had endured over the past few weeks were all felt to be worth it when they arrived at the home which had been selected for them. It was a large house and the Jewish couple who lived there welcomed them with open arms. Moor was squashed against an ample bosom and ushered into a cosy living room with a roaring fire. Aaron had his bundles lifted away and his hands shaken warmly by two of the happiest looking people he had ever met. Their names were Ezra and Hannah Eddelman and they made life more than bearable for Aaron and Moor from the start.

After introductions had been made, they were shown to a small but cosy bedroom with two feather beds in alcoves at either side of a fireplace. An old wooden armchair sat to one side of the fire which was burning brightly, and a large floor cushion lay on the other side. A candlestick and a basin and ewer sat on a small table with a colourful cloth, and above it, the window shutters were closed. The neat private room was a welcome change from the dormitory they'd shared over the past month.

'This looks good, doesn't it Moor?' said Aaron, turning to the lad.

'Mm, yes,' said Moor, taking in the comfortable surroundings.

'There is a closet there for your clothes and water in the jug so you can freshen up then come back beside us for a meal. You must be cold and hungry,' said Ezra.

'Thank you. We will come through in a few minutes,' answered Aaron as Ezra left the room.

Moor flopped down on the cushion by the fire. 'I think I might like it here after all,' he said smiling.

The next morning, Ezra asked Aaron what he wanted to do.

'Well, first of all I need to change my Danish money into Polish coins,' he decided. Then I'd like it if you could show us around the Jewish community. I need to look for a place to set up a tailoring business. That is my trade and Moor will be my apprentice.

'In that case, our first destination will be Spider Goldbaum. He will change your money.'

'Spider?' queried Aaron.

'Yes. That's not his real name, I fancy, but everyone calls him that. You will soon see why.'

It was a bright morning and the rain had stopped as Ezra, Aaron and Moor left the house, wrapped up against the cold. They made their way along the busy, filthy streets, Ezra being greeted by many of the passers-by, and turned into a dark alleyway. 'Go up those steps and through the door at the top,' Ezra directed when they reached a wooden outside stairway. 'I'll wait for you here. My knees don't like climbing stairs nowadays.'

Intrigued, Aaron and Moor climbed the steps and reached a half-open door with *Goldbaum* scratched upon the wood. Aaron knocked on the door. There was no answer so he tapped again, then pushed open the door and he and Moor stepped inside. It took a few moments for their eyes to become accustomed to the gloom. The stale room was small and bare, apart from a table facing them with someone seated behind it. There was no fire to offer any heat or light, the floor was filthy with mud and dust and long cobwebs hung from the low rafters. Stepping forward, they could see the man who indeed looked like a great spider. He wore a big brown coat slung over his shoulders on top of multiple layers of old clothing. The coat sleeves hanging down gave the appearance of extra arms. His face was almost covered by a large, battered hat and his long straggly hair and beard made it difficult to make out his features. He had dark beady eyes above a large nose, and they stared up at Aaron without blinking. His long, skinny fingers on dirty hands attached to long, skinny arms were constantly moving. They scuttled around the piles of coins on his table, fingering and caressing them, straightening columns and rearranging pouches.

Aaron held out his three pouches of coins. 'This is Danish money. Would you change it to Polish coins, please?' he asked.

The pouches were grabbed and the skinny fingers tipped the money out and immediately started sorting it into piles. After much fingering and moving the piles around, the man took different coins from some of his pouches beside him and announced, 'Here,' and shoved the money towards Aaron.

'I would like my leather pouches back,' said Aaron. They were pushed towards him roughly. 'I hope you have given me an honest exchange for my money,' he added, shovelling the unfamiliar coins into the bags and securing them to his belt inside his cloak.

'Take it or leave it. I have to make a living,' came the gruff reply.

Aaron glared at the glinting eyes and turned on his heel. 'Come Moor,' he said and they hurried down the stairs, glad to be outside once more.

'What a creepy man,' said Moor with a shudder when they met up with Ezra.

'I know, he is most unpleasant, but he usually gives a fair deal,' said the old gentleman. 'And he's the only money changer we have. Now, what next?'

'Would you manage to show us around the town and perhaps you know of somewhere to rent?' Aaron asked.

Ezra nodded. 'Come along then,' he said briskly and led them around the cobbled streets, past fruit, vegetable, and fish vendors. Behind doors in small wooden buildings with their shutters open, he pointed out a baker's shop, a cobbler, a potter's workshop, a butchery, a wood turner's shop and then they came to a small tailoring business. Aaron looked at the clothing on display on the window sill. He wasn't impressed by the stitching and there was no style or decoration to the garments. They passed on down the street.

'My tailoring is superior to that man's work,' Aaron said to Ezra, once they were out of earshot.

'All the more reason for you to set up in business as soon as possible,' he stated. 'Come, I know where there is a house which may suit you,' and they carried on past more dwellings when Aaron's eye was caught by a display of wooden pattens.

'Ah, these are what we need, Moor,' he said. 'Let's find some which fit over our shoes to keep us off this mud.' The purchases were duly made and Moor and Aaron hobbled off tentatively on the wooden platforms which elevated them a little above the mire. They laughed together at their new height and Ezra joked that they were moving up in the world already.

When they reached the last building in the row, Ezra stopped and pointed to it. 'This has just been vacated as the craftsman has moved to bigger premises. He was a carpenter, so there should be a reasonable size workroom. The owner of the property is in this house here,' He pointed to the neighbouring dwelling. 'Shall we see if anyone is at home?'

'Certainly. This looks promising,' said Aaron and hugged Moor around the shoulders.

An elderly man answered their knock and appeared delighted that someone was interested in his property next door. He turned back to retrieve a key which he used to open the front door of the neighbouring house and led the way inside. There was a large workroom directly in front of them which had shelves along one wall and a small fireplace. Aaron looked around feeling his spirits rise. This appeared ideal and he could display garments on the deep windowsill or set up a stall at the front door. A door led into a further room which contained a larger fireplace with hobs and spit and two bed alcoves. This was the only other room and would be used for living and sleeping.

A back door led out into an area with a privy which was shared by the other families in the street. It consisted of a hut divided into two, one side for men and one for women, with a long wooden seat in each with several holes for sitting over. The deposits were dug out once a week making the place far from fragrant and offering little privacy. A deep gutter on the other side of the communal privy was used for emptying chamber pots and dirty water.

Aaron and Moor grimaced to each other when they saw this place. 'Let's hope the wind is blowing mostly in the opposite direction,' Aaron remarked to Moor with a smile.

Rent was discussed with the landlord and he and Aaron shook hands on the price. 'You can move in straight away,' said the old man. 'What is your business?'

'I am a tailor. Aaron Levey. I have made fine clothes for the aristocracy in Denmark as well as being happy to sew everyday clothing for the townsfolk,' answered Aaron.

'We already have a tailor down the way a bit, but it is always good to have competition,' he replied. 'I am happy to make your acquaintance,

Levey. I'll collect the rent before Shabbat each week.' He handed the key to Aaron and departed, leaving the three standing in the workshop area.

'Well, young man, are you happy with this?' asked Ezra, smiling.

'I certainly am. I'm sure we'll manage to get our business off the ground here. Are you happy too, Moor?' he asked, turning to the lad.

'Yes, Aaron. We need to shop for feather beds though.'

Ezra and Aaron laughed at this.

'We'll need a lot more than just feather beds,' replied Aaron, 'but we can start purchasing right away.'

'Come back to the house with me meantime, and get yourselves fed and warmed again. Hannah will have a meal ready I'm sure, and you can decide what you need to do next.'

*

True to his word, Aaron showed Marta's trinkets to Moor once they were unpacked.

The ring fitted on one of the lad's fingers and he whooped in delight. 'Can I wear this all the time?' he asked.

'Of course, but it will probably get too small for you as you grow. However, once you have a sweetheart, you can give her the brooch and necklace and you may want the ring for her wedding band. It probably belonged to your grandmother.'

Moor sat quietly thinking and looking at his ring.

*

The Eddelmans were kindly and helpful and Hannah in particular made a fuss of Moor, baking him special treats and delighting in hearing his chatter. Aaron and Moor stayed with them for another week while they worked to make their new place habitable. A broom was purchased and

Moor swept out the rooms while Aaron located a trader who sold feather beds and pillows. They collected those and put them in the wooden frames in the alcoves. A table and chairs, blankets, dishes and spoons, candles and chamber pots, log basket, tinder box and cooking vessels, a kettle and various other items considered necessary were purchased and proudly positioned in the new home.

'I need a large work table and two stools now,' Aaron decided next. 'The big question is, where am I going to get the materials I need for tailoring?' he thought aloud.

He found the carpenter who'd recently moved out to larger premises, and the man was pleased to offer Aaron a suitable table. As luck would have it, he was in the process of making one, just the right size, and all that was needed was for the legs to be fitted. It would be ready the next day and Aaron and Moor could collect it and carry it through the cobbled streets to their own residence.

'Do you have any wood for sale, for my fire?' Aaron asked the carpenter.

'I always have off-cuts and shavings,' he answered. 'If you care to call in from time to time to take them off my hands, you are welcome to them for the price of a tankard or two at the inn.'

So that was settled.

Next evening, after supper at the Eddelman house, Aaron asked the old couple about their background. It transpired they had no family of their own left, as they themselves had had to flee during the plague outbreak from the northern Germanic state where they'd lived previously. Their offspring had perished in a holocaust similar to the one in Cologne.

'I don't know why *we* managed to escape to Poland and our children had to die,' said Ezra, shaking his head and wiping away tears. 'We are old and yet we live. God must have work for us still.'

'That is why we offer our home as a temporary haven to refugees like yourselves who come across the border to safety,' said Hannah, patting her husband's hand.

'Have you had many people stay with you?' asked Aaron.

'Yes, all sorts. Families, couples, single men and women. We try to treat them as we would our own kin,' answered Ezra.

'Well, Moor and I feel very glad to be with you,' said Aaron. 'Your generosity has been a Godsend.'

Moor nodded his head vigorously in confirmation. 'I'll miss your baking, Mistress Eddelman. Aaron is good at soups and stews but you make the best cake.'

'Well, you are welcome to come here for a piece of cake anytime, my dear,' answered Hannah, smiling with pleasure. 'You could also try the bakehouse on the other side of the Jewish quarter. It has a very good reputation.'

'We'll remember that,' said Moor. 'I'll need some sweetening after toiling for Aaron each day. No more play for me, I'm going to be a full time apprentice now,' he groaned, holding his forehead in mock pain.

They all laughed and Aaron punched him on the arm in fun. 'Unless I can buy some materials somewhere, I won't be needing an apprentice,' he said.

'There is a large market in the city centre, quite a bit away from the Jewish sector. There are always food stalls each day but on Thursdays, Fridays and Saturdays, the merchants bring goods from far and wide. Surely you'd find someone with the cloth that you need there?' suggested Hannah.

'That sounds like a good plan,' replied Aaron. 'It's Thursday the day after tomorrow, so Moor and I will set off early in the morning. We can borrow a handcart from Adi, you know, the carpenter, and walk over to the market.'

Moor gave another groan and was promptly tickled by Aaron until he was helpless with laughter.

*

Thursday at dawn found the two pushing the handcart over the cobbles towards the city centre. It was a cold, grey morning and mist hung around the streets making the air damp and chill. As the cart rumbled along, Aaron voiced his plans to Moor. 'We'll buy good quality cloth and start as we mean to go on. The other tailor can cater for the cheaper end of the market and we will aim to sell only the finest of garments.'

'You need someone like Count Holstein to buy something... then you'd get more business... just like in Copenhagen,' said Moor starting to get breathless with all the pushing.

'That's right. Hmm. I'll have to give that some thought,' replied Aaron. 'Perhaps Ezra or Hannah might know of someone who'd buy superior garments. I must ask them tonight.'

It took the best part of an hour for them to reach the market place. A watery-looking sun was attempting to burn away the mist and there was a happy clamour as men and women set up their goods for sale. There were hand-woven baskets, assorted second-hand clothes, candles, cheeses, bread, rabbits and chickens and all manner of food and household goods.

Aaron looked about then decided to ask for help. He approached a chilled-looking man stepping from foot to foot and blowing into his curled hands beside his table displaying pots, pans and knives. 'Excuse me, but do you happen to know if there is a trader here who sells cloth?'

'There's usually a mercer over there,' the man replied, pointing to the opposite side of the square. 'Sometimes there is an eastern gentleman, like your young man there,' he pointed to Moor, 'with colourful materials. My wife always covets his cloth. Too expensive for me though,' he added.

'Thank you. I'll try over there,' said Aaron. His mind was racing. Could the eastern gentleman possibly be Raju?

They trundled the cart across the square and sure enough, there was a stall with bolts of cloth. The trader was delighted to sell Aaron a supply of good quality woollen cloth in black, brown, grey and a dark wine colour. He also purchased quantities of linen, muslin, needles and thread. There was no sign of anyone selling silks or expensive fabrics.

'Does anyone here sell beads and lace or fur for trimmings?' enquired Aaron of the stallholder.

'You might get what you're looking for further along this side,' answered the man, directing them to a woman sitting making lace with her bobbins on a cushion on her lap.

Pushing the now laden cart over to the woman, Aaron went to look at the goods on display. He purchased a quantity of lace and a pouch full of fancy beads and spangles.

'Do you know if there is a tanner here?' he asked after he'd paid for his purchases.

'Keep on going down this side and you should come to Marek,' she replied. 'He's Polish,' she added.

Thanking her, Aaron pushed on with Moor and it occurred to him for the first time that he'd been able to understand everyone he'd spoken to so far. They must have been Germanic or Danish in origin, but he wouldn't understand the Polish tongue. Locating the tanner with his leather goods, Aaron searched the stall until he found some long leather thongs which he could use for fastenings and some scraps of leather which could also be useful for collars and decoration. Then his eye settled on what he most wanted: fur. The man came over to assist Aaron.

'Marek?' Aaron addressed him with a smile, and handed over the items he'd chosen. Pointing to the fur hats and fur-trimmed gloves, he asked, 'Do you have any pieces of fur?'

The man did not understand however and brought over a hat and some pairs of gloves for Aaron.

'No, no,' Aaron said, shaking his head. He pointed to himself then pointed to the bolts of cloth on the handcart. He mimicked sewing and, picking up the fur hat, held it around his neck like a collar.

Marek immediately understood and laughed at Aaron's antics. He reached behind his table and produced a basket of assorted small pieces of fur. Some were little scraps while others were a decent size such as squirrel tails and rabbit pelts. Aaron nodded vigorously with delight.

'How much?' he asked, and held out in his palm what he considered to be a fair price.

Marek shook his head and obviously wanted more. Aaron added a few more coins. They haggled happily like this for some minutes then came to an agreement. Shaking hands on it, Marek handed over the furs in exchange for the money. Aaron grinned to him and waved a goodbye salute.

'Can we buy something to eat now?' begged Moor who needed sustenance after all his pushing.

'Yes, choose what you'd like from the stalls on the way out. It's getting busy here now. We need to get on our way back home. '

They stopped and had some fried fish and hot wine, then Aaron bought Moor a pot of roast chestnuts from the hot brazier of a roadside vendor. Feeling warmer and refreshed, they set off on their return journey.

Aaron was excited about his purchases. 'I can't wait to start fashioning some cloaks and kirtles,' he gasped as they pushed the heavy cart along. 'I've been studying what the people here wear... and have so many ideas for trimmings... but I'd better stick to some plain things to begin with... to see how well they are received.'

*

Aaron and Moor moved out of the Eddelman house and into their own, following Shabbat. Aaron immediately started to cut out material for a woollen cloak and instructed Moor on cutting out the lining. Within a few days, there was a small pile of clothing for display, so Aaron opened the shutters of his front window and placing a small bench underneath on the street side, he laid the garments over the wide windowsill and arranged some to drape down to the bench. He had kept his designs plain and neat, with tiny stitching and the material was of high quality. He then wrote a sign on some parchment which Ezra had given him. It read,

Quality Tailoring

For Men and Women

Enquire Within

Placing the sign on the bench outside, he went indoors to his workshop to await customers. Many people stopped, read his notice and fingered the garments but walked on.

'I mustn't expect too much yet,' said Aaron to Moor, trying to keep his spirits up. 'I know, I'd planned to make a new cloak for Ezra and a skirt for Hannah to thank them for their hospitality. I might as well do it now before we get too busy. Bring down the grey wool, Moor, and I'll get started on the cloak. I think the dark wine would be nice for Hannah. What do you think?'

Moor agreed. He could feel Aaron's anxiety, and had an idea. 'Why don't we open the door, so that the people can see us at work? I know it will be cold but we can wrap up well, stoke up the fire and perhaps it will encourage folks to come inside.'

'Excellent suggestion, Moor!' Aaron opened the door straight away then ran over to the fireplace and added a few lumps of wood to the embers. 'Here, put this other tunic on top of yours,' he ordered handing one to the lad as he pulled one of his own over his head.

Moor was busy cutting out material for Ezra's collar and Aaron was already stitching the cloak together when a man entered.

'Er... I liked the look of that surcote you have on display. Could I have one made please?'

Aaron was thrilled. 'Certainly sir. Come over to the shelves here and select your material.' He chose the brown wool. 'I could do a leather trim if you'd like that, sir. Something a bit different for you?'

'That sounds interesting. Yes, why not,' replied the man and stood happily while Aaron took his measurements. 'I would like it as soon as possible. I could come back in a week's time. Would you have it ready by then?'

'I will have it ready for you in two days.' replied Aaron.

'In two days!' exclaimed the man. 'Well, well. The other tailor takes forever. I look forward to seeing what you make for me.'

'See, it worked!' said Moor excitedly once their first customer had gone. 'We'll soon have more work than we can handle.'

'Well, I better get started on it right now,' said Aaron, folding up the grey material for later and unfolding the bolt of brown wool cloth to spread across his side of the table.

They didn't exactly end up with more work than they could handle, but over the next few weeks more and more people looked inside the workshop and Aaron usually managed to secure an order for garments. He always suggested some addition such as a fur or leather trim or a beaded collar and most customers agreed to the decoration and were delighted with the results.

Ezra and Hannah were also pleased with the cloak and skirt that Aaron had made for them. 'I will recommend you to all of my friends,' said Hannah with sincerity. 'This skirt is so soft and warm. I will appreciate it greatly over these winter months.'

'It is but a token of my appreciation for all that you gave to Moor and me when we arrived in this new country. I will continue to make you gifts of clothing from time to time,' declared Aaron.

'Oh, but that is too much, ' remonstrated Ezra. 'It was our choice and pleasure to welcome you both.'

'As it is my choice and pleasure to give of my skills to my friends,' was the reply.

Aaron was satisfied with the way his business was building with people now returning for additional clothing. He was also pleased with the way Moor had taken to working with cloth. He was a quick learner being precise and neat with any task Aaron gave him and was now allowed to make linen shifts and underclothes by himself as well as muslin petticoats. The material was depleting rapidly so Aaron decided it was time to return to the market to replenish their stocks.

On the next Friday morning, they pushed the handcart over icy cobbles and slithered around on the frozen road on their way to the market. This time, Aaron knew exactly who to visit for his required purchases and duly collected all that he required. While he was piling bolts of woollen material on to the handcart, the trader said, 'I recall that you were interested in buying colourful fabrics, yes?'

'Yes,' said Aaron, stopping for a moment.

'Well, that eastern gentleman I told you about has his goods under cover over there in the corner today,' he said pointing out the direction.

'Thank you, I'll pay him a visit. I'm much obliged to you,' Aaron replied and finished packing the cart.

Hardly able to believe that it could possibly be Raju selling his silks, he made his way with Moor over to the corner as directed. However, instead of the familiar friend in turban and pantaloons, there was a dark-skinned trader warmly wrapped in a long cloak, turning on the charm for the ladies. He did indeed have some colourful cloth for sale. Aaron felt his heart sink as his disappointment registered. He stopped nearby and, asking Moor to stay with the cart for a minute, he walked over and fingered the material. Making his choice from the selection on display, he signalled for the cart to be brought over. He made his transaction with the mercer and adding the bales to the cart he and Moor set off again over the cobbles, bumping their way back towards the cooked fish seller for some sustenance.

They ate hungrily in silence but Moor picked up on Aaron's mood change.

'Is something... the matter?' he puffed as they once more trundled along.

'Oh, it was just seeing that dark-skinned trader,' came the answer after a moment. 'I thought it might be Raju. He was a good friend to us... and we travelled on his ship. You won't remember, Moor... you were just a baby,' panted out Aaron as they scrambled along.

'I would like to hear about him,' puffed Moor.

Aaron told him a little about their adventure aboard the *Rashima* as they slipped and slithered home.

They came to a halt outside their workshop and Aaron was about to open the door when a young man rushed up and shouted, 'Levey?'

'Yes, that's me,' answered Aaron, and pushed open the door. 'What's the matter?'

'I'll tell you what the matter is!' shouted the man. 'You've taken my trade, that's what the matter is, and I have a wife and children to feed.' He stood looking pitiful and shaking his head.

'Come inside,' said Aaron. 'You can explain what you mean in private. Moor,' he said quietly to the lad, 'would you start bringing in the cloth, please? Now, tell me who you are and how I have taken your trade,' he continued to the stranger.

'My name is Abe Cohen and I have the tailoring business further along the street. At least, I used to have a business until you started up, but now, everyone seems to go to you.'

'Well, I'm afraid that is their choice,' said Aaron quietly. 'I haven't deliberately stolen your customers. I've just provided good quality clothes with good workmanship.'

'That's the thing,' said Cohen, his shoulders slumping, 'I was doing my apprenticeship with a good tailor in *Mainz* at the time when the Black Death broke out – when the Jews were accused. I was lucky to escape with my wife overland to this country. Most of my friends weren't so lucky. I never had the chance to learn the finer points of tailoring, but as there wasn't any tailor here, I opened my workshop and did my best. Until now, that is.'

Aaron listened to the man's story and felt sorry for him. He stood thinking as he watched Moor struggling to bring in the bolts of silk. 'Just give me a moment while I help the lad carry in this fabric. It's a bit much for one person to manage. Sit down, I have a proposition for you.'

Cohen sat down as directed, wondering what his competitor was going to propose, and watched with envy as the fine, brightly coloured silks and other expensive materials were quickly brought into the workshop.

'Now, Cohen,' said Aaron, stopping to get his breath back. 'How would you like to come and work with me? '

Moor's back straightened sharply when he heard this. His mouth opened and closed but he didn't say a word... just looked from Aaron to Cohen and back.

'I could do with another pair of hands as business is picking up and as you can see, I have a choice stock of materials.'

'I ... I hadn't expected this... I... I don't know what to say,' Cohen replied.

'I already have one excellent apprentice in Moor here,' and Aaron indicated Moor, who nodded to Cohen. 'If you are prepared to learn from me and sew to my standards, I'll pay you a good wage. What do you say?'

'I think I would be a fool if I didn't say yes,' said Cohen, putting out his hand to Aaron.

'Then welcome to our workshop. If we bring your table along here, you could have your own space to work and I'll teach you all I know.'

'Thank you, thank you. I didn't expect things to turn out like this,' gasped Cohen, pumping Aaron's hand. 'Wait 'til I tell my wife, Anna. Thank you.' He shook Aaron's hand again and made his departure with a sprightly step.

'Well, what an amazing day this has been!' mused Aaron. 'I've got the materials I've longed for, and now we have a new would-be master tailor joining us! We shall have an evening of good dining and celebration indeed.'

CHAPTER EIGHTEEN

Winter Wonder

As the following day was the Jewish Sabbath, Aaron and Moor did not do any work. Aaron was embracing the Jewish faith once more and with Ezra and Hannah's help was doing his best to follow the religious requirements. He and Moor both wore the little kippahs on the crown of their heads and attended gatherings in a local hall where there were readings from the Talmud, prayers and singing. The community were collecting money each week towards building a synagogue and were almost at the stage where work on a building could commence. Moor was happy to conform to Aaron's religion and enjoyed seeing Aaron wearing his tasselled prayer shawl and taking part in all the required rituals. Moor truly felt part of a community for the first time in his short life while Aaron felt his early memories of Judaism being rekindled. He too felt at home. His one regret was that he didn't have a wife and family of his own. He had been too busy dealing with tragedy and changes over the years, not to mention running his tailoring trade. *Never mind,* he thought, *Moor is like a son to me and perhaps I should start looking for a nice Jewish wife, now that I have an established business.* His thoughts returned to his boyhood sweetheart Satis, and he wondered if she was alive somewhere. He sighed. 'Probably not,' he said out loud. 'I'll be an old man of thirty years soon, I guess, so time is running out. I better start looking for the right woman.'

That Sunday found Moor and Aaron helping Abe to bring his worktable and small stock of materials into their workshop. The weather was now too cold to leave the shop door open, but clientele entered without any enticement other than the recommendation that they had received from friends. Within a few weeks, Abe had settled in well and was a keen apprentice to Aaron. It was decided that he would carry on fashioning the simple skirts, kirtles, tunics and cloaks – but now with much neater stitching and finishing as he'd been shown – while Aaron concentrated on more expensive garments with leather, fur or bead adornment.

'We could do with someone to tidy up the place,' announced Moor one day as he picked up the scraps and trimmings that were dropped on the floor. It was their practice to lay a large piece of muslin on the dirt floor under the tables, to prevent garments from getting marked as they worked, sometimes with the long skirts or coats draped over their knees. 'I'm too busy to stop sewing and sweep up often. We need a woman to help us out.'

'Good idea,' replied Aaron. 'And while she's at it, she could keep the fires going – it's a nuisance having to keep getting up – and it would be good to have a meal cooked for us in the evening, wouldn't it? I'm getting tired of having to make food after a long day in here.'

Abe and Moor generally took turns at fixing the fires and making hot drinks during the day, but Abe went home to Anna each evening.

'What you need is a good wife like mine, Aaron,' said Abe with a smile.

'I've been thinking along these lines myself,' came the reply. 'Do you know of any suitable young woman who could put up with Moor and me?' he said, half in jest.

'Well, I don't know if she would be able put up with you as a husband,' joked back Abe, 'but Adi, you know, the carpenter, has a daughter who might be happy to work for you.'

'Is that right? Well, joking apart, Moor's correct. We do need someone to clean this workshop and tend the fires and it would be wonderful if she'd do some cooking. I will have a word with Adi tomorrow.'

The conversation with Adi the next day went well. His daughter Bina, of around nineteen years of age, was willing to come in each day to sweep and tidy the workshop and house. She'd come in the late morning for a short time and again at the end of the working day, when she'd also prepare a meal for Aaron and Moor. The fires would still have to be tended by Abe and Moor, but that was acceptable.

From the start, it was obvious that Bina was attracted to Aaron and did everything she could to show him that she was a good prospect. It had come to her on the grapevine that Aaron was looking for a wife. She was clean and tidy in herself and kept the house and shop in neat order, unobtrusively sweeping up any discarded scraps of material, threads and the mud which was constantly walked in. She cooked appetising kosher food and Aaron was not oblivious to her subtle advances, but made no move to further their relationship. Something he could not explain that was deep inside prevented him from encouraging anything other than an employer-employee situation between them.

The business continued to grow, despite or perhaps largely due to the freezing winter weather. More and more customers placed orders for thick cloaks and skirts as well as warm undershirts. Aaron and his helpers had to work late into the dark evenings on many occasions to finish making garments by the promised time.

One morning, they awoke to find that snow had fallen thickly overnight and was piled up high against the door at the front. It plopped on to the workshop floor when Aaron pulled open the heavy wooden door, and he promptly swept it outside again. No-one was about. It was bitterly cold and the sky in the far distance was leaden with the promise of a further snowfall, but the crisp whiteness blanketed the grey cobblestones, rooftops and walls, freshening the air and creating a soft light.

Aaron suddenly had the urge to run in the snow, playing as he had once done as a child. 'I don't think we will have any urgent business this morning,' he said when Moor appeared at the door behind him. 'The snow is too deep for passers-by. 'Why don't we take some time off from sewing and go out for a brisk walk in the snow?'

'No working?' queried Moor.

'No. This morning we shall play,' Aaron announced. 'Hurry up and get your warmest clothes on. We'll put pattens on over our boots and that might help us get through the snow.'

In a short while, they were making the first footsteps outside in the street, trying to walk where the snow was less deep. Their progress was slow and their breath formed in steamy puffs as they laughed and threw snowballs at each other.

'We'll call in at Abe's house and tell him not to come to the workshop until the afternoon,' said Aaron.

Abe was delighted to have time off to spend with his children. 'I'll see you later then,' he called as the two trudged off along the street, cheeks glowing.

They walked for a while, enjoying the crisp air and the sight of the clean whiteness over everything. Seeing Moor jumping in a drift and kicking up the snow reminded Aaron of the time he'd celebrated the Midwinter Solstice in the woods with Ulrich, while King gambolled around.

People were beginning to come out of their homes and sweep the snow from around their doorways. Children appeared with trays or pieces of wood to sit on, prepared for sliding fun.

Aaron and Moor walked into streets they'd never had time to explore before. The comforting aroma of baking bread and spiced cakes drifted towards them.

'That smells good,' Aaron said. 'Perhaps it's from that bakehouse that Hannah mentioned ages ago. Shall we go and see if it is, and if they have something tasty for hungry snow walkers?'

Moor laughed and nodded his agreement. They turned a corner and found a baking establishment with the door ajar and candlelight and sweet smells enticing them inside. A woman was stacking loaves onto a shelf behind the counter on which was displayed a selection of buns and cakes, fresh from the oven.

'Yes, what can I get you?' asked the woman turning to them with a smile.

Aaron suddenly had no voice.

'Yes?' she asked again.

Moor gave Aaron a nudge. 'Can I have a bun, please?'

Aaron was staring at the eyes of the woman. His tongue stuck to the roof of his mouth as he struggled to ask,' S... Satis?'

The woman stood completely still as she stared at the speaker. 'Yes... I'm Satis.' The man's eyes looked familiar somehow but that beard and hat... then her face blanched and her hand flew to her mouth. 'Can it be... Oh, is it... Aaron?' She staggered and clutched at the counter.

Aaron was nodding wildly as he rushed around the counter to her, then stopped, not quite knowing whether to grab her in his arms as he'd dreamt of doing for as long as he could remember, or should he...

The decision was taken out of his hands as she threw her arms around him laughing and crying at the same time.

Moor stood staring, transfixed by this show of emotion.

'I thought you were...' Aaron started but was interrupted.

214

'And I thought you were...'

'How did you get here? Are your parents alive too?

'Father, Mother, come quickly, see who's here!' called Satis.

The next few minutes were a flurry of hugs and exclamations as they were all reunited. With eyes shining with excitement, Aaron suddenly remembered Moor. 'Oh, everyone, this is Moor, he is my ward,' he said, putting his arm around the boy's shoulders. 'I...I can't believe we've been here for months and haven't all met up before now.'

'Have you been going to the meetings in the hall?' Satis asked.

'Yes, but I didn't see you there.'

'We weren't looking for each other, I suppose.'

'Perhaps we went at different times.'

Satis' mother gave her husband a look and said loudly to her daughter and Aaron, 'You two go through to the living room and have a hot drink and chat by the fire. I'll get something to please this young man while your father gets back to his oven.'

'Oh, er, yes. Wonderful to see you again Aaron and know you are safe. I'll hear all your stories later. Er... Must get back to work,' and with a swish of white apron and flour, the baker left the room.

'Off you two go then,' ushered Satis' mother, flapping her hands at them. 'Now what will it be, Moor? A sugared bun, gingerbread or apple cake?'

*

The rest of the morning disappeared in a haze of happiness for Aaron. When he and Moor took their leave over an hour later, it was with a promise to return the next evening for supper. He couldn't keep the grin from his face all the way back to the workshop.

Aaron raked at the embers of the fire and coaxed it back into life with some twigs and then logs.

Moor was looking inside the calico bag that Satis' mother had thrust into his arms when they left. 'Oh, Aaron, look what Mrs. Kopel has given us! Fruit cake and spicy buns. Can we have some with our meal?'

Aaron was crouched in front of the fire, gazing into the flames, oblivious to his surroundings.

'Aaron, cakes, Aaron,' but Aaron just sat where he was, deaf to Moor's excitement. Moor shook his head and went off to fill the kettle to put on the fire to heat. He prepared a light meal of bread and cold meat and shook Aaron's arm to bring him to the table.

'What? Oh, food, yes,' Aaron muttered and made his way to the table. Sitting with a silly grin on his face, he leaned an elbow on the table and with his chin in his hand, gazed into space.

'Aaron, don't you want to eat anything?' asked Moor who was devouring his food. 'Aaron!'

'Oh, what?' came the reply as he stirred.

'Food. Eat,' ordered Moor.

'I... I don't think I could eat a bite,' answered Aaron. 'My belly's all a-flutter.'

Moor shrugged and delved into the calico bag. 'I'll have some cake then.'

'Yes, you and Abe can have it all,' and he went back to his daydreaming.

He was still sitting in the same position when Abe thumped in, in a swirl of white, leaving a wet trail on the floor from his boots. Brushing the snow off his cloak he hung it up on a peg behind the door. 'Snow's on again,' he said and went over to the fireplace to warm his hands. 'I'll get on with that brown skirt for Mrs. Nachman when my fingers have thawed.' He turned towards Aaron who gave no response.

'He's acting strange,' said Moor from his worktable. 'He's been sitting like that ever since we came back from visiting people he knew from before. He said he can't eat anything. His belly's all a-flutter,' and he mimicked Aaron. 'The lady gave us cakes so you can help yourself.'

'Hold on a minute. Slow down,' said Abe. 'Where did you go? What people?'

So Moor related as best he could, how they had walked and played in the snow and then gone to the bakehouse at the other side of the town. He was more interested in talking about the array of buns and cakes he'd seen, but Abe managed to glean that Aaron had met up with a young lady from his past.

'From the look of him,' he nodded towards Aaron, 'it's not a stomach upset that's bothering him, it's a girl.' He dug into the bag of cakes. 'Is there one for me here?'

Moor made a face, and shrugged. 'Yes, help yourself. What do you mean about a girl?'

'The man's in *love*, Moor,' he answered taking a bite from a bun then gave Aaron a shove on the shoulder. 'Come on, boss. It's time to get on with some work.'

Aaron straightened up and grinned at Abe. 'I've met up with Satis again. I can't believe it. I must tell you all about her,' and he settled down at his worktable and told Abe and Moor how Satis and her parents had escaped from *Koln* thanks to Aaron's warning. 'They went on a different road from my family and eventually managed to board a ship which was going in the opposite direction on the Rhine from the way I travelled. Then they had an awful journey across land hidden in the back of a farmer's cart under straw. The farmer, who helped them, looked after them at his home for a short while then they walked for weeks across country, as much as possible when it was darker and they slept under hedges during the day. The weather was very cold and the journey must have been tortuous. When they eventually found themselves in Poland, fortunately the authorities handed them over to the Jewish community here.'

'How amazing that you have met up once more,' said Abe, smiling. 'Is Satis special then? I've never heard you mention her before.'

'Yes, she's very special,' he answered blushing red. 'I... I thought she was dead. I thought I was the only one to survive the burnings in *Koln* but thank God I was wrong. Satis and her mother and father were chosen to live too,' and tears came into his eyes.

There wasn't much sewing done that afternoon. They all just sat discussing Aaron's news and rejoicing with him. Abe and Moor enjoyed the buns and cake.

*

Aaron wasn't aware of the ground beneath his feet or any of his surroundings as he hurried to visit Satis the following evening. Her mother opened the door and ushered him into their cosy living room, where she gave Satis a nod and pointed look, then excused herself and left them alone.

Satis rose from her seat when he entered and stood hesitantly twisting a handkerchief in her fingers. Aaron stepped forward ready to enfold her in his arms, but she reached up a hand to stop him.

'Aaron, oh Aaron,' she gasped.

'Wh… what is the matter my dearest?' he asked, his elation turning to concern.

'Oh, Aaron, I should have told you yesterday,' she hesitated, looking at him, her eyes brimming with tears. 'I... I was so amazed to see you again. I forgot. I should have told you then.'

'Told me what?' urged Aaron, gripping her hands in his.

'I am already betrothed to someone,' she whispered, hanging her head and pulling away from him. She slumped back into the chair.

The words hit Aaron like black icicles thumping into his heart.

'Betrothed.' His mouth went dry. 'To someone else.' The words seemed to come from outside of him.

'But... I love you. I have loved you all my life... ever since you used to serve me in the bakehouse when I was a young boy.' Aaron stood, unable to move, his hands opened like a beggar.

'And I have always loved you too,' Satis answered, rising to hold his hands. I thought you were dead.' Her words tumbled out. 'I turned down offers of marriage in the past but decided I must make a home life for myself. I want to have children.'

'Then you must break this betrothal. I will marry you and *we* will have children,' he entreated.

Satis shook her head. 'I cannot break this, the contracts have been signed.'

Aaron gripped her arms. 'Contracts signed? Then un-sign them. Break them! If you feel the same way about me as I do about you, you will want this.'

He gazed into her eyes, pleading for hope.

'I *do* want to be with you. It is all I've ever dreamed of but I don't know if I can break this betrothal. I will speak with my parents and the gentleman concerned. I am so sorry. Why did it have to happen like this? Why could we not have met sooner?' Her words rushed out. 'Oh, I'm so sorry, Aaron.'

219

Just at that, there was a tap at the door and Satis' mother entered bearing a tray with drinks and cake.

'I'm sorry. I have to go,' Aaron muttered as he turned away from Satis and nodding to her mother, hurried from the house.

He didn't remember walking home. His despair was the deepest he'd ever felt. All the dark memories of his life came hurtling back – his family being wrenched from him forever; losing Ulrich, then Marta; betrayals – on and on his mind threw up sadness from his past. Just when he thought he'd found true happiness at last, it was taken from him. He staggered into the house and barged through to the back room where Moor relaxed by the fire. He started up as Aaron swept past him and threw himself on to his bed, his face turning to the wall.

'Whoa! What's happened?'

When there was no answer, Moor ran over and laid his hand on Aaron's back. 'What is it, what's happened?' he asked again but just felt the body beneath his hand heave as it was racked with sobs. He sat beside Aaron for a while, just being a comforting presence until the heartbreak subsided.

*

CHAPTER NINETEEN

Attack

Aaron returned to work the following day with a heavy heart and no interest in his business. Abe and Moor tried their best to cheer him up but knew that only time would heal his hurt. Aaron tried his best to busy himself in his sewing but every now and then he would find himself staring blindly out of the window, longing for what could have been. *Why was life so cruel? Why had God brought Satis and him together if they could not marry? How would he ever manage to carry on living in this place, knowing she was near?* With his thoughts in turmoil, he worked through the day mechanically. He was so glad when evening came. Abe took his leave with just a nod from Aaron who closed the door almost on Abe's heels. Moor realised that his guardian was deeply upset and did not try to engage him in conversation, but set about putting a kettle on the hob. Bina knocked on the door and entered as usual, ready to prepare their food but to her astonishment, Aaron stepped forward and held up a hand to stop her.

'I'm sorry, Bina, but we won't be needing you here anymore. I will settle up what is owing to you. Moor and I can manage on our own, thank you.'

'Have I done something wrong? What has happened?' Her face showed her shock and she pulled her shawl tighter around her.

'No, no, you have always done your best for us. It… it is just that… Oh, I am sorry but please just go!' and Aaron made to move towards the door, but she turned, tears sliding down her cheeks and bustled out, slamming it behind her.

Moor rounded on him. 'What on earth did you do that for? You know she has been a great help to us! You've hurt her with your words!'

'Don't say another thing! You heard me. We'll manage.'

He turned away and busied himself creating a meal for the two of them. He knew he'd acted disgracefully but was not yet able to feel apologetic. His heart hurt too much and he could not bear to see anyone.

*

The meal was partaken in a strained silence and Moor quickly took his leave from the table, washed his utensils, stoked up the fire and announced that he was going for a walk to clear his head.

Aaron did not answer but sat staring into space.

A short while later, there came a loud angry thumping on the door. Aaron was stirred from his thoughts, but did not move.

'Levey! Open this door!' and the banging continued.

'Go away. I don't want to speak to anyone,' Aaron returned.

'You'll speak to me, so help me!' came the answer and the door burst open as a man barged in and rushed towards Aaron sitting at the table.

'Get out! What the...?'

But his words were silenced as the man grabbed him by the collar and dragged him towards his face.

'What do you mean by trying to take my future wife from me? Eh? Eh?' and he shook Aaron roughly. 'Everything was fine until you turned up!'

'I ... I didn't know anything about you! I knew Satis when we were young in *Koln*.'

'Well now she doesn't want to know *me*! She wants to break our betrothal, thanks to you!' and as he threw Aaron backwards, Aaron's leg caught on the chair and he fell awkwardly to the floor yelling out in pain.

'Shut your whimpering mouth, Levey!'

But Aaron could not hold in his gasps and cries of agony.

'I told you to SHUT UP!' And he proceeded to kick Aaron in his side and on his head again and again as he shouted, 'Shut... up... your... noise!'

When Aaron lay still and quiet, the man came to himself and realised what he had done in his temper and made a rush for the doorway. Moor had returned and was just about to enter. He was shocked to see this stranger pushing past him but was more shocked when he saw the state of his adored guardian.

CHAPTER TWENTY

Reparation

It was a few weeks before Aaron had recovered enough to return to work at his sewing table. Thanks to Moor running for help to Abe and Anna, they'd managed to get him comfortable in bed. Anna bathed his wounds and she sent Moor to the apothecary for some arnica and a tincture for the pain. There was an unexpected visit later that evening when Satis and her father arrived at the house. Satis was distraught when she saw the state Aaron was in. Daniel, her betrothed, had come round and confessed what he'd done in anger, and begged her forgiveness. Any feelings she'd held for him disappeared with the realisation that he could perhaps do the same to her in the future. Satis was horrified that he could inflict such injury and her father promised to visit the Rabbi the following day to have the betrothal contract annulled. She begged to be allowed to stay with Anna and Moor to assist in nursing Aaron overnight, and her father granted this.

Anna suggested that they take turns to sit with him throughout the night in case he took a turn for the worse, so Moor made up a make-shift bed by the fireplace for himself. Aaron had a fitful sleep that first night and when he tossed and turned, the painful bruises made him cry out. Anna and Satis did what they could to bring him comfort. His poor face swelled up and his eyes were almost closed and blackened.

It was three days before Aaron regained full consciousness. To the relief of his carers, although very dazed, he seemed not to be suffering from anything worse than a few cracked ribs and a very sore head. He thought he was dreaming when he saw his beloved Satis at his side. She had tears in her eyes and assured him of her devotion and begged him to rest.

After much consultation, officials at the synagogue agreed to make the betrothal null and void. The young man concerned could not face Aaron, but wrote a letter of sincere apology which he pushed under the door of the shop.

It read,

Sir,

I write begging your forgiveness for my unspeakable attack upon your person. I have no excuse to give. I acted out of jealousy and anger upon hearing that my wife-to-be no longer cared for me and chose you instead as her lover. My rage clouded my vision and caused me to act in a most appalling way.

I have now had time to collect my thoughts and realise that it would be best for all concerned if I voluntarily departed from this town and made my home elsewhere. I would not be happy marrying someone who did not care for me, so have agreed to the annulment of our betrothal vows.

I hope that you have no lasting injury and recover full vigour quickly. It is my wish to make reparation for my behaviour therefore I enclose a sum of money. I hope this will in some way compensate for your loss of earnings while you recuperate and also for the pain and suffering I have inflicted upon you.

Yours very sincerely,
Daniel Mossbaum

The Rabbi tried to encourage Aaron to have his attacker, brought to trial, but Aaron said that as he was recovering well and there had been no real harm done, he did not want to press charges as the man in question had lost a lot already. He had lost his love, his reputation and now he was having to move away and start afresh. Aaron knew how hard that had been for him, so it would be doubly hard for Mossbaum carrying the assault of an innocent man on his conscience.

Word soon got around that the tailor, Levey, had been badly beaten up and also the circumstances surrounding the attack. Well-wishers were constantly enquiring after him so Moor and Abe were kept very busy both with custom and passing on news of Aaron's improving condition.

Aaron sent Moor to call on Bina and ask if she would kindly come to visit him. She came back with Moor but was a bit reluctant at first to meet with Aaron following his abrupt dismissal of her previously. However, when she saw the bruises on his face and the careful, slow way he moved, she gasped and her hands flew up to her mouth.

'Oh, Aaron, Aaron. What can I do to help?'

'Oh, Bina,' mumbled Aaron through swollen lips, 'I just want to apologise for my rudeness to you.'

'There is no need. I heard what happened. I mean… with you and the girl from the bakehouse.'

Aaron nodded and gave a sigh. 'That did not excuse the way I treated you.'

'How wonderful for you both to have found each other after all this time.'

Aaron could tell from her eyes that she was being sincere.

'Yes, it has turned out well, after all.' He hesitated then spoke again. 'Bina, would you consider coming back to work for me, as before?'

'Of course,' she replied, without hesitation. 'Shall I start tomorrow?'

'That would be perfect, thank you. Forgive me for not rising to shake your hand, but I still ache all over. I am really and truly grateful to have you as such a loyal friend.'

'Oh, I haven't done anything so far. It is Anna, Satis and Moor who have been watching over you I understand.'

'Indeed. They have been wonderful. Thank you again for putting up with such a grumpy wretch.'

'Forget it! I have only ever known you as a warm and kindly man. I will leave you in peace now but will be back tomorrow.'

*

It was therefore no surprise that a wedding took place within six months. The betrothal ceremony came first when the marriage contract was signed by the two witnesses, Abe and Adi. It was followed a week later by the marriage ceremony itself. This took place under a chuppah where Aaron stood proudly, dressed in grand clothes while his beautiful, veiled bride circled around him three times in the ancient ritual which signified righteousness, justice and loving kindness. Vows were exchanged, a gold ring presented to Satis by Aaron and blessings were read by the rabbi. There then followed the traditional 'breaking of the glass', when the groom placed a nuptial glass in a napkin and broke it with his right foot. This was as a reminder that despite the joy of the occasion, the Jews still mourned the destruction of their temple in Jerusalem. Next came the dancing and celebration as guests danced for the happy couple. Aaron and his bride were the last to dance together before being seated for a grand feast.

CHAPTER TWENTY ONE

Looking Back

Many years later

'Grandfather?' whispered David. 'Grandmother asked me to put some more logs on the fire for you. She is resting now but will see you at supper.'

Aaron stirred from his dozing and lifting his head, smiled at his grandson. 'Thank you,' he said gently to this kindly lad. Was he fourteen or fifteen now? Aaron found it harder these days to keep track of the members of his family. It was much easier to lose himself in his memories. He watched the young boy through blurred vision as he attended to the fire. His eyesight had been failing for many years now and it had hurt him to have to give up his tailoring. It had been one of his proudest moments when he'd placed the sign saying *Levey and Son* over his new workshop. After his marriage, Satis had suggested that it might be an idea to adopt Moor officially and give him their surname. Aaron had been overwhelmed at her generous suggestion and Moor was thrilled at the prospect. Aaron smiled to himself as he recalled the day he officially became Moor's father. He'd given his 'son' a small book of Jewish prayers and pressed inside was the copper beech leaf that he'd kept all those years since Marta's death. 'Thanks again, Marta, for looking out for Moor and helping us to find safety and become a real family,' he whispered.

'Did you say something, Grandfather?' asked David, turning from the fireplace.

'Um... No, no. I was just remembering the day that your Uncle Moor became a Levey and was truly part of the family at last.'

His thoughts drifted off again. People rarely tended to pick Moor out as a foreigner any more as most of the Jews had dark hair and some had darker skin than others.

His mind turned to the son and daughter that he and Satis went on to have, called Jerod after Aaron's father and Talitha, after Satis' mother, who died a year after their marriage. Her father continued to run the bakery business and Satis worked there as often as she could. When they were old enough, Jerod and Talitha took over the bakehouse which eventually Aaron gave to them on the death of Satis' father. They were both now married and apart from David, their offspring all enjoyed working in the expanded bakery business.

'Grandfather? I was talking to Uncle Moor today. He is pleased that I am getting on so well at the tailoring. He still comes into the workshop from time to time to check that everyone is keeping up your standards. He said I must take my love of it from you as my father doesn't like sewing, he prefers the bakery.'

Aaron laughed. 'I am so glad that the Levey name will carry on in the tailoring world as well as in the bakeries. *Levey Tailoring* now announced the two shops overseen by Moor. I am very proud of you, David.'

'Thank you, Grandfather.'

'I was just around your age when I first became accomplished at cutting cloth.'

David sat down on the rug. 'Grandfather... Uncle Moor said that you and Grandmother escaped being burned alive in Cologne. Is that true?'

As Aaron sat gazing into the fire, the memories came vividly flooding back. 'Yes, it is true.' He nodded slowly. 'I can remember it all as though it just happened recently.'

'Will you tell me about it?' came the eager question.

'Yes. I think it's about time you knew your family history. Why don't you come to see me after your work and chores someday soon, and I'll tell you all about my life and how I met your grandmother.'

'I've finished my work and chores for today,' David said quickly. 'Why don't you tell me some of your story now?'

Aaron stared into the face of this handsome boy whose personality reminded him so much of his young self. 'Very well... I was living in Koln – or Cologne as you may have heard of it – with my parents and two younger sisters, Abigail and Dorit,' he halted for a moment, deep in thought, 'when the Great Death – as the plague was known – came to our city. We lived in a small house with just two rooms and Father's workshop, not a grand house like this one here in Poland.'

He continued telling the lad about the horrors of that time when the family had to flee, leaving out none of the gruesome details.

The door opened and Jerod's wife, Chana, entered. 'So this is where you've been hiding, David. I hope you're not tiring your Grandfather.'

The boy shook his head.

'Not at all, Chana,' Aaron answered. 'I've been telling my grandson about my early life in the Germanic state.'

'I hope you're not filling his head with frightening stories, old Aaron.'

'It is time the lad knew the truth,' he replied quietly.

'Come away now, David,' ordered Chana, turning to the door. 'Leave your grandfather to have some rest before supper.'

The boy rose and patted Aaron's arm and whispered, 'Thank you, Grandfather. I will be back tomorrow to hear more.' He followed his mother from the room.

Aaron nodded and turned back to gaze into the fire, his mind conjuring up the faces of Ulrich, Marta, Jen, Sigrid and Berta. 'Such dear, dear people,' he murmured aloud. Alina, Tomas, Anya, Ezra, Hannah and Abe were next to walk through his thoughts. 'We were chosen to be friends,' he said, smiling. 'We will meet again and these friendships will last throughout eternity.'

*

And we know that God causes all things to work together for good to those who love God, to those who are called according to His purpose.

Romans 8:28